IMMORTAL
FAITH

A novel of vampires and unholy love

Shelley Adina

Moonshell
Books

Moonshell Books, Inc.
PO Box 752
Redwood Estates, CA 95044
www.shelleyadina.com

Publisher's Note: This is a work of fiction. Names, characters, places, and incidents are a product of the author's imagination. Locales and public names are sometimes used for atmospheric purposes. Any resemblance to actual people, living or dead, or to businesses, companies, events, institutions, or locales is completely coincidental.

Book Layout ©2013 BookDesignTemplates.com
Cover design by Kalen O'Donnell at art.kalenodonnell.com
Author font by Anthony Piraino at OneButtonMouse.com

Immortal Faith / Shelley Adina – 2nd ed.
ISBN 978-0615520957

For Jennifer Skully and Kimberly Hunter,
who loved it from the first page

1

The baby chick, hatched just yesterday and half the size of my palm, peeped as I stroked its downy yellow back with one finger. The two halves of its tiny beak crossed at the tips, which was why it had been peeping. It couldn't pick up the feed and it was hungry.

Mamm would be out any moment, but I couldn't help myself—I had to do something for it, even if all I had to offer was the warmth of my hands. I knew it had to be culled; if it managed to grow up and have chicks of its own, it would pass on the defect. On an Old Order Mennonite farm, even a tiny scrap of life such as this still had to do its best and pull its weight, and my mother had no tolerance for things that didn't pull their weight.

Unless we were speaking of my youngest brother, Jonah.

Sometimes you didn't know until a creature was half grown that it would need to be culled. When one of the young roosters decided it was going to challenge Dat for the rule of the farmyard, and attacked his leg in a fury of male aggression, Dat simply pulled it off his boot and ended that discussion with a quick twist. "I'll not have that bird passing on his bad seed," was all he'd said, and we had chicken and dumplings for dinner that night.

Jonah and Caleb laughed and called me softheaded as well as softhearted because I couldn't bring myself to do some of the things that were necessary on a working farm. And while I knew God had a purpose for every animal and human here—even Jonah—and we all had to fill our places ... I gazed down at the defenseless fluffball in my hand. We were taught to strive after perfection, but couldn't there be a little room for mercy, too?

But questioning was a sure path to a bad spirit, which led to discontent and pride. *Father, forgive me for my resentful thoughts.*

"Sophia, are you out here?"

"*Ja, Mamm.*"

The sunlight streaming in the barn door darkened briefly, throwing my mother's body into silhouette and shining through her *kapp* to show the smooth braided bun beneath it. "You're not mooning over those chicks, are you? You know we can't keep the ones that aren't up to standard."

"I know."

"You'll have to learn to do this some day." Her tone softened as she joined me at the pen where the broody hens lived until the chicks were big enough to go out into the barn. "When you're married and have a fine farm of your own, you'll be overrun with rickety, good-for-nothing birds if you don't cull the bad ones."

No one I knew kept chickens as pets, but in the rare moments that I sat down on the back steps and one would jump into my lap, I would swear that, like my baby sister, they wanted to be cuddled. I wished I could keep this one as a pet.

"She's not bad," I said softly. The chick had settled in my palm, and I covered it with my other hand. "It isn't her fault she's not perfect."

"And would you have a yard full of cross-beaks that can't eat their food? That grow up spindly and thin and won't fill the stomachs of your family?"

"No." I sighed. We had this same conversation every spring, and every spring I hated it just as much. The part about getting married and having my own farm hadn't come up before, though. I wondered what had brought that on.

"Sophia." Mamm held out her hand. Gently, I put the chick into it and turned away. With no sound but a sudden rustle of the dark blue cotton of her sleeves, it was over. "Are there any more?"

"The one with the yellow spot on its head can't walk. There, by the Wyandotte mama." Another rustle of movement. "I'll bury them, Mamm."

"Don't be long bringing in the eggs. I want to speak to you."

After I'd done my sad duty, I comforted myself watching the rest of the chicks tumble over each other, nip food away from their companions, and collapse in happy abandon for a nap under their mamas' wings, which kept them warm on this sullen day in the hind part of April. The chicks could not know what had happened to the others, and their innocence was a joy in itself. But how fair was it that they'd only escaped because they met a standard they didn't even know existed?

The chicken barn was sectioned off from the field horses' stalls and the neat area where the buggies and tack were stored. That part belonged to Dat and the boys. This part belonged in name to Mamm, and in reality to me. It was dry, cozy, and safe, and on rainy days the birds made themselves comfortable in the deep bedding of wood shavings or perched on the hay bales stacked along the wall. For me, it felt peaceful and industrious at the same time, as the hens got on with the business of laying, raising chicks, and eating. Once I'd collected the eggs, I walked slowly across the yard, drying now as spring advanced, to the kitchen door.

What did Mamm want to speak to me about? We talked all day long. As the second eldest girl in the family, and since graduating from eighth grade three summers ago, I was her biggest help. That had been my older sister Hannah's place, but no longer. During her season of *Rumspringa*, of running around, last year, Hannah had said in her letters that she'd fallen in love with life in Council Bluffs and would wait a little longer to come back to Mitternacht. Why wouldn't she? She could stay out all night if she wanted. Talk to a boy without a dozen relatives leaping to conclusions and then into wedding plans. Learn how to drive a car like the *Englisch*, and even go to high school.

That was all well and good—for her. But she shouldn't wait too long to decide whether she was coming back. My father had taken to falling into silence whenever her name was mentioned, and that was not so good. The thought of having to treat my own sister as *Englisch* made my skin go cold and coiled a sick knot of apprehension in my stomach. What crazy girl would sacrifice her family and her church just to stay out late and drive a car?

I ran warm water into the sink and began to wash the eggs while Mamm put a couple more sticks of wood in the stove and sliced into the pile of scrubbed potatoes on the counter. Dat and the boys were out planting, now that winter had released its iron grip on the ground and the days were long enough, and they'd be hungry as bears when they came in.

"What did you want to talk to me about?"

On the rug my grandmother had braided as a bride when she'd come to Mitternacht, baby Miriam kicked her legs with great energy, and Mamm glanced at her to make sure she wasn't going anywhere. At this rate, she'd roll over and start crawling, without any of the in-between. My mother seemed to be taking an awfully long time to reply.

Oh, dear.

I ran the last several hours through my head, and when nothing popped up that would rate a talking-to, I ran through yesterday, too. I'd dropped an egg on the way out of the barn, but the birds had eaten it so fast there couldn't have been any evidence left to tell the tale.

This silence couldn't have anything to do with marriage and new farms, could it? I was only sixteen. I hadn't even gone on *Rumspringa* yet, like several of my friends had. Didn't even know if I wanted to. Then what—

"Gabriel Langford helped your father and brothers with the planting yesterday," she began with a "this isn't important but I thought I'd pass it on" kind of tone.

"That was kind of him," I said, "though I'm sure he has plenty to do in Joshua Hodder's fields."

"He does. Which is why it meant something, Sophia, for him to finish there and then do nearly a full day's work here."

"Why would he do that? Does Joshua think that if he works him to death, he'll be less likely to want to join church?"

"That boy's capacity for work puts even your father to shame," Mamm said. "Not to mention his willingness to try his hand at anything, from planting to construction."

"Have the men got a competition going to see who can wear him out first?" I was only half joking. My friends and I complained to each other that even if Gabriel Langford was the one we most wanted to bump into, with him it was the least likely to happen. He worked from dawn until dark, and when he wasn't working, he was taking *Deitsch* lessons with Bishop Stolz, and when he wasn't doing that, he was in meeting. Head bowed, glossy black hair combed, clothes spotless, he occupied his bench in a way that made heads turn.

Well, the heads of all my friends, anyway. I never would have believed it would be so hard to keep one's gaze facing front and not let it slide to the men's side of the meetinghouse during worship. To ignore those long-lashed eyes and beautiful cheekbones turned up toward the preacher. To pretend not to see the sunlight make its way through a curtain or a window and light up that skin. A blemish would never dare appear on his face. What an awful thought.

Some of the boys—cornfed nobodies who had the mistaken idea they were somebody—had tried to pick a fight with him when he first came last winter, calling him "Gabrielle" and telling people he wrote poetry. That had lasted about five minutes. The boys said that Adam Hertzfeld had broken his collarbone falling out of the haymow, but his sister Katie, my best friend, told me the truth. After that no one accused anyone of writing poetry. Those boys kept their mouths shut and tried to look friendly when Joshua hired Gabriel out to their fathers' farms.

"There's no competition that I know of." My mother gave me a look. "A hard worker he might be, but he's still *Englisch* and no daughter of ours will be thinking thoughts about him."

She'd brought him up, not me. "I'm not thinking thoughts." Was that a lie? Just in case, I sent up a breath of a prayer for forgiveness. "I just wondered if he planned to join church. Have you heard anything?"

"I haven't heard a word about his plans, nor do I want to," Mamm said with disregard for the life of any *Englisch*, which from her tone of voice, had nothing to do with hers, now or in the hereafter. Even though the alfalfa Gabriel had put in our fields would go to feed our cows and make the milk we sold to the cooperative every week. "Plans are nothing. When he actually kneels in front of the bishop and the church and gives his life to God, then his plans will have some substance. In the meantime, you're not to behave as if he's plain. No talking with him among the *Youngie* after Singing, no accepting a ride on a rainy day, nothing. Understood?"

"Can I say *guder mariye* if I pass him on the road?"

Narrow eyes examined my face to see if I was talking back. Maybe I was. Or maybe I honestly wanted to know. The words had just popped out and it was too late to unsay them.

"Just good morning," Mamm said at last, evidently not finding what she was looking for. "Nothing more than you would say to any *Englisch* in town. A plain woman is always modest and polite, especially to people outside the church."

I don't think my lips moved in unison with hers, but they could have. I'd heard those words approximately ten thousand, five hundred and eighty times during the course of my life.

"And why are we discussing Gabriel Langford anyway?" Mamm asked. "I wanted to talk about something else."

Thank goodness. "What?"

"After meeting on Sunday, David Fischer asked your father for permission to walk out with you. What do you think about that?"

I dropped an egg into the soapy water and heard the sickening sound of a crack. "Me?!"

"Sophia Brucker, watch yourself!"

"Sorry." I pulled the plug and let the broken yolk wash down the drain, then picked the shell fragments out of the trap. "Are you sure? David Fischer? This isn't Dat's idea of a joke, is it? Who asks the parents' permission anymore?"

Mamm allowed herself a smile. "When it comes to the subject of courtship, your father does not make jokes. Just ask me. And there's nothing wrong with asking his permission. I think it was a fine way to show respect and have everything above board. After all, it's David. Why should that surprise you?"

My mouth opened and closed like a fish on a riverbank. *Surprised* didn't even begin to cover it. *Astonished* might be a start. Me and David? That was crazy. We'd known each other since we were babies and I thought of him as another of my brothers—when I thought of him at all. There was no room in my brain for David when Gabriel haunted it. Oh, if only he were plain! Every girl in Mitternacht over the age of twelve would give her eyeteeth to walk out with him.

"Gabriel has to be planning to join church," Katie had said after that very same meeting. No wonder I hadn't seen David, if he'd been lying in wait for Dat by the hitching rail in the Millers' lane. "No one would devote so much of himself to work and worship if he didn't."

I couldn't think of any other reason, either. Converts were rare in Mitternacht, and as for good-looking single male converts ... well, there had never been one in *my* lifetime. But even if that was God's will for Gabriel, I didn't dare let hope blossom in my chest and warm me with possibility. The simple fact was that there were lots more girls in our district than ordinary brown-haired, gray-eyed me. Girls like merry, laughing Katie or Ellie Stolz, whose parents had left her a bed-and-breakfast when they died, even though her aunt ran it. Or Rebecca Hodder, who was tall, beautiful, and eighteen and lived right there where Gabriel was boarding. The fact that she had run through every boy under twenty-one within a twelve-mile radius just made it seem more inevitable that she'd settle on him ... when he joined church.

"Sophia? I asked you what you thought of David Fischer."

What *did* I think? With Gabriel in the neighborhood, did anyone think about David? "I ... I don't know."

"Well, if he offered you a ride home from Singing, would you go?"

I stopped pretending to clean the sink and turned away to dry my hands on a dishtowel. "I don't know."

"Sophia."

"I'm telling true, Mamm. I don't know what I'd say. I—I've never thought of David like that. He might as well be my brother."

"He is your brother in God." She took the towel from me and dried her own hands. "He's worth ten of Gabriel Langford."

How fair was this? "You just finished saying what a hard worker Gabriel is. You don't really know him."

"My point exactly. None of us know him, except maybe Joshua Hodder. *Ja*, he is a hard worker and seems to be committed to the church, but I've seen it before. People get romantical notions about plain living—until they actually have to do it. Then they're running for their hair dryers and radios."

"He's been here since November and hasn't run yet."

"Maybe not, but I'll believe it when I see it. Meantime, aren't you going to ask me what else your father said to David?"

I could see where this was going. "What did he say?"

"He said it was up to you. That you were old enough to make up your own mind." Again the narrow look, but it held no displeasure this time. Instead, I saw concern in my mother's face. "Is it too soon, *liewi*? Would you rather Dat told the boys to go away and come again in a year?"

I had to smile at that. "You know no one would listen to him. All of us see each other all the time. It was nice of David to ask, though. Even though it embarrasses me."

"There's nothing to be embarrassed about," Mamm said firmly, and lifted the stove lid to check the coals. "Your father asked my Dat if he could court me, and he never regretted it." The smile fought its way free again, and I had to laugh at how she didn't say which *he* she meant. My parents adored each other, though it would take an educated family eye to see it. The way Mamm always gave him the choicest piece of the roast, or made dumplings fried in bacon and onions just because he loved them. The way he always handed her out of the buggy as if she were a queen, even before he saw to Daisy, our mare. I'd seen many a man take care of his livestock and *then* worry about whether his wife was ankle deep in mud beside the buggy.

A tiny bit of a wonder about whether David would put his horse or his girl first whisked through my brain before I chased it away. I was going to have a hard enough time treating him the way I'd always treated him—as a friend, a brother, someone who also sang parts outside of meeting—now that he'd made his feelings public.

Dat was as closed-mouthed as a rat trap, but if there were any guarantees in this world, it would be that a private matter between men would get out sooner rather than later.

When I didn't speak, Mamm finally said, "Ah well. You go and weed those front beds and think about it. There's no rush. But I won't ask your brother to wait for you Sunday after Singing."

Smiling as if this was hugely funny, Mamm got out the frying pan and I escaped into the muddy, bare garden, where the weeds were the first things to sprout.

Sunday after Singing ... when I would see Gabriel again.

Eternal life.

Isn't this what every Christian longs for? And yet, having attained it, I am still a little confused. When the gift was given to me at the age of nineteen, I was filled with joy. Endless ages in which to praise my Creator! To worship Him while the stars wheeled overhead and the seasons turned. The fact that I was not doing so in front of a throne, or in the company of beings made of spirit and light, puzzled me at first, but then, like any creature, I adapted. Not that I would ever intimate that the Bible was mistaken. But reality being different from prophecy, and I being a realist, I simply got on with what I was given.

Eternal life.

I'm still finding it strange, even after two centuries.

2

As it turned out, I didn't even have to wait until the Singing to see Gabriel. The next morning I caught a ride into Mitternacht with my younger brother Jonah, who was apprenticed to William Stolz at the carpentry shop. They made barrels, doors, barn trusses—or whatever the customer could draw on a piece of paper. I don't know how much skill my brother had at turning people's ideas into solid, usable things, but William Stolz had a gift from God. You should see the Noah's ark he made for Miriam when she was born. Every animal had a personality, from the curious, outstretched neck of the giraffe to the grumpy, hunched-up body of the bear, who had clearly just been awakened from his winter sleep.

I hopped down from the buggy in front of the fabric store. "*Denki*, Jonah. I just need to pick up a few things, and then I'm meeting Katie for lunch and going home with her."

He just grunted, all his attention stolen by the bus full of tourists that had just roared to a halt next to us and sat there, blowing exhaust everywhere as though it had sprinted all the way from Council Bluffs. Daisy side-stepped nervously and Jonah turned her head toward Taft Avenue. "It's okay, girl. Just ignore the big ugly thing. It won't hurt you."

"Oh, look at the Aim-ish!" A quartet of girls about my age spilled down the steps, holding up camera phones in exactly the way a medieval priest I'd seen in a book warded off the devil with a cross.

Well, if they wanted to ward me away, I was happy to oblige. We were not Amish, though folks often confused us with them. Our *kapps* were different, and so were our dresses, if a person only paid attention. And so were many of our beliefs. I turned my head away from the nasty intrusive lenses and hurried up the steps into the little courtyard where the fabric shop was while Daisy and Jonah beat a smart retreat down the road.

"Hey, he was cute. Needs to lose the hat, though."

"He's too young for you."

"Don't run away, girlfriend. I just wanted a picture."

"They don't like getting their picture taken, Ashley. Don't you know anything?"

"Why not?"

"Because of their cutting-edge fashion sense?" asked the third girl. "Nice apron, Grandma Moses." The fourth girl laughed.

"I think she heard you."

Did they think I was deaf? Did they think the whole town was? There were some people who were sincerely interested in our way of life. And there were some who just thought we were entertainment for their benefit. I let the door close behind me with a feeling of relief.

"Hey, Sophia, how are you?"

Lilian Borchardt may have been *Englisch*, but she was also a friend of my mother's and had lived in Mitternacht all her life. A *kapp* and apron were as normal to her as they were to any of us, and she had a great eye for color. Half the quilts for sale in plain yards that fronted the highway had a little of Lilian in their design—and of course, the cottons had come from her shop.

"I'm fine, thanks. You?"

"I smell spring in the air, and that makes me happy. Placed my first order for summer cottons, and that makes me even happier."

In another month I'd be trading my dark green and purple winter dresses for summer cottons myself. "Keep an eye open for a nice pale blue for me, then. So. I need enough batting for two queen-size quilts and a king. We spent the winter piecing the tops, and my mother is ready to put them together now."

"Let me get it for you. That much, I'll need to pull out of the back."

She disappeared around a corner, and like a curtain being pulled, the sun came out from behind a cloud and filled the shop with brilliance. My feet seemed to move by themselves. After a long, dark winter, the thought of the sun on my skin was too tempting.

Outside in the courtyard, I tipped my face up and closed my eyes against the light. The warmth on my face felt wonderful, like a blessing—a promise—from God that there would be an end to the mud and the glazing of ice on the puddles and the sheer mess of spring.

"You look like you are waiting for a kiss," a soft male voice said, inches from my ear.

I must have jumped half a foot. With a gasp, I whirled to see Gabriel Langford leaning against one of the bookshop's wheeled shelving units outside its door.

My lungs contracted and the blood rushed out of my brain and into my cheeks. "Wha—what are you doing here?" Had he really said that to me? No. He couldn't have. We'd never spoken as much as two words together, and certainly none as intimate as—No. I'd imagined it.

"*Guder mariye* to you, too," he said mildly, and an even hotter wave of embarrassment rolled over my cheeks, my neck, and halfway down my arms. What an idiot I was. Why didn't I just sink into a hole in the ground? Or run?

That was it. Run. "*Guder mariye.* I have to get—" With an inarticulate wave, I practically fell into the fabric store as the door gave way far too easily under my hands.

"Oh, sorry, Sophia." Lilian caught me before I fell flat on my face on her varnished plank floor. "I was just coming to get you. I've got the batting on the counter."

"Thanks," I choked out, and took a deep breath. What was the matter with me? *Get hold of yourself, girl. Gabriel said good morning. You said good morning back. Sort of. Never mind. It's done.*

But it was not done. When I pushed through the door with an enormous plastic bag containing three beds' worth of batting bumping against my knees, he was still lounging on the rolling bookshelf. He closed the book he'd been paging through with a snap.

Waterloo: Napoleon's Last Campaign.

The title registered on my eyes, but didn't filter through to my brain. That was too busy shrieking, *He waited for you!* We'd already exhausted the conversational limits Mamm had set. *Now what are you going to do?* I had no idea. But I knew what I wanted to do.

The clouds closed over the sun and the gloom we'd lived with for a couple of weeks closed back in. The breeze sneaked down the neck of my dress and I shivered. I wished I had a hand free to wrap my black knitted shawl closer.

"May I carry that for you?" He levered himself off the bookshelf and reached for the bag.

"No, it's fine. Really."

"Is someone waiting for you with the buggy?"

"Yes. I mean, no. I mean, not at the moment." Good grief. After one experience talking to me, he was going to go running back to Rebecca Hodder with a sigh of relief. "I'm meeting my best friend. She has her dad's buggy."

"Please let me. This bag is as big as you are."

Since it looked like a giant snowball, I gulped. *Somebody* was going to be giving up dessert for the rest of the year. "It's not heavy."

"Luckily for me." He swung it out of my hands and over his shoulder. "There. I look like Father Christmas, doing my rounds four months late."

Father Christmas? Oh. Santa Claus. Well, imaginary figures never looked like this. How was it possible for one person to have inherited such gifts? And how had I never noticed the deep dimple that creased his cheek when he smiled?

Because he didn't smile much. Except now. At me.

Who had already said more than the two words I was allowed to.

The smile faded, leaving a look of concern in dark, long-lashed eyes that made my knees go weak. I straightened them and kept walking toward the restaurant where I was to meet Katie.

"Did I offend you just now? Talking about Santa Claus? I know we don't believe in such nonsense, but it was a joke."

We? "I know."

"Having a bad day?"

The sympathy in his voice was enough to make a girl dissolve like sugar in a glass of water. "No." The opposite, in fact. I couldn't remember a day more miraculous than this, ever.

"Well, if you're not offended and you're not having a bad day, that only leaves me one conclusion."

The pause grew so long that the blood beat into my cheeks again. "What's that?"

"You just heard that David Fischer was going to call me out for talking to you, and you're determined to save my life."

The ridiculousness of it—nonviolence is drummed into us from birth, with the odd exception—surprised a laugh out of me, and before I knew it, he was laughing too. Did I mention he had a dimple when he smiled? That's nothing to what happened to his face when he laughed. Another dimple danced at the corner of his mouth, and his eyes crinkled at the corners as his whole face filled with delight.

Well, after that, doing what Mamm said seemed not only silly, but downright rude. "David Fischer has no say over who I talk to," I informed him. "And where did you hear such a thing, anyway?"

"Oh, word travels, you know." He shook his head. "Not that I'm afraid of him. But he is friends with Caleb, and Caleb visits Jonah at the carpentry shop, and there are all those sharp objects lying about."

"Caleb doesn't care who I talk to, either."

"Now, there you are wrong. I was warned away from you just yesterday, in fact, after meeting."

"What?" Of all the—!

"He was just being loyal. I took it gracefully, as is my wont."

I'd never heard anyone actually use that word. "You sound like a book."

"Do you like books?"

"The kind with pages and covers, sure."

He looked down at his black pants and hefted the bag to the other shoulder. "I'm covered."

"Yes, you are. You look a right fine plain man." Now was the time to say it. *But you're not a plain man, and I'm not supposed to have anything to do with you until you are.*

Go on. Say it, Sophia.

I looked sideways at him and the words turned to ash on my tongue.

"So, is it true?" he asked.

"Is what true?" Submission in one's appearance was a sign of submission in the inner man. That's why women wore prayer coverings, and why both sexes dressed in sober, unadorned clothes that put modesty and practicality before fashion. Did that mean Gabriel had already submitted himself to God—and the public proof of it was only a matter of time?

"That you and David are going to be walking out."

Poor David. I'd forgotten him again. I wanted to say, "No, of course not. I'm completely free and available and would you like to drive me home?" But I didn't. That would be presumptuous and vain.

"He asked my father if he could. That's all."

"Oh." The light went out of his face. Another breeze sneaked down my collar and this time I did pull my shawl closer, tucking the ends into my apron. We crossed the street and I counted the buildings until the Harvest Moon Diner, where I was to meet Katie. Four buildings. How many seconds would it take me to bring that smile back?

"May I tell you something?" he said quietly, and I changed my mind. Gabriel smiling was a lovely sight. But Gabriel serious, with all the concentration of those dark eyes on me, was enough to steal the breath from my body.

"Of course," I said. At least, I think my lips moved.

"On Sunday, all of us who have been following instruction will be at the meetinghouse." He paused to let that sink in.

When it did, my mouth fell open. "You mean—"

With a nod, he said, "Yes. I am going to be baptized and join the church. After Sunday I shall be one of you. And then ..."

His deep gaze met mine and I forgot everything. The town, the wind, the cars whizzing past—everything faded into silence and there was only those two words, as unfinished as a promise and just as sure.

And then ...

"Sophia!" I heard familiar syllables but they held no meaning. "Sophia! You're ages early. Oh, hi, Gabriel."

Slowly, hearing returned and connected itself with brain. A diesel truck went by, its tires hissing on the asphalt as it spattered through the puddles. Sight expanded, and there was Katie over Gabriel's shoulder, the strings of her *kapp* loose and her front hair all *strubley*, as if she'd been blown across the street by the wind. She looked from Gabriel to me and about a hundred silent questions fell into the gap.

"Katie Hertzfeld," he said solemnly. He handed me the bag of batting. "Here you go, Sophia. Joshua Hodder sends his regards to your father, and thanks him for teaching me about planting alfalfa."

The powers of speech were taking their time to return. I took the bag and he loped away down the sidewalk, ramming his wide-brimmed black hat on more firmly in case the wind tweaked it off his head.

"What did he do, carry this big bag over from the fabric shop for you?" Katie didn't wait for me to confirm the obvious. "Rebecca Hodder says he's always doing things like that. He even gets up early to build the fire in the kitchen stove for her. I'm positive it's only a matter of time before he goes to the bishop. And then watch the free-for-all start."

I nodded, pushed the restaurant door open, and promptly got both myself and the bag stuck in the too-small space between the exterior and interior glass doors.

"Sophia, you crazy girl. Let me go past you. I'll hold this one."

What had possessed me to go to the store so early, and have to lug the big, unwieldy thing all over town? I should have met Katie first, had lunch, and then gone for it.

Then I wouldn't have seen him. And not seeing him, not hearing those words, would have ruined my life.

"Personally, I think Rebecca Hodder's got him all sewn up." Katie dropped into a fake red leather booth and picked up the menu. "It's kind of inevitable, when you think about it."

I heaved the bag under the table and sat opposite her. The menu could have been written in Egyptian for all the sense it made to me. "Probably."

"Did he say anything about his plans? What did you two talk about?"

"Nothing very much." That was the absolute truth. "I told him he looked plain."

"All the boys should look so," Katie said on a sigh, as if she were some romantic heroine. "Did I tell you I heard Ellie the other day, praying 'Please God, let him come to church.' Crazy girl."

I frowned at the menu, where the words finally managed to swim together into coherence. "What do you think? Should we try the lasagna?" Mamm never made such things. I had a shameful passion for restaurant food—the kind we didn't get at home. My parents considered it a sin to pay for something you could make in your own kitchen.

The waitress came and took our orders, and reappeared with the plates a few minutes later. "So," Katie said, digging into her salad, "did you hear the news?"

I looked up from my lasagna and reached for the Parmesan cheese. "About Gabriel?"

"No. Have you got a one-track mind?" I barely stopped myself from rolling my eyes. She was a fine one to talk. "You didn't hear, then. About Abram Troyer's cow."

"Oh, there's a headline." I shook cheese onto my pasta.

Katie blinked at me, clearly shocked. "You don't think it's terrible?"

Um. Something wasn't right. "About a cow? What's so terrible about that? Did it break down a fence?"

She put down her fork and her gaze locked with mine. "Sophia, someone cut his cow's throat right there in his barn and left the poor thing there to bleed to death."

The tomato sauce congealed in my mouth and I barely got it down. "What?"

She sat back. "I knew you mustn't have heard. Isn't it shocking? Right there by the milking pen, and no one heard a thing. Not even when the poor creature was—" She made a slashing gesture that was much more graphic than words.

"Who—what—" I felt sick with dismay for the poor animal. "Who would do such a thing?"

"No one knows. I passed Cara Troyer on the road on the way in. She told me her father and the boys heard the beast's moaning when they went in to milk at five, but there was nothing to do by then but just butcher it. Completely the wrong time of year, but what choice did they have?"

"Who or what could have—an animal, maybe?" I looked down at my lasagna, layered with tomato sauce, and wished I'd ordered a salad instead. "Somebody said they saw a coyote running by the road out Myerling way."

"A coyote wouldn't tear an animal's throat out and leave it to lie. And especially not inside a closed barn."

I pushed my plate away. "This is lovely lunch conversation. Are you doing your hair differently?"

Thankfully, Katie took the hint. "Just a tiny braid on both sides. I got tired of rolling it. Everyone does that." I touched my own, neatly twisted up at the sides and tucked under my *kapp*. "Yours looks nice, though," she added hastily, in case I'd been offended or hurt. "You have cheekbones, unlike me. Rolls just make my face look wider."

"Vanity and vexation of spirit," I told her with affection.

"You know I have none of the first and plenty of the second when it comes to my hair," she sighed. "I wish I knew how Rebecca does it. She could walk through a blizzard and come out the other side looking as though she'd just spent an hour in front of the mirror."

Rebecca Hodder had a yard of rippling blond hair. I squelched a surge of envy. "The awful part is that she isn't vain. If that mirror gets five minutes of her time every day, I'd be surprised."

"Even with Gabriel in the house?" Katie shrugged and resigned herself to unruly curls that not even a *kapp* could tame. "It's not like I can compete with her, anyway."

"That would be wrong, for a start. For seconds, you know what some are saying."

"That she's a flirt? I think that's a price I'd be willing to pay if I could have her hair and skin."

"God gives us the gifts that please Him," I reminded her. "Don't be envious, *meine freinde*. Besides, there's nothing wrong with the rest of you. Want to know a secret?"

Her eyes lit up and she leaned toward me across the table. "What?"

"I saw my brother Caleb making eyes at you two Sundays ago."

She sat back, her face a study in astonishment. "You did not."

"I could have been mistaken, but I don't think so. He stared at you for about ten seconds as if he'd never seen you before. The real you. The one I know."

For a moment, her eyes unfocused, as if she were looking deep into her memory to see if what I said was true. Then her shoulders drooped. "It couldn't have been me. Guess who was sitting right next to me?"

I couldn't remember.

"Rebecca," Katie said flatly. "It was probably her he was mooning over."

"He's already had his turn. Last summer he drove her over to Myerling to a building party and nothing came of it."

But Katie and I shared more than a lifetime of friendship and the fact that we both belonged to the same gang of *Youngie.* We shared a common belief that to hope for something other than one's eternal salvation was a sure way not to get it. "No," she said, "I won't think that way. You're just being nice because you're my best friend. Besides, I know Caleb's taste. He likes tall, slender girls, not short ones who eat too many dumplings at dinner."

"He likes dumplings."

"Speaking of, is there something wrong with your noodles?"

I shook my head, the vision of Abram Troyer's poor cow flooding back into memory. "No, not a bit. I need to lay off the fattening things myself. I'm this close to having to let out all the seams in my dresses."

Which was nearly true. But the real reason lurked deep inside my head, echoing in the pauses in my conversation, tantalizing me with a future that dangled just out of my reach.

And then ...

During the first of what they called the World Wars, my fellow drivers in the English ambulance corps had an expression for those whose injuries were of the soul rather than of the body. *The walking wounded.*

She is like that.

I cannot make her out. One moment her spirit shines from her eyes and the world around her is permeated with joy. The next she is utterly quenched, as though a thundercloud thick with rain and threat has passed over her, leaving just the obedient shell of a person.

I've seen many such women, but she is different. So much potential there, kept so deeply hidden away.

I must know the cause. It calls to me.

3

After lunch, Katie went to get her dad's buggy. I stood on the sidewalk, feeling a little exposed all by myself, but thankful that at least I could savor those few minutes with Gabriel with no one to see or judge.

When a horse drew up in front of me, my body was already in motion before my mind caught up to the fact that those weren't Katie's hands on the reins.

"*Guder mariye*, Sophia," my uncle Paul said.

With a gasp that I hoped he hadn't heard, I stopped my forward momentum by bending over the bag of batting and pretending to check that it was still tied shut. "*Guder mariye, Onkel.*"

"Are you waiting for a ride?"

"Yes. Ka—"

"Are you going home? I can take you."

I would not look up. If I did, I would see his face, and I couldn't bear that. To see his eyes. "That's kind of you, *Onkel*, but I'm with Katie Hertzfeld. She should be here in a little minute."

The horse backed up a step, stamping, as if her driver had tightened his hands on the reins. Goodness, my own hands were freezing. I could hardly move them over the knot in the carrying handles.

"Having a little girl time, then, hey? Does your mother know you're here?"

Did he think I was playing hooky from housework? "Of course she does. I'm taking this home to her."

"I can take it for you, and get it out of your way so you can have your girl time."

"*Neh, danke.*"

"It's no trouble." He laid the driving lines down and stuck one leg out of the buggy. "We'll just put it in the back, and you can come over and get it later."

Never. No. Mein Gott, help me now.

The good Lord must have had a spare moment of silence—long enough to hear my desperation, because Katie clattered around the corner at a spanking pace and drew up next to my mother's brother, effectively blocking him in. "*Guder mariye*, brother Gingrich. We'll only be in your way for a second."

I threw the bag of batting into the back of the closed buggy and scrambled onto the leather-covered bench next to her. "Nice to see you, *Onkel*."

"Enjoy your time together ..." He might have said more, but Katie slapped the reins over Schatzi's back and he took off so abruptly I had to grab the bench to keep from falling over.

"Why the hurry?" I asked her, hoping my relief and gratitude didn't show.

"We took longer than I thought over lunch. I promised Dat I'd have the buggy back by two." *Thank you, Gott.* "I hope your uncle didn't think I was rude."

"I'm sure he didn't. He was probably on his way somewhere anyway."

Why did I keep up the pretense, even with my best friend? The weight of silence pressed on my chest, demanding relief, but I could not give in. One didn't talk about one's family in public. Well, people did all the time, but not like this. It was one thing to remark that so-and-so must think her pickles were perfection because she served them at every single meal, or that if such-and-such cared as much about his barn as he did his cows, he would give it a coat of paint. It was quite another to hint that—

"Sophia, can I ask you something?"

"Of course." I was about to add, *Anything*, but closed my mouth before the lie escaped.

"Is it true about David Fischer?"

My spine sagged with the sudden release of tension. "What about him?"

She eyed me for a second. "Hm. Maybe it isn't, then."

With a sigh, I gave up trying to be cagey. "Yes, it is. He asked Dat if he could court me last week after meeting."

If she hadn't had the reins in both hands, and if we hadn't been trotting down the side of the highway, she'd have hugged me. As it was, she gave a squeal and shot a big grin my way. "That's wonderful good, Sophia! But why so quiet about it? I waited through a whole lunch and you didn't say a word. If Caleb had gone to my father, I'd have died of embarrassment and then run across two fields to tell you."

"And had the brethren on your doorstep for messing up their neat planting."

"But you know what I mean." She pulled Schatzi to a halt at the four-way stop that marked the halfway point, then flapped the reins over his back. "Don't you like him?"

"Of course I like him. But imagine if it were you. Don't you think it would be like courting Adam?" She made a face. "Exactly."

"Well, there's no rule that says you have to go with the first boy who asks you," she said at last. "I mean, if you really don't think it's right."

"But that's the part that's hard." The truth finally came boiling up. "I've known David my whole life. How can I hurt his feelings by saying I don't want to, especially when it's gotten out and people will be watching us?"

"Adam told me, but I don't think it's gone any further."

"But Gabriel Langford said—" I stopped and barely restrained myself from clapping a hand to my mouth.

Katie gave me the look I'd been dreading ever since he'd left us at the door of the Harvest Moon. "Now it comes out. Since when are you talking about such an interesting subject with Gabriel Langford?"

"I wasn't. Honest."

"If you don't tell me right now, I'm going to stop in that next driveway and we won't move until you do."

She would, too. And with my luck, the old wreck wouldn't start up again. "I'm telling you true. All he said was that he'd heard David would call him out for talking to me. It was a joke. But it still means the news is out."

"*Ja.*" She fell silent for a moment. "If any calling out is going to happen, it'll be your mother, if she hears you've been talking to a boy who isn't plain."

"I know," I said with a sigh. "I just hope no one but you saw him in town."

We crested the hill and our farm came into view behind the maples that lined the creek. "Thanks for the ride."

"I wasn't about to let your uncle take you," she said. "I'd never have gotten the story out of you then."

I breathed thanks to God for that. "See you Sunday at Singing. Supper is at our place, then we're all going to Millers'. Caleb said there might be a hundred—the Myerling gang is coming, and some from near Council Bluffs."

Schatzi's hoofbeats faded as he climbed out of the dip formed by the creek that ran along one side of our farm. I bumped the bag of batting down a lane that had never seemed quite this long before.

And then I wished it had been twice as long. My uncle's black buggy sat in the yard like a big ugly spider, his horse placidly cropping the grass next to the house. He had taken the short way here.

For about two seconds, I actually considered stashing the batting in the barn and taking off across the fields to Katie's. I'd probably get there right about when she did. But then sanity returned. Mamm knew when and with whom I was coming back, and if I didn't turn up, the questions would soon become impossible to answer. And with Gabriel thrown into today's mix, questions were the last thing I needed.

So. Daniel had survived the lion's den. I could survive five minutes in the kitchen. There were so many chores to be done that finding an excuse to escape would be easy.

I struggled in the back door with the bag, which meant that he jumped to his feet to hold the door. "*Danke, Onkel.*"

"You made it," he said, as if Katie's driving skills were so bad he wasn't sure he'd ever see me again. "Had enough girl talk, eh?"

"Katie had to get the buggy back to her dad. Mamm, where do you want this?"

"In the laundry room. Thanks for bringing it in. You could have saved Katie coming around the long way if you'd caught a ride back with Paul."

"I didn't want to put him out," I called from the hallway. "And Katie doesn't mind." I rolled the bag under the worktable, where Mamm's neat piles of fabric quarters told everyone she'd finished piecing another quilt. If only I could stay in here! "Mamm, do you want me to do this basket of ironing?"

"Eventually, but right now I need you to do something else."

The Lord's ear was turned toward me today. Maybe I should pray that Mamm and Dat would let me walk out with Gabriel after Sunday.

In the kitchen, I filched a cookie off the plate on the table. "What do you need?"

"I want you to go over to your uncle's place with him and fetch back my big speckled roaster. With the potluck here after meeting on Sunday I'll need it for the beef roast."

The bottom dropped out of my stomach. As if he'd read my mind, he smiled at me and said, "If I'd known your mother needed it, I'd have brought it with me."

"I'm glad you thought to drop in." Mamm smiled at him with affection as she sat across the table from him with her own cup of coffee.

For the hundredth time, I wondered why it was he who had stayed in Mitternacht, instead of their older brother Joseph, who had moved to an Old Order community in Ontario, far away in eastern Canada. Then I'd only have to see him once every couple of years, instead of—my mind shuddered away. "But aren't we going to wash the floors? You'll need me to help move the furniture."

"You're only going to the next place, Sophia, not to Mitternacht. If you leave now, you'll be back in half an hour."

"But we wanted to get it done before Dat and Caleb got home."

Mamm gave me The Look. "The longer you stop to talk, the less time we have. Your uncle is ready to leave."

Daniel survived the lions' den. I hadn't taken off my shawl yet, so there wasn't even a moment's respite, or a way to get out of the trap. "*Ja,* Mamm."

I'd barely got my feet into the buggy before he'd turned it around and we were trotting down the lane. "If we only have half an hour, we'd best hurry," he said, as if he thought I needed an explanation for his haste. But I didn't. I knew.

"She was serious," I said stiffly. "She expects me back in thirty minutes. Jonah will be home from school to help move the furniture. It will take all of us."

"I'm happy you can come for a visit. Too bad it can't be longer."

"We were there two Saturdays ago, helping *Aendi* Sallie clean for the potluck."

"*Ja, liewi*, but that was different."

I hated it when he called me that. I ground my teeth together and refused to speak for the rest of the short trip. My feet dragged on the kitchen steps as he opened the door and waved me into the house. As I passed him, his hand dropped from the air and I scooted out from under before he could touch me.

"Where's the roaster?"

"Your aunt put it in the oven to dry and forgot about it. When she went to do some baking she found it plenty hot." He still stood between me and the door.

"Where is it now?"

"Back in the oven, *liewi*."

Did he think that putting himself out to locate the pan in his own kitchen would make him guilty of doing women's work? I didn't want to turn my back on him, but the moments ticked loudly away in the silence. "Where is *Aendi* Sallie?"

"Visiting her sister up by Council Bluffs. I've been without a woman's sweet company since yesterday."

Now I knew why he'd come over. I could consider myself lucky that Mamm hadn't asked him to stay for dinner.

Hurrying now, I bent and pulled the black speckled roaster out of the oven, but I wasn't quick enough. His denim pants caught on the back of my dress as he pinned me against the oven door, and rucked it up several inches. "You've grown up into very sweet company," he whispered against the back of my *kapp*. My fingers tightened on the handles of the roaster. "Why don't you come over like you used to?"

"If you don't back away from me, I swear I will tell."

He actually had the gall to chuckle. "Now, what kind of unwomanly, disrespectful talk is that?" Slowly, he began to pull the ends of my shawl out of my apron. "You must take this off and stay."

"I'll tell Mamm." I forced the words out, suffocating. "You'll go before the church and be put out."

"And who will believe you?" He pulled the shawl from my shoulders and tossed it over the back of a chair. "You've never said a word before, like a good girl."

"I'm saying it now. Stop it! This is wrong. It must end. Today."

My hands on the cold burners, I tried to push away from the stove, but his weight against my back only grew heavier. "Stop talking like those *Englisch*. You don't want it to end. In fact, you've been coming to me all this time, trying to get me to go upstairs with you." Two large hands, rough with field work, bracketed my waist. "No one but me knows what a bad girl you are."

Too late, I saw my danger, and the blood ran cold under my skin. "You wouldn't dare."

His face was so close to my ear I could hear his breathing. Could hear the drag of his beard against the cape that covered my dress. "Who will be first to race to tell the bishop?" he whispered on a gust of onion breath, and his mouth touched my earlobe.

Something seemed to snap inside me. Talk would be useless. What I had dreaded, what had given me nightmares since the age of nine, would happen in the next twenty minutes—unless I stopped submitting and pretending and evading and did something.

But what? Revulsion crept on my skin with every breath he panted in my ear. I could not use violence, throwing an elbow or swinging the roaster for a weapon as though I were scuffling with Caleb in the barn. He would have me up before the bishop in a moment for violence. His hands moved over my chest and I twisted with a cry, arms crossing over my breasts instinctively, trying to force his away.

Help ... help me, mein Gott, please ...

"Paul? Sophia?" A voice that belonged to neither of us cut through the silence.

My uncle released me with a suddenness that made me gasp. In a blur, I snatched up my shawl and stuffed it in the roaster, pushing past whoever had come to the kitchen door. A hand reached out and grabbed me.

"Sophia? What's going on? Are you all right?"

Through a blur of tears as hot as shame, I saw Gabriel Langford's horrified eyes. I jerked out of his grip and practically fell down the steps into the cold air. I pelted across the yard, dodged between the barn and the garden fence, and lit out across the fields as if Satan himself were after me.

"Sophia! Wait!"

I'd run out of breath on the far side of the first field. In the distance, I could see the roofline of our barn, the trees that fringed the creek clouded with pale-green shoots. My entire being was focused on getting there and hiding, like a fox going to earth. The faint voice behind me goosed my steps back into a jog. I had to stay ahead of him. Facing him was impossible.

"Sophia, stop!"

The cold afternoon wind finally penetrated my clothes. I put the roaster down in the dirt and swung the shawl around me, pulling it so tight the pattern lengthened and distorted across my chest as I tucked the ends in. When I looked up again, Gabriel had crossed half the field, running flat out in my footsteps. Even in my extremity, I had run in the furrow between the rows of fresh planting. The thought of Dat's wrath kept me from spoiling his field.

And other things.

He was some runner, that Gabriel. But I was past appreciating the beauty of him. Anything I had once hoped for had crumbled into the dust of utter humiliation. I turned away, picked up the roaster, and trudged on. If running away didn't work, maybe if I made it clear I didn't want to talk to him, he'd give up.

"Sophia." His voice right behind me killed even that pathetic hope.

"Leave me alone."

"What *was* that?" He wasn't even breathing hard. His voice was as calm as if we were strolling on a lawn. Jogging the last few yards, he closed the gap.

"I don't know what you mean." Plod. Plod. The soil felt heavy on my shoes.

"I think you do. Please." He crossed into the next furrow so he could walk beside me. When I still refused to speak, he touched my arm.

I wrenched away, and hopped like an awkward crane across the rows to the windrow, where the hard ground under the poplars had never been broken by horse and plow. "I said, leave me alone!"

What did he expect from me? To fall into his arms and tell him everything? I couldn't bear for him to even look at me, much less speak. I had hoped my shameful secret would stay hidden behind closed eyes and closed doors. That no one would find out while I struggled to escape the trap my uncle had sprung.

I needed time. Time to hide and think, and he was taking even that away from me.

"I'll leave you as soon as you tell me that what happened in there wasn't what I think it was."

"It's none of your business."

Still keeping his boots in the prints my black oxfords had made, he joined me under the poplars. Their bare branches rustled overhead in the captious wind, whispering.

"I think you *are* my business," he said so softly it might have been a secret, told among the trees.

4

Goaded beyond control by dead dreams that insisted on resurrecting themselves and tormenting me, I turned on him. "Don't say that. Don't make fun of me. You can't be that cruel."

"I'm not making fun. Far from it. I want to know what he was doing that is making you so upset that you run away."

I set my mouth in a firm line that wouldn't let any words escape, and trudged on.

"All right, then, I'll say it. It was lucky Joshua Hodder sent me over to find out when your uncle wants me to whitewash his milking pen. Otherwise a terrible thing might have happened to you. Am I right?"

Had God prompted Joshua Hodder? Was He listening to my frantic prayers for help at last? And the price I had to pay was the loss of that look of delight in Gabriel's face when he set eyes on me? Because I hadn't once been able to look up. I kept my gaze averted, watching the poplars as they marched past on my right, one by one.

"Sophia, look at me." Gently, he took my arm and my feet stopped their mindless tromping in the direction of home. The roaster drooped from my fingers.

"I can't," I whispered.

Why do you bother? Go chase Rebecca Hodder with her rippling gold hair, or any other good plain girl who isn't covered in an old man's handprints. Whose soul isn't smeared with lies and omissions.

"Yes, you can." As gently as though he touched the defenseless back of a baby chick, he lifted my chin with a fingertip until I had no choice but to look into his face. The Bible says that the eyes are the windows of the soul—and in his case, the windows were wide open and the lamplight was blazing out.

Gabriel's gaze practically scorched my face. How was it possible for him to be so angry on my behalf—and yet so full of pain? Of sorrow, even? My lips trembled and I looked down, focusing on the top hook of his shirt. Why hadn't I worn my black visiting bonnet? At least its wide brim would have given me somewhere to hide.

"You must tell me if it's true," he said at last. "And then the bishop needs to know. You cannot let him get away with this."

I shook my head and tried to unblock the words backed up in my throat. "Nothing happened."

"And if I hadn't come over?"

"I can handle it my own way."

"This is a matter for the church, Sophia."

"What is?" I looked up, couldn't hold his gaze, and turned to look at the fields instead. "Nothing happened."

He made a sound of frustration. I knew I was being stubborn. But I had no choice. "Perhaps not now, this time. In any case, keeping silence is the same as telling a lie."

The sheer injustice of this goaded me to honesty. "What do you want me to say, Gabriel? We're meant to put the unity of the *Gmay* first. It would cause nothing but pain and shame in my family, not to mention a big scandal in the church. Do you want me to be the cause of that?"

"You aren't the cause," he said gently. "He is, with his wickedness and depravity."

"The result is the same. Besides, he'll just tell them I came to him." My own frustration trembled in my throat. "They'll listen to him. My uncle has been a deacon, before he moved here. The only reason he hasn't been elected to that place here is because the lot hasn't fallen on him."

"Maybe God is telling us he is not worthy."

"I'm not going to judge. I'm just going to stay away from him."

"And we saw how well that worked. You're a better person than I, it seems," he said, his voice rough with bitterness.

"No," I said sadly. That was impossible. "I'm just plain."

"And I'm not, is that what you're saying?"

"Well, you aren't, are you?"

"Not now, perhaps. But after Sunday I will be."

"I'll pray that God takes away your anger, then, Gabriel."

"You'd do better to pray that God would take away your uncle." Shocked, I stared at him. He seemed to realize all at once how bad it sounded. "He could send him on a trip."

"Maybe He will. He has His reasons for everything."

"You can't really believe God is allowing your uncle to—to do this to you. The Lord is not cruel. Especially not to the innocent."

"No," I said slowly. But whether He allowed it or not, it was happening. And had been for seven years—since the summer when Mamm and Dat had gone to be with Grossmammi when she died in Ohio. They'd left us kids with Paul and *Aendi* Sallie. That was the last summer I'd spent being a kid. Ever since, I'd felt like prey, except for the times I was in school or at home. But out in public? Nowhere was safe.

I'd become an expert at making sure I was hardly ever alone. The problem with this was that sometimes I liked to be alone. Mamm thought I liked gardening, for instance. I just didn't tell her that it was the only place for miles around that I could be outside and yet feel safe enough to be by myself.

And I did like it, now. The smell of the earth, the chickens hunting for worms and bugs in my wake, the sight of healthy green shoots coming up and responding to the sun—they calmed me and restored my belief in God's faithfulness.

"But all the same," I went on slowly, "it's God's will that we put Him and His church before ourselves. So that's what I'm doing."

A muscle flexed in his jaw and I realized he was trying to keep his words inside, where they could do no harm. But unsaid words could sometimes wound the person who wouldn't speak them.

"Thank you for caring about it, Gabriel," I said. "But please don't say anything. Promise me."

It took him a good two minutes to work up to it as we began to walk again. "All right," he said at last. "I promise. But I want you to promise me something in return."

We climbed the last swale, the trees along the creek the only barrier between us and my family's vigilant eyes. "I don't want Mamm to see you," I told him. "We have to say goodbye here."

He ignored me. "Promise me that if you need me, you'll call."

I raised an eyebrow at him. Sometimes he was just so *Englisch*. "How? None of us have phones, and if I needed someone, running to the pay phone up the road is the last thing I'd do."

"Call for me in your heart." Again, I had the sensation of falling into those deep, dark eyes. "I will hear you."

"That's very romantic, but not very practical."

"I mean it. Promise me."

Boys. Sometimes they just didn't make any sense. But it was clear he wasn't going to go until I did what he wanted. "Fine, I promise. Now, will you go?"

"I'll see you Sunday." He stepped away from me. "We will talk some more then."

If he were baptized, I wouldn't get within ten feet of him, the sea of *kapps* would be so deep. "Sure."

I turned away and kept my gaze on the safety of our yard. I didn't look back, even though I knew he stood there watching me go.

On Sunday, I couldn't look at my uncle as he shook the elders' hands. I turned away and found my seat among my friends, hoping I might blend into our crowd of black dresses and black shawls like a hen among its flock. While Mamm and I had cleaned the house from top to bottom on Friday and Saturday, Dat and Caleb and Jonah had been busy down at the meetinghouse with the other men, sweeping and polishing the floors and every single bench and lamp inside.

And now, the plain clapboard building had been transformed into a holy place, where the baptism would be performed. As we sang the first hymn, I let the very edge of my gaze wander from the familiar words in the hymnbook over to the men's side.

Though I was halfway back and he sat at the front, I could see a sliver of his profile. It was enough.

Meeting began at nine, and by eleven o'clock the bishop glanced at the others and I knew it was time. The service had that sense of anticipation, of consecration, that I sometimes felt during the twice yearly communion service, even if I wasn't baptized yet and couldn't partake. There was that same sense of holiness. *"This drink in remembrance of me."* The water and the blood purified His people—and today it would be the water in the culmination of many weeks of instruction.

Katie had seen Bishop Stolz and the two preachers walking up the Hodders' lane to meet with Gabriel and Joshua Hodder, who would stand in the place of a parent. Poor Gabriel. I could hardly imagine taking such an enormous step with none of my family around me. I mean, I knew he was an orphan; gossip had ferreted that out right away. But somehow it had never hit home to me that he was facing this experience with no one at his side—no mother blinking back tears, no father standing silently by as the bishop rehearsed the vows and took him through the Confession.

Bishop Stolz cleared his throat and I snapped back to attention. "Are there any here who are willing to take the step of baptism?"

Susanna Miller stood up. So did Katie's eldest brother William and two men in their twenties from Myerling whose names I couldn't remember. Some relation of the Millers, I thought. And then, just when I thought I would pass out, I remembered to breathe as Gabriel got to his feet, head bowed.

The bishop murmured something that must have been an instruction to kneel, because they sank to their knees in a row in front of him. Then he looked into each person's eyes. "Do you believe in the Almighty God, in Christ Jesus his Son, and in the Holy Spirit?"

"Y—" Gabriel coughed and tried again, his voice joining the others. "*Ja.*"

"Are you willing to renounce Satan and all his works, the world, and your own will, and promise to be true to God unto death?"

Now all five voices came strongly in unison. "*Ja.*"

The elder took a breath. "Are you willing to submit yourself to scripture, and to all the rules of the church, even unto death?"

"*Ja,*" they said as one.

I felt my own throat closing as practical considerations faded and tears began to swim in my eyes. I blinked them back. I didn't want to miss a single moment.

He stepped toward Gabriel and cupped his hands over his head. I craned my neck to see between people's heads, risking Mamm's disapproval at being so nosy and forward.

"Upon your faith, which you have confessed, you are baptized in the name of the Father—" One of the deacons poured a little water from a pitcher into his hands, which trickled onto Gabriel's head. "—the Son—" More water. "—and the Holy Spirit." A final stream of water poured through his hands, where I imagined it splashing over Gabriel's wet hair and soaking into his shirt. "Amen."

Then the woman in front of me shifted on the bench and I could no longer see. I heard the elder say the same words to each of the others, and heard the water gurgling out of the pitcher in the dead silence. Quietly, the bishop's wife made her way to join her husband, and stood in front of Susanna Miller. Bishop Stolz held out a hand and said loudly enough for even the people at the back to hear, "In the name of the Lord and the Brethren, I extend the right hand of fellowship to you. Rise up."

Thank goodness! This part I could see. As the elder shook Gabriel's hand and kissed him, Fraa Stolz gave the same words to Susanna, lifted her up, and gave her the holy kiss as well. The bishop did the same for the three remaining men, and then it was done.

Gabriel was now my brother in Christ, and a full member of our church. For those moments, all I could think of was how shiny and clean his soul must feel. And then, as the final hymn ended and the bishop dismissed us, the thing I had feared began to happen.

The flood of white organdy *kapps* began flowing toward the front of the barn, like moths to a burning flame. And really, who could blame them? Some things were inevitable—the swing of the sun through the sky; the turn of the seasons, the falling of leaves.

The bishop may as well have ended the service by declaring hunting season officially open.

And now I am made new.

I have been baptized before, of course, but neither the Church of England nor the Episcopalian Church of New York are like this. After decades of running and searching on three continents, I believe God has finally led me to the place where He wants me. Here, among plain people who live in a way I was once used to, I can serve Him. I will give the gift of life back to Him daily.

He has also given me a revelation. It was not by accident that Joshua Hodder sent me to the Gingrich farm on Thursday. The Lord's timing is perfect, and because of it I think I now know the secret wound she carries—that thing that blots out her light with its evil.

I am filled with holy fire as we drive to the Brucker home for lunch. I can hardly contain it as I move among His people, smiling and shaking hands, but I must. *Vengeance is mine, saith the Lord.* And I am His instrument, guided by His hand.

Wait. There she is. Barely. It angers me that he has made her look so ... diminished. She works with her group of friends, setting plates and dishes of food out on tables as though she truly believes she is invisible. Am I the only one who sees her? Who understands the fierce, loyal spirit banked behind those meek and downcast eyes? Another thing we have in common.

Ah. There he is. Her uncle stands by the barn door, conversing with the men as they unhitch their horses, while looking at none of them. He is watching her.

And she knows it.

She is hiding in plain sight.

Now that I think about it, she has become very good at that. I never see her alone. She is always with someone—family, friends. David Fischer told Adam that this was one of the things that had prevented him from speaking for months. How can you declare yourself to someone who is never alone? And sending a message through one of her friends would just result in a gale of giggles and ribbing.

He was finally forced to go to her father, who at least could be trusted to keep his mouth shut on such a personal subject.

I don't think I need go to her father. I have found her alone twice already. Is the connection between us—the mutual knowledge of her secret—enough to dispense with these social obligations? God has made His will clear to me. I am not sure of her, though. She was so angry with me. Will that send her running to David, who is as uncomplicated as a piece of string—and as perceptive?

I take my place at the table. She will not sit; she is busy serving and will probably eat after everyone else has finished. I'm glad the newly baptized do not sit in some special place near the elders. That would be prideful. I do not feel proud—on the contrary, I feel humble and clean, and filled with the knowledge of God's will. That certainty is like a cup of cold, clear water on a hot day.

Part of me wants to sit with the men, close enough to Paul Gingrich to hear him talking. Close enough to keep an eye on him. But on the other hand, hearing his hypocrisy and knowing that he wants to stare at her would just make me so angry it would splinter my sense of peace.

Because I am at peace.

As I find a place with the young men who have accepted me into their circle, I know what I must do.

He laughs at something someone has said. He should laugh. He will be serving God in a way he never dreamed of.

His will be done.

5

That Sunday was the hardest I'd ever spent. After the emotional few days I'd had, culminating in the baptism service, the meal afterward was like being on a rope swing—and falling off right at the top of the arc. Despite the fact that there were at least a hundred people at the long tables outside, I could feel my uncle's gaze on me. I hated that he had the upper hand. With his standing in the district, and the simple fact that he was a man of property and I was a girl of, well, nothing, the bishop would believe him, no questions asked.

By dinnertime, most of the adults had hitched up their buggies and headed home. But our lane was still crowded with the buggies of the *Youngie*, who would have supper at our place before we all headed over to

Millers' for the Singing. The spring day had decided to take back its warmth, so the boys moved the trestle tables into our big living room. The women had washed the lunch dishes earlier, so while Katie and Rebecca raced each other down each side of the tables, seeing who could set out the neat row of plates the fastest, I went out to the root cellar to get a couple of jars of Mamm's beet pickles.

I found Adam Hertzfeld and David out there on the back lawn, deep in discussion. They looked up when I ran down the porch steps with a flashlight. "Hi, Sophia."

"Hi, David. Adam, Katie was looking for you. She says the apple pie she made is under the seat in your buggy, and could you bring it in for her."

With a cocky grin, he nodded. "Why don't you walk over there with me? I want to show you what I did to it."

"Adam—" David began.

"Would you relax? I'm not going to steal your girl."

Even in the last light of day, I could see poor David hunch his shoulders in embarrassment. "I didn't mean that."

"Sophia wants to see. Right, Sophia?"

"See what? I have to get some pickles out of the cellar."

"It'll only take a minute. And you've got a flash. That's even better."

Adam could be as persistent as an alarm clock, and the more you ignored him, the louder he got. "All right. I guess I can get the pie while I'm at it. David, are you coming?"

"I don't like what he's done," David mumbled. "I'll pass."

That didn't sound very good. A minute later, I saw what he meant as I gaped at the interior of Adam's buggy. "What on earth?"

"Isn't it great?" He sounded so proud as I played the flashlight beam over the burgundy velvet interior, which had been tacked so that the stereo speakers set flush in the walls could be covered with a pair of matching curtains. "It plays CDs, too, not just the radio. The whole thing runs on a battery pack under the seat."

Katie had never said a word. Maybe this was as much of a surprise to her as it was to me—or maybe she was avoiding the subject out of embarrassment. I mean, Adam had never had a reputation for being studious and devout, but this was something else. Something I'd never expected, even from him. "So you're going on *Rumspringa*, hey? What do your parents say?"

"What can they say? I haven't been baptized yet, and I used my own money. They gave me this buggy a year ago, but it took me this long to plan out what I wanted to do with it."

"I thought you gave your wages to your dad."

"Most of them. But it's me who's putting in the work at the RV factory, so I should get to keep some of it, at least."

That wasn't why Adam had gone to work in that factory in Myerling. It was because the farm was going to his older brother, and he had to have a way to support himself if he was going to look for a wife. Of course, the kind of girl who would go riding in a souped-up buggy like this probably wasn't wife material anyway.

"What do you think, Sophia?" David's voice came out of the trees. The grass whispered against his boots as he joined us. "Think you'll want to go riding with Adam now?"

"I think that he's been spending way too much time learning to upholster dining units." I gave the plushy, padded wall a push with my hand and ignored the second question, which didn't deserve a reply. "Did you do this yourself?"

"Of course. But I had to order that material from Council Bluffs. You don't find red velvet like this in Borchardt's."

"I guess not."

"So, Sophia, want to go over to Furniss with me next weekend? I hear there's a hoedown happening."

Something in the tone of his voice told me this was less an invitation to me than a challenge to David—and I'd had just about enough of being used for one week, thank you.

"I wouldn't be caught dead at a hoedown, Adam Hertzfeld, and you know it." Who wanted to drive all that way just to get drunk and pass out? Ugh.

"Is that because you're afraid to be cool?"

I shone the flashlight in his face, and the smirk fell off his mouth as he squinted and batted at my hand. "Yeah—I'm afraid to be so cool I freeze to death in a muddy field, you idiot. Everyone knows what goes on at those hoedowns. I'd rather go to Singing with my friends."

"You'd rather chase Gabriel Langford with your friends, you mean." Beside me, David sucked in a breath through his nose, but his mouth stayed firmly shut. Adam shot him a glance filled with contempt. "You've got your work cut out for you if you want to take this one home," he said.

"Sophia can make up her own mind," David said finally. "Just because she turned you and your fancy buggy down, doesn't mean she's chasing ... anybody else."

"I'm standing right here," I informed them. "You don't need to talk about me like I'm not."

"I just meant—" David began.

"Sophia!" My mother stood on the front veranda, her hands on her hips. "Sophia, what happened to the pickles?"

"Coming, Mamm," I called. Then I looked back. I was never going to have anything with Gabriel Langford. It had been a long shot before. Now that he knew my secret, all I wanted to do was hide myself away from those deep eyes that saw far too much. So I took the plunge. "David, maybe you'd have room in your buggy for one extra on the way home from Millers'?"

I didn't need the flashlight to see the smile that broke out on his face.

Because planting was in full swing and people would have to be up and at work early the next morning, there weren't as many kids from away as there would be, say, in January. But the Millers' basement room was still full of at least eighty of us, boys at one long table and girls at the other. Some of those had heard about Adam's buggy and had stayed outside to listen to worldly music. Dan Hodder, one of Rebecca's cousins, finally started singing without them in hopes that they'd hear us through the open ground-level windows and straggle in.

I didn't care two hoots about Adam or his silly buggy. What was the point of having something that was neither plain nor worldly? It didn't fit in your world or anyone else's. What I cared about was right in this room. Gabriel sat halfway down the table, across the narrow aisle from Rebecca. If he wanted to, he could lean back and speak to her. I tried not to look, but I couldn't help noticing how pale he was. Wasn't he feeling well? Or was it just the effects of a long, emotional day?

David followed the direction of my gaze and parked himself on his bench, practically back to back with me. A second later, a couple of the girls put their heads together and pointed it out to their friends. By morning, the word would have raced all the way to Myerling that Gabriel was courting Rebecca and David was courting me.

The very thought made me focus on the words in the hymnbook as if I were trying to memorize it a syllable at a time. Then, on the second verse of *"Gin flottes Leben fuhren wir,"* my fear took form. Gabriel leaned back and whispered something in Rebecca's ear. She smiled and I missed a high note. Then she elbowed him gently into his place, and I missed another one. Katie gave me a look over the top of her book and I practically drilled a hole through the pages of mine, I stared at it so hard.

How much more proof do you need that you were a fool to nurture your little hopes?

The fragile green shoots shriveled up in the cold wind of reality. It wasn't even the fact that he knew my secret. I'd fully expected him to disappear out of my life because of it. And half of me wanted him to disappear. But on top of it, gossip was right. Rebecca Hodder had him sewn up before he was even out of the bag, and that public little show was the knot in the end of the thread.

My singing dried away to a whisper, and then I just mouthed the words while my throat swelled painfully. I would not cry in front of everyone. And don't think it was pride. Not at all. What did I have to be proud of? But Gabriel didn't need to know how much he'd hurt the part of me that loved his smile, either.

By the time David leaned back during the third verse of *"O Gott Vater, wir loben Dich"* and whispered, "Think I should go get Adam?" I'd made up my mind. I nodded, knowing full well everyone would think he was whispering sweet nothings and I was agreeing to some secret meeting later. Let them think that. They could think we'd be opening the couch for all I cared. It would serve them right. At least someone thought I was good enough for him.

When Joanna Miller and her sisters began laying out bowls of chips and dip, and plates full of cut-up vegetables, the Singing ended and we trooped upstairs. Conversation and laughter rose to fill the high-ceilinged rooms. Someone told a joke and I laughed as if it was the funniest thing I ever heard. One of the new ones, Will Esch, said his dad had given him his horse and buggy yesterday, the day after his sixteenth birthday, and I smiled until my cheeks bunched. Oh yes, I was the life of the party, and there was David, hovering around me like a hummingbird around a honeysuckle vine, smiling as if everything I said was the cleverest thing he'd ever heard.

Pretending you don't care sure can make your face hurt.

I used to like going to Singing. But if they were all going to be like this until Gabriel and Rebecca put us out of our misery and had their wedding date published, then I'd find something else to do on Sunday nights. Maybe I'd change my tune and go to that hoedown with Adam—it was far enough away to be interesting and maybe I'd even try a drink of alcohol. At least then my life would contain one thing completely unconnected with Gabriel Langford.

"Ready to go?" David said beside me.

"Sure." I'd been ready since the second hymn.

We made our *denkes* to the Millers, who had stayed out of sight in the kitchen in order to let their daughters act as hostesses. At least ten pairs of eyes watched us out the front door—and then David held the door for me on top of it. Why hadn't he just gone and got the buggy? Did he have to make this huge public statement about it? Because the only thing it would get both of us was—

"There go the lovebirds!" Adam called, cracking up the rest of his friends. "David, want some advice on what to do next?"

"Watch yourself, Sophia," Cara Troyer called, hardly able to keep her face straight. "He doesn't have a courting buggy. You know what could happen in a closed one."

"Are you kidding?" Caleb hollered. "That's his dad's. Nothing's going to happen in that old thing."

"Ewwwww!" chorused a bunch of girls led by Cara, right on cue.

I couldn't take it. I ran down the steps and along the lane. Which was his? Who cared? Skip the buggy—skip David—I could walk home.

"Sophia, wait!"

Another day, another boy to run away from. I slowed, my oxfords crunching on the gravel as I turned to let him catch up. "Next time, just go get the horse and I'll meet you at the road." This wasn't how courting was supposed to be. It should be like when Gabriel carried the batting for me, all light and incandescence and anticipation.

Not ... like a balloon leaking air, leaving you flat and worn out.

"Sorry," he said. "But they'll do it anyway. Better here than at meeting, I suppose." He pulled up the horse next to where I stood. "Hop in."

Well, that answered that question. I wasn't going to be handed into the buggy like a queen anytime soon. I hopped in, tucking my skirt around me with way more attention that it deserved. David flapped the lines and we rolled out onto the road.

"What's his name?" I nodded at the roan.

"Roan. He's my dad's. We couldn't afford a courting buggy."

"That's okay. After all that, I'd be too embarrassed to ride in it. I wish people would mind their own business."

"They don't mean anything by it. It's all in good fun."
He didn't look like he was having fun. I stole a glance at
him. Poor David. I wasn't being much of a companion. In
fact, he was probably wondering where this self-centered,
depressing girl had come from.

So I couldn't have what I wanted. Who did I think I
was to take it out on him? It wasn't his fault that he was
simply the person he'd always been.

"So," I said in a topic-changing tone, "have you and
your father got all the planting done?"

He sat a little straighter. "Yes. The warm weather
we've had the last couple of days has really helped."

"I didn't think our yard would ever dry up, but the
damp seems to have gone out of it since Wednesday."
The day I'd met Gabriel in town. *Stop thinking about
that.* He guided Roan around the right turn at the stop
sign, and in the night's silence I could hear the creek
rushing. Roan set a good pace. We were nearly home.

I'd heard of companionable silences. But this just
seemed awkward. What was wrong with me? I'd known
David my whole life. Why couldn't I think of a single
thing to talk about? A person couldn't discuss the
weather indefinitely on their very first drive home with a
boy. Did this happen with every couple?

I bet it wouldn't with Gabriel.

Stop it.

Roan trotted up our lane and David pulled him up in
the yard. Obligingly, the light in my parents' room went
out. If I hadn't been so uncomfortable, I'd have smiled.

David cleared his throat. "Well, here we are."

"Thank you for the ride."

"Maybe we can do the same from the volleyball game Friday."

"Oh, is there one? Where?"

"Cara said to put the word out it's at their place. If it rains, they'll set up in the barn, but it should stay nice until then."

The barn. Where the cow had died. What was Cara thinking? Hastily, I dragged my thoughts back to the weather. "I'll let Katie and the rest of the girls know." I hopped down. "And it would be nice to ride together. Thanks again. Good night."

"Good night, Sophia."

I should be grateful for small mercies. At least he hadn't tried to kiss me.

Now that I know how I am to serve God and promote the peace of the community He has brought me to, my only task is to choose a time and place. If it is far away, I possess transportation. If it is close by, I need only opportunity. I have to think carefully.

Fortunately, there is a rhythm to this work that helps to calm my mind. Dip the brush in the bucket of whitewash. Slap it along the boards of the milking pen. Catch the drips along the bottom. Repeat.

It will need to be soon. Already I can feel the desperate humming in my veins—the dullness in my thinking—the weakness that I hate. This practical side of eternal life is something I've had to accept, but I've never quite become used to it. It is a simple fact of biology that blood cells die.

My metabolism may be altered from what it was before, but the engine that drives it—my blood—needs to be replenished at intervals with living cells that this immortal body does not seem to produce on its own.

I am not sure how this plays into the promise of the Revelation, but I must accept His will for me and do the best I can. I have learned that the strength and renewal I feel from the blood of a cow does not come close to that of a human being. I had known the two substances were different—but knowing and experiencing that difference are two separate things.

For many years I could not bring myself to break the sixth commandment. I would try to renew my inner man with the blood of small creatures—even descending in despair to the rodents in the bowels of the ship during the sea crossing from Southampton to New York a century ago. But it soon became clear that if I was to serve God in the way He wanted, being reduced to hunting like a hyena at night in alleyways because I no longer had the strength to go out in the daytime was not conforming to His will.

That first taste of human blood was unforgettable— the heat, the rush of strength, the tingle that crested deep inside as my very tissues flushed crimson with health. After that, I fell to my knees and begged forgiveness for my blindness and unwillingness.

I still make mistakes. The blood of the leukemia patient at the sanatorium in Connecticut laid me flat for a week. And I learned the hard way not to leave the empty husks where they could be found too easily, and to have reliable transportation close at hand. Those were difficult years of abrupt departures and manhunts—until I found

His earthly kingdom, His saints scattered in their quiet communities across many states. Even yet, I struggle with the sixth commandment on those bright days when I see His people going about their work, glorifying God with each task they do. How can I be the death of one of these lambs?

And here, in the milking pen, the answer comes to me. I am not responsible for the death of His lambs. I'm responsible for the death of the wolf that circles the door of the sheepfold, seeking to devour and destroy for his own selfish purposes. Where there are sheep, there will always be wolves to prey on them.

I know my mission now.

As though my thoughts conjure him out of thin air, I hear the crunch of rubber boots on the gravel, and Paul Gingrich joins me in the barn. "*Wie geht's*, young Gabriel?"

"It's going very well." I keep my tone low, respectful. I try not to look at him directly, to challenge the wolf. He knows I saw something in his kitchen, though he will not ask. He has kept his conversations strictly on the subject of whitewash and my work habits since I began this job. "I should be finished by tomorrow afternoon."

"I've heard you're a good worker, but maybe that's just to impress the girls, hey?"

The words are genial, but his eyes are not. I have seen too much of this world to be baited. "I like to work."

"Do you? Be careful it doesn't make you proud. God put us on this earth to labor for our bread."

"So He did."

"There will be no prideful ways on this farm. No shirking of work. Like when you ran off the other day."

This is the second time he has brought it up. I answer as I did before. "I hadn't actually started work, Paul. Joshua Hodder just sent me over to get instructions."

"Then you should have done as he asked you, not come strolling back hours later when I was in the middle of milking. I don't know what you were used to before, but this is a good plain farm. I don't hold with fancy *Englisch* ways."

Again, I ignored the bait. "I'm sorry."

"You're as thoughtless as that niece of mine. Making her friend drive her home when it would have been sensible to come home with me. Wasting her mother's time."

So he really does intend to talk about her. Shall I play with him a bit? Make him afraid? He is blustering and stupid, pawing at the ground, but even a wolf knows when it's in danger. Under his hat, I again glimpse the light in his eyes—the eyes of a hunted creature convinced that it is the hunter.

"Perhaps she wanted to ride with her friend." My tone is mild. Innocent. "Girls do."

"What do you know about girls, hey?" he demands. "Thinking of getting married?"

"Some day."

"If you're thinking of our Sophia, you'd best think again. She'll have none of your fancy ways."

"I'm plain now."

"On the surface, maybe, but it's clear to any man you don't understand humility or order. You just stay away from my niece."

"I think it's for her to say."

His eyes practically bug out under his black brows. "What did you say to me?"

"I didn't realize you were deaf. I'll speak up."

Hot blood floods his face. I swallow with need and look away, and he takes it as fear. My muscles tense, so that when he crowds me against the newly whitewashed wall, I don't actually brush the wet paint. Despite my hunger and weakness, I am immovable, and this only serves to madden him further.

"You watch your tongue with me, boy," he growls, his face so close a fleck of spit lands on my cheek. "A word from me will put her family on guard about you, and then you'll never have a chance with her. In fact, I'll just tell her mother what an insolent, disrespectful boy you are. What a disgrace for a person who's only been baptized for a day."

Our eyes lock and I fight to keep my expression neutral. He does not know that his time as the hunter is over.

IMMORTAL FAITH

6

The light woke me.

For a second I lay and stared at the ceiling of my room, wondering what was different and why I'd come out of a dead sleep so easily, as though someone had stood next to me and called my name. Usually my mother had to shake me by the shoulder to wake me for milking. Then I saw it. A circle of light played across the ceiling and danced down the side of the dresser my *Grossdaadi* had made for his bride before their wedding.

I threw back the covers and ran to the side of the window, where I could see, but whoever was out there couldn't see my white nightgown. It was after three, the night impenetrable in the way it had before the world turned toward the sun. I'd heard about courting couples, of course, and how the girl would leave a lantern in her window so the boy would know she was waiting for him. While her parents supposedly slept, they could talk in the kitchen for hours and no one would say a word.

But it had never happened to me. And I wasn't sure how I felt about running to answer when some boy called. I mean, doing that might say more than I intended, if it were the wrong boy. What if it was David out there, come back for the kiss I'd denied him last night?

What if it wasn't?

There comes a time in every girl's life when she just has to take a risk.

I pulled up the sash as quietly as I could, thankful that it hadn't been painted shut like the one in my sister Hannah's room, when she'd been caught sneaking out once too often.

The light flashed under the cherry tree. "Who's that?" I whispered as loudly as I dared. Mamm and Dat slept at the end of the hall, on the other side of the house, but my mother could hear a whisper through two walls, and that was a fact.

I swear, an eternity passed in the next second. Was it David? Or ...?

"Gabriel," came the quiet reply. "Can you come down?"

I drew back without answering, though my body wanted to shout Yes! to the whole world. I closed the window and flung my shawl over my nightie, then snatched up my shoes and ran on tiptoe down the hall. Past the boys' room, down the stairs—skipping the third and seventh from the top, which squeaked—through the kitchen, and out the back, holding the screen door carefully so it wouldn't slam.

On the ground outside, I rammed my feet into my shoes, then crossed the lawn to the cherry tree. "Where are you?"

"Here." His pale shirt swam into my night vision, and the starlight glinted off his teeth as he smiled. "I wasn't sure you'd come."

"Why did you?"

"Because I had to."

I stopped myself from throwing my arms around him—barely. As it was, I sort of hitched toward him and then halted, grateful that the dark had hidden it. "What will Rebecca think of that?" How cool I sounded. I surprised myself.

"Why would she care?" When I didn't answer, he chuckled. "Come, Sophia. You don't really think she has a say in what I do."

Oh, sure. And not thinking that had kept me awake most of Sunday night. "Everyone thinks you two are courting."

"Then everyone would be wrong. It's not her cherry tree I'm standing under, is it?"

"No." I finally allowed myself to smile and be glad he was there. "So you couldn't help yourself, huh?"

"I needed to know you're not still angry with me."

What had happened to the pain and loss of the last two days? They seemed to have dissipated the way the fog does when the sun burns through, simply because he was standing in front of me, solid and real. "No," I said at last. "I'm not angry."

"That's good. Because now your uncle has forbidden me to see you."

I jerked my head up, still swimming against the urge to put my arms around him. "What? What business is it of his?"

"He seemed to think you were his business. I have a feeling it was all about that nothing you told me was going on."

"I don't want to talk about him." That would ruin everything. Maybe it already had. My heart had begun to pound, and the spring air felt thick in my throat. I took a step back toward the house.

"Hey." His hands settled on my upper arms, and I felt a jolt—as though he'd run across a carpet scuffing his feet before he touched me. "We won't. We have much more interesting things to talk about than a sour old man who didn't get to live out his dreams."

"What?"

But he'd already turned, his hand sliding down my arm, trailing electricity as it went, to take mine in a firm grip. His fingers interlocked with mine as though we were meant to fit together that way, his on top, mine trustingly below, palm to palm. His skin felt hot—alive—as though he'd been working instead of sleeping before he'd come to me. With a grin, he said, "Come on. Let's walk and watch the sun come up."

"That won't be for hours yet."

"You say that like it's a bad thing."

That surprised a laugh out of me, and I skipped a step to keep up with his long-legged stride. My eyes had adjusted to the dark now, and the freshly seeded field seemed bright under the setting half-moon. That meant I could see him better—the smile he couldn't seem to keep off his face, the bounce in his step. Energy pulsed between us—or at least, it seemed that way to me. Maybe it was completely one-sided. All in my imagination. I needed to find out.

"Gabriel, have you had good news? Is that why you're so awake in the middle of the night?"

With a laugh, he squeezed my hand. "I'm just glad to be with you."

Not one-sided. Oh, the relief! Did he really mean it? Was it possible?

"That's quite a compliment, but that can't be all of it."

He shook my hand, waggling it back and forth between us. "I feel really good. Energized, as the *Englisch* say. I'm happy and I'm with a pretty girl under the moon. Isn't that enough?"

He thought I was pretty! And he actually had the nerve to say so aloud. What a wonder. "Goodness. You'll make my head swell, and then I won't be able to get back into my room."

His smile dimmed, as though someone had turned down the flame in a lamp a quarter turn. "It would be impossible for you to be proud. Even though you have the most reason to be, you're not. Sometimes you're so modest you disappear altogether."

"You say that like it's a bad thing," I quoted back at him. I didn't know whether to be pleased—because that would be vain—or embarrassed. I touched my hot cheek. Well, then. Embarrassed.

"It's not a bad thing. It's one of the things that makes you special." He squeezed my hand again, and we began to climb the rise out of the creek bottom, toward the windbreak of poplars where we'd walked the other day.

How strange these fields looked at night. How mysterious, hiding secrets even in broad acres of moonlight. It could almost be a different country. A country where we were the only creatures with life singing in our veins, one with the stars and with the seeds stirring deep under the soil. A country where a girl could actually feel special, for a little while.

"So how was the ride home with David?" he asked, when we reached the windbreak and were strolling slowly along the track.

"Jealous?" Was that flirting? I hadn't known I could even do it. But teasing him felt so natural—in a very nonsisterly way.

"Fiercely," he said with mock solemnity. "I hope you had a miserable time."

"Oh, I did. He didn't even kiss me good night."

"An opportunity lost." I giggled, tickled at the way he spoke. "What?"

"You sound like a book. Most boys would have been like the *Englisch* and said, 'What a loser.'"

"The result of a classical education, I'm afraid."

"I don't even know what that is."

"Latin, Greek, lots of literature."

Goodness. Even in the *Englisch* high school, they didn't teach things like that. Or so I'd read in the paper. "Really? Were you in university in your old life?"

"For a while."

A couple of years ago, I had wanted to go to high school, to learn more and read thicker books and be able to talk with people about more than planting and putting up vegetables. But I'd put that desire on the altar of sacrifice and reminded myself that my place was here, among my family and the people of God. But Gabriel had obviously been to high school, and more—to university. Did he think I was stupid for not even knowing what a classical education was? My face heated again. "How old are you, Gabriel?"

He hesitated. "Nineteen. I would have been twenty in June."

"Would have been?" I may not know much, but at least I knew my tenses. "You still can be. It's a month away."

"So it is."

"But you didn't go to school around here. You sound—I mean, you have a little accent."

"I was born in England."

Ah. That explained why he didn't sound like us—not that *Deitsch* is easy to pick up if you don't grow up with it. He had traveled. Seen world. All this on top of his education. Could any two people be more different? "So are there plain churches in England, too?"

"At the time, there might have been. I don't know about now. I was just glad to find the people here. I finally feel as if I fit in somewhere."

"Lucky you." Oh, dear. Had I really said that out loud? And how could a well-traveled man fit in here, in tiny Mitternacht, Iowa?

"Don't you feel that way? You've grown up here."

"I used to." Before I turned nine. And there lay the biggest difference between us.

"What changed?"

I pushed through the branches of the windbreak and emerged in my uncle's hay field. "Look. The hay is already as high as my ankles." The fronds of meadowsweet, grass, and stray alfalfa that had blown over from our field brushed my bare calves in cold greeting.

"Sophia."

"I said I don't want to talk about it, Gabriel."

"I know. I'm sorry. I don't want to make you unhappy."

"Then let's talk about something else."

"May I just say one thing?" He came up beside me and reclaimed my hand.

"One. And then we talk about the weather, *ja?*"

He didn't laugh. Didn't even smile. Instead, he reeled me in, sliding his hands up my arms and pulling me against his chest. Pictures—memories—flashed in the dark, blocking out even his face. I stiffened. "*Neh.*" I got my hands up against his shirt and pushed. "No."

Without a word, he did as I asked. "I just want you to know that I would never do anything to hurt you."

I didn't know what to say. Was this some variation on This is going to hurt me more than it hurts you?

"Do you believe me?"

I turned away and pretended to watch the moon fall slowly toward the horizon while I breathed, waiting for my heart to slow down. *Gabriel's arms. Not his. Don't let him spoil this the way he's spoiled everything else.*

"Even if you don't, I mean it. I want to protect you. To keep anyone from hurting you and dimming that light in you."

"I appreciate the thought, Gabriel." Even if action was impossible.

"It's more than a thought. Or even a promise."

"Can we not discuss it?" He let out a long breath at my hard-headedness. "Tell me about England."

"Why?"

"Because I've never met anyone from there before. And because I like to hear you talk. What place did you grow up in?"

"All right. You win. I was born in Surrey at Langford, my family's estate, but I was sent to school in London when I was eight, at a place called Sparrow Hill."

"All by yourself?"

"There were two hundred other boys there," he replied in a dry tone.

I couldn't believe it. "Your family sent you to school in some strange city all on your own? A little boy?"

He took two steps. Three. "My parents went with me before the term began. And you have to understand, it was normal then, for people in our position."

"Rich people, you mean?"

"I suppose you could say that."

"Where are your parents now?" Then I remembered. "Oh, Gabriel, I'm sorry. That was stupid. What I meant was, how long have you been without them?"

"Years. The winter was very hard in my second year at Oxford, and they both died of pneumonia."

"Really? That would have been the winter before last?"

He looked at me, but his face was half shadowed in the dark. "Is that all it's been? It seems like centuries to me."

"I'm so sorry. I guess no matter how good the doctors are, sometimes they just can't help people in certain situations, can they?"

"No. What about you? Have you always lived here?"

"Born and raised. But our family has moved around a little. My mother's other brother went to a settlement in Ontario, and he's promised that I can come visit someday. But it's a long way." I veered away from the subject of Mamm's brothers. "You must miss them. Your parents, I mean."

"Sometimes." Easily, he let me do the veering. "Christmas is the worst. I can't tell you how glad I was to be at Hodders' this year. It gave me some happy memories to overlay the old ones."

"I love Christmas. Mamm and Hannah and I used to bake and cook for weeks beforehand. One year I made shortbread and—"

"Who's Hannah?"

I realized too late that the rush of memory had carried me out into deep waters. "My older sister."

"I didn't even know you had an older sister. Where is she? Or is she—Sophia, I'm sorry. Did she die?"

"Only as far as Dat is concerned. She's in Council Bluffs. She moved there when she was running around and she just ... hasn't came back."

"Are you in contact with her?"

"Oh, yes. She owes me a letter." And my reply would be a lot thinner than some of them. Suddenly my life was full of things I couldn't talk about.

"But your dad shuns her? She's not under the ban, is she?"

"No, of course not. She was never baptized. But Dat has stopped talking about her, and Mamm doesn't ask me if I've had a letter in front of him anymore. She only does it when we're alone in the kitchen, or when we're doing laundry."

"So she doesn't write to her, either?"

"She used to, but I think she made Hannah feel pretty guilty about not choosing the church, you know? I think Hannah got offended, and then the letters stopped coming."

"That's too bad. I'm glad you're still in contact with her, anyway. Leaving the door open if she wants to come back."

It was nice of him to put it that way. "I don't think she will. She has an *Englisch* boyfriend and drives a car, and she's taking classes at that college there."

Somehow we'd come to a stop at the high point in the hay field without me realizing that I was no longer moving. He said, "Do you ever want those things?" very quietly.

"I don't know." When he said nothing, just waited, I filled the silence. "I don't want Dat refusing to say my name." Which wasn't much of an answer, but it was the best I could do.

"I wouldn't, either." He almost sounded relieved. Did where I stood with the church matter to him that much?

I mean, he was newly baptized. I suppose the new ones want everyone to make the same choice they have. It would probably be my choice, too, eventually. The safe choice.

I took a breath. "Look." Over the top of Katie's father's hill off to the east, a line of gray was beginning to form where the sky met the fields. "The sun will be up soon. Don't you need to be back for milking?"

"We have a few minutes yet."

"Maybe from the Hodders' point of view, but not from my father's. He's up at first light, and if he finds me out in the yard in my nightie, it won't be very easy to explain."

He laughed, and when I swatted him—it might be funny to a man, but not to me—he put an arm around my shoulders and gave me a squeeze. "All right. We'll go back. If we run into your father, I'll do the talking."

The walk back over the fields seemed to take only seconds. I suppose it always does when you're trying to hang onto every moment and impress it on your memory so you don't forget a single thing. The scent of crushed grass, the crisp tang of unwarmed air, a whiff of cotton and soap as his body temperature rose with the exercise and carried it to me.

With a tingly feeling of relief, I saw that the lantern hadn't yet been lit in my parents' room. Best to keep our voices low, though, just in case.

"Well, good morning," I whispered, turning to him as we came to a stop where we'd started, under the cherry tree.

"Good morning. When can I see you again?"

"Gabriel, you see me all the time."

"I mean ... like this. Alone."

"There's a volleyball game on Fri—" I stopped. When he looked into my face, waiting for me to go on, I swallowed. "I was mad at you, so I told David he could take me home."

His lips twitched. "Then since you are no longer mad at me, perhaps I can take you there."

How absurd. I clapped a hand over my mouth to keep the giggle from escaping. "Wouldn't that look fine—coming with one boy and leaving with another. I don't think so."

"Then I'll come afterward, at night." He took my hands and pulled me toward him.

My blood seemed to set off sparks in my veins, as if being close to him ignited me. "What are we doing?" I breathed.

"I must see you," he said, as if this were an answer. "If it can't be in public, then it will be in private." I could feel the heat from his body through my flannel nightie and knitted shawl, as though I were standing next to a stove.

"Why?" I whispered. "Why me?"

As if in answer, he tilted his head and captured my mouth with his.

7

When I was twelve, Dat took us to see the ocean at Cape Cod. I stood in the water up to my waist, an old dress pinned between my legs so it wouldn't float up and expose my homemade underwear, and looked back toward Hannah on the shore, who hadn't been brave enough to wade in. A huge wave crashed into me and knocked me over, pulling me under with a roar and erasing every sense except the need to breathe.

Kissing Gabriel was like that.

Hearing and sight faded into the darkness, but like a blind person, touch and taste surged in to make up for their lack. He tasted like toothpaste and something else— something I couldn't identify but I knew I would never forget. His mouth was soft and yet firm at the same time, teasing me—promising things I didn't know the meaning of, but making me realize I wanted to learn.

I had never realized a boy's mouth could say so much when it wasn't speaking.

There were a lot of things I had never realized. Among them were how fast my temperature could rise to match his, and how little it took to wrap my body around his, as if our clothes and skins could melt together and make us a new kind of being.

Lips off, laps off, hands off.

Dat's voice echoed in my head, as if my brain had just woken up and realized what my body was up to. I dragged my mouth from his and pulled back, hands lingering on his shirt. Cold air rushed between us.

"Gabriel—"

"Whoa." He shook his head a little. I felt like doing the same—shaking some sense into it. "My word."

"We can't—I—I have to go."

When our hands slid apart and finally separated, I felt as though my heart was being torn out of my ribcage. I couldn't look back or I'd never be able to leave him a second time. Instead, I ran across the lawn and around into the shadow of the house.

Somehow I made it back up to my room without being discovered. I'm not sure how; maybe the stairs didn't creak because my bare feet never actually touched them. Hours and shapes had lost all meaning while I kissed Gabriel Langford ... and it took me a while to become familiar with everyday things again.

I was still sitting on my bed, dazed with reliving those amazing, precious moments, when the door opened and lamplight flooded in. I squinted and felt the jolt as I fell back into my own life.

"Up already?" Dat leaned around the door. "You must be as anxious for milking as those cows."

"I ... *ja*. I'll be right down."

My body put clothes on and my hands tied my kitchen apron without any help from my brain. That was still out in the orchard, feeling his mouth move on mine—feeling the softness of his lips ... the work-hardened planes of his back and shoulders ... the strength of his arms as they wrapped around my waist.

The fear that had made me push him away out in the field must have gone where old fears go when you grow out of them. Because nothing had seemed more natural— or more magical—than to go into his arms, to turn my face up to his, to invite his kisses as though I deserved them.

I braided my hair automatically, pinned it up, and set an old frayed *kapp* over it with the mindlessness of long habit. And then I walked downstairs, feeling the satiny smoothness of the round banister under my hand. As smooth as his fingers, twined with mine.

Once outside, I glanced back at the orchard, at the cherry tree. But it was no longer the outpost of our special country. It would be transformed at night, when he came again, and we would rule it in solitary glory, just the two of us.

In the barn, I found Caleb and Dat already hard at work, their hands moving under the cows' bellies in an easy rhythm. I took a milking stool and got down to business, putting Gabriel and the wonder of his kisses in a special box in my head. I wouldn't spoil them by mixing them in with the painful ordinariness of the milking pen, the smell of manure and hay and warm cows, and the grunts of the men as they hefted the pails of milk over to the tank that held it for the collective in Mitternacht.

At the sound of thudding boots outside, Dat lifted his head. "Who's that?"

I leaned around the post of the stall in time to see Adam Hertzfeld fall in the door and glance around wildly, as if he didn't see us with the cows right in front of him. Dat pushed the cow away and stood up. "Is everything all right, young Adam?"

Adam's chest heaved and his breath rasped in the sudden silence. His hat was gone, his hair ruffled up on end. "You've got to come."

Now Caleb stood. "Come where? What happened to you?"

"Not me. It's Paul Gingrich." His face was as white as the paint on the walls, only tinged with green. "You've got to come."

Dat crossed the pen and took his upper arms in both hands, giving them a gentle shake. "Make sense, Adam Hertzfeld. Is Paul ill?"

"It's worse than that. I can't—" He tore himself out of Dat's grip and spun to a pile of soiled hay, where he fell to his hands and knees and retched.

Dat gestured at me. "Sophia, see to him. Caleb, Jonah, come with me."

He and my brothers pushed past me. I ran to the water pail and filled the tin cup. "Here."

Adam gulped the water down. "I've got to go."

"Are you sure you're all right?"

He gave me a hard look, and I realized that I might have seen the last of the boyish jokester Adam had been. "I'm fine. But Paul won't ever be all right again."

In my mind, he hadn't been all right for years. My breath backed up in my throat and I struggled to force my lungs to drag in air. But I had to know. "What happened to him, Adam? You must tell me."

"I don't know. But Troyers' cow was a mercy compared to this."

With that, he flung himself out the door. I stood on the cement floor, torn between my duty to stay and milk, and my desperate need to know what had happened. Maybe my uncle was still alive. Maybe he was not. But if another hour passed without knowing, I would burn up from the inside.

I ran out of the barn on Adam's heels. Through the orchard, into the dip, then up the other side to the hay field. Panting, out of breath, I retraced the path where Gabriel and I had walked, all unknowing, less than ninety minutes before. Had Paul been up for milking then? Had he met some dreadful fate while Gabriel and I kissed under the cherry tree?

Only an evil person would be happy if he had. And I was not evil. But part of what drove me across the field behind Adam was the sense that if it were true, then freedom hung just out of reach. I needed to know so that I could grasp it, and never let go again.

Heaving, the two of us staggered into the Gingrich yard, where the only evidence of life was the sound of hushed voices coming from the barn.

"Will you be all right?" I asked Adam. Whatever was in there, it had already made him throw up. He ignored me completely, as if his weakness were relegated to the past, when he'd been a child, and was never to be mentioned again.

Wordlessly, I followed him into the barn, all the way to the back, where the milking pen was. As I stepped inside, the smell hit me. The smell of cold iron. And then I saw it. Red blood, drying now to brown. Fans of it on the walls, droplets flung against the white paint to spatter and drip. And in the middle, my uncle's body, his throat ripped out and a gaping hole in the leg of his pants, where his thigh had been torn into by—what? Teeth? A knife?

"What is she doing here?" my father roared.

Caleb grabbed me and shoved me roughly out into the yard. "Get out of here, Sophia. This is no place for you."

I staggered away, my stomach heaving up into my throat. I would not let it. I would control myself.

"Sophia!" Dat shouted. "Make yourself useful. Go to the phone box and call the police."

A task. That would take my mind off what my insides threatened to do. There was no point in running anymore. I had seen enough dead animals to know that. But still, the urgency in my father's voice propelled me down the lane and along the half mile of road to the pay phone. Thank the good *Gott* that a 9-1-1 call didn't cost anything, because there wasn't a cent in my pockets and it was a long walk back.

"Nine one one, what is your emergency?"

"It's my uncle. He's out in the barn. Something terrible has happened to him. He's dead."

"Your name, please?"

"Sophia Brucker."

"Address?"

"Mine or my uncle's?"

"The location of the emergency, miss."

"Twenty-seven fifteen Highway Thirty, Mitternacht."

"Nearest cross street?"

It took me a second to remember where I was. "Old Cooper Road."

"Are you in any danger, miss?"

Not now. The realization began to burn at the edges of my fear and horror. "No. I'm at the phone box on the highway and there's no one here."

"Phone box?" The official voice lightened into that of an ordinary woman. "Wait—are you calling from a Mennonite farm? The deceased is Mennonite?"

Did it make a difference? "Yes."

"All right, Miss Brucker. I'm going to send the sheriff and an ambulance. Could you stand at the end of the driveway and flag them?"

"Yes. Thank you." I almost told her there was no hurry, but bit it back in case she thought I was heartless. I hung up the phone and pushed open the louvered doors.

A moment later the sound of a galloping hooves made me lift my head. My mouth fell open at the sight of Mamm tearing toward me in the two-seater, Miriam strapped across her chest in the folds of her shawl. Her *kapp* hung down her back, having blown off, and her eyes were wild.

Ach, mein Gott. She does not know.

"Sophia!" she shouted. "What are you doing? Where is your father? And the boys? I've been frantic!"

Help me now. Where was Dat when I needed him? It was his place to carry this news, not mine.

"Sophia, I asked you a question!" She hauled back on Daisy's reins and skidded to a stop with a clatter of hooves, next to the phone box. The open buggy bounced on its springs, creaking.

"They're all at Uncle Paul's," I said. "Oh, Mamm." My eyes filled with tears, scalding hot in the cool air of morning. "Dat sent me to the phone to call nine-one-one."

Her face set, as if she were bracing herself. "Why?"

"It's Uncle Paul. Mamm—he—he—" I took a breath and just said it. "He's dead. Out in the barn."

The color fell out of her face. "Paul is dead?" Far away, the howl of the siren rose and fell. "How? I just spoke to him yesterday. He didn't say anything about not feeling well." Her hands tightened on the reins and she flapped them over Daisy's back. "Git up, girl."

"No, Mamm, don't—"

But she was already ten yards away, moving at a brisk clip, as though she'd forgotten I was standing there. She was already out of sight over the hill when the ambulance rounded the curve. It screeched to a stop when I waved my arms.

The glass window dropped and the driver leaned out. "Is this the Gingrich farm? Are you the one who called nine-one-one?" The siren switched off in mid-screech, dropping silence on the fields as though we'd all gone deaf.

"No. Yes. I mean, it's that way another half mile." I pointed. "But I'm the one who called." His window was already halfway up when I added, "You don't need to turn the siren on."

He glared at me and the siren whooped back into life as the ambulance pulled away. It had no sooner wailed out of sight than the sheriff's black-and-white car roared past me in its wake without even stopping. I hesitated on the gravel shoulder. The last place I wanted to be was my uncle's yard, with the police and everyone there. And yet, our house would be empty, with no one to go to for a hug and a good cry.

I could go to Katie's, but she had her own chores to do and her mother wouldn't appreciate my need for a hug. And Gabriel? The Hodder farm was two miles away and that was if you went straight across country. My heart cried out for him, but what was between us was so new ... what if he was the kind of person who didn't handle the ceremonies of death well? Yes, I wanted to be safe at his side. But at the same time, this was a family matter. And the circumstances were so ugly. I wanted to keep our special country just that—special. Separate. Unconnected with so much horror.

And besides, what if the police wanted to talk to me?

With a sigh, I realized there was only one thing left for me to do. The thing I should have done so that the sight of my uncle's mutilated body wouldn't haunt me every time I closed my eyes.

Milk the cows.

I was still milking when Caleb brought the sheriff's deputy to find me. "Sophia, this is Deputy Palermo. He wants to talk to all of us. I'll finish here."

I massaged my aching hands as I got up and yielded my stool to Caleb. "Where's Jonah?"

"With Dat. They've gone out to Myerling to get Aendi Sallie."

"With all these cows to milk? Why didn't he come back with you?"

The sheriff cleared his throat and I bit back my incredulity. Trust Jonah to weasel out of actual work while pretending to do the right thing. One of these days someone besides me was going to figure him out, and he wasn't going to like it one bit.

"Is there somewhere we can go so I can ask you some questions?" the sheriff asked as I joined him.

I nodded. "Come into the kitchen. I made coffee before I came out here."

Though the morning wasn't cold, the sheriff wrapped both hands around the white stoneware mug and shook his head when I offered him cream. I added a generous splash to my own and took my usual chair at the table, halfway down. Moving stiffly, as if sitting at our kitchen table would somehow lessen his position of authority, Deputy Palermo lowered himself into Dat's chair.

He took out a pen and notebook and flipped to a fresh page. "Before we start, please accept my condolences for your loss."

I didn't know what to say. I couldn't tell an outsider that Uncle Paul had gone to his eternal reward and condolences weren't necessary—especially when I wasn't altogether sure what kind of reward it was. So I said nothing.

After a moment, the deputy took a sip of coffee and went on, "Just for the record, your full name is ...?"

"Sophia Karina Brucker. Karina with a K."

"Age?"

"Sixteen."

"And this is your place of residence?"

"Yes."

"You were the one who placed the 9-1-1 call?"

"Yes. I was out by the pay phone when you drove by."

He took another sip. "Sorry. I didn't see you."

If he had, it probably wouldn't have registered anyway. I suppose one girl in a black apron and *kapp* looks very much like another to outsiders.

"Why were you at your uncle's place this morning?"

If it had been *his* uncle, wouldn't he have gone? "A friend of ours came while we were milking. I guess my uncle had hired him to do something or other, and when he went over, he found him ... there. He ran to get us and we all went over to see if—" *It was really true.* "—we could do anything to help."

"And?"

The warm cup felt good between my aching hands. "There wasn't." I took a breath. "Do you know what happened to him? Is it the same thing that killed Troyers' cow?"

He swallowed a big gulp of coffee, his Adam's apple moving up and down with surprise. "Troyers' cow?"

Of course he wouldn't have heard what we all knew. "About a week ago it was, John Troyer went out to his milking pen and found a cow with its throat chewed up, just the same way. Like an animal did it. Maybe it came in the barn and my uncle cornered it and it attacked him trying to get away."

He wrote something in the notebook. Several somethings. "I'll look into that possibility. What time did you and your dad and brothers get over there?"

"We get up at four-thirty for milking. Adam came just after we got out to the barn. So, maybe four forty-five?"

"And what about this Adam Hertzfeld? What was he doing there so early?"

"I don't know. Getting ready to start work, I guess."

"That seems pretty early."

"Not on the farm," I told him, dryness creeping into my tone. "Twenty cows have to be milked before the trucks come for the milk at eight."

"And Adam was helping Mr. Gingrich milk?"

"I don't know. Probably. My uncle hired people to help him because he and my aunt don't have boys. You'd have to ask him, though."

"Oh, I will, believe me. Do you know if this kid had anything against your uncle?"

"Adam?" I gawked at him. "Of course not. He's a bit of a joker but all he wants is a good laugh. I don't think he's capable of holding a grudge against anybody. That's unforgiveness."

"Is there anyone who might have a reason to ... injure Mr. Gingrich?"

Only me. "I don't understand why you're asking me this. Shouldn't you be out there with shotguns and traps, looking for that animal?"

He drained the cup and clacked it on the table. I jumped as if he'd taken out his gun and shot the ceiling. "We're doing everything we can, Miss Brucker. Gathering information and asking questions is the first step."

Oh, dear. "I'm sorry. I didn't mean to tell you how to do your job. It's just that—we're *all* in shock right now."

"I'm very sorry." He reached into the chest pocket of his khaki jacket and took out a card. "If you think of anything else, please give me a call at this number." His gaze darted around the kitchen and took in the hall, too. "Or stop by the office if you happen to be in Mitternacht."

I took the card and slipped it into the pocket of my work dress. He shook my hand and left, the roar of his big police-car engine foreign to our quiet yard.

Later that day, I dropped the dress in the dirty-clothes hamper, and when we did laundry next, the card was still in the pocket.

The funeral slipped into its third hour.

IMMORTAL FAITH

The deacon finished his sermon and sat, and Bishop Stolz announced another hymn—one about the martyrs of old and their suffering. My aunt and uncle's house was so full that we *Youngie* were sitting on benches in the kitchen, which meant that the casseroles and trays of food had to go outside, under a tarp, until it was time to serve.

Guilt is like mud. The more you try to wipe it away, the more it gets all over you.

I sat directly in what would have been my Aunt Sallie's line of sight, if she had looked up. But she never did, not once during that interminable service. Instead, she stared at the spotless plank floor as if she might eventually see an explanation. She did not sing when the deacon called the hymns; in fact, her face looked as if it would waver and crack if she allowed her lips to quiver. Like the ice in the pond in March, she was hard on the outside and probably spongy with grief on the inside.

I had done this. I had wished him ... away ... and now our entire community grieved.

My fault. I was a horrible person. I didn't deserve to be here.

And I couldn't find it in my sinful self to be sorry.

Dear Sophia,

Sorry it's been so long since my last letter. I know you don't like it when I type them, but if I didn't, it would take even longer and you'd like that even less. (I'm smiling.)

Midterms are over finally! I think I did pretty well. They weren't any harder than the GED exam so I'm seeing a light at the end of the freshman tunnel. It's surprising how much I learned in our little one-room school—stuff that some of the kids here don't even know.

I have a couple of roommates but they keep to themselves pretty much. One's a history major and the other something to do with computers. Lots of math. Yuck. They stay up late watching movies on their computers and playing games on them. Their eyes are going to go square, I think. But it looks like fun. I watch the movies too, sometimes. I have a lot to catch up on.

How are Mamm and the boys? Give them a hug for me, and Dat too if he'll let you. I know they want me to come home and join church, but to be honest, I don't think I can. The world is such a big place and there's so much to learn about it. And I'm finding I can serve God just as well in a pair of jeans as I can in kapp and apron.

I think you should go rumspringing, little sister. A different view would be good for you. You need to be able to make an informed decision. I don't think God wants us to follow along our well-worn track just because it's there. I think He wants us to use the brain he gave us and choose. I know Dat thinks I'm going to hell because I don't choose the track he chose, but I don't think I am. Jesus was Jewish, not Mennonite, and he got to Heaven just fine.

I'll let this do for now. I miss you and love you. Write soon and let me know all the news. Has Malachi Hodder gotten over his broken heart and starting courting someone else yet?

Love, Hannah

8

I couldn't bring myself to go to the grave, either.

Instead, my buddies and some of the neighbors offered to stay home from the burial to help rearrange the benches and set up the tables for the meal, and I accepted gratefully. Every household had brought tablecloths, so we smoothed those over all the tables and began setting out rolls and pickles, plates and cutlery, and filling pitchers of water.

Before long the procession of buggies began to trickle back into the yard and we got busy with all the food. After that I lost track of the time—which was good. The busier I was, the less time I had to think. To feel.

Joy was wrong.

Grief was impossible.

What was left? Guilt.

All I had to balance that was work, which under the circumstances, I suppose, was a blessing. Maybe if I worked hard, God would add that to my heavenly treasure. I didn't think it had a hope of outweighing the massive negative on the other side of the account, but all I could do was try.

Darkness had fallen by the time everyone had shaken Aunt Sallie's hand and said their last farewells. My parents lingered in the kitchen with Aunt Sallie and my Uncle Joseph and Aunt Irene, who had arrived yesterday on the train from Canada with their three daughters. I kept myself busy washing the last of the coffee cups from the dining table, where we had all been sitting and talking, until my folks were ready to walk home across the fields.

"Sallie, do you have any plans about how you're going to manage the farm?" Uncle Joseph finally said when conversation had petered out from the sheer weight of the day.

"I don't know." Her voice had a rough edge, the way Mamm's gets when she's talked too much. But Aunt Sallie had said hardly a word. "It would have gone to Benjamin if ..." Her voice choked off, but we all knew the ending. *If he had lived.* My oldest cousin had died in a buggy accident ten years ago, and the brother next in line, Michael, no longer walked with God. Sallie's two girls were married and gone to their own farms on the other side of Myerling.

"You could keep it for little Peter," Mamm suggested. He was my cousin Carrie's oldest boy, but he was only a toddler. "It's a fine farm, and Carrie and her husband wouldn't have to worry about providing for him."

"But what do I do with it in the twenty years until he's ready for it?" Sallie heaved a sigh. "I can't milk all those cows myself, nor plant the acres, nor go to the auctions when the equipment wears out."

"We can help there," Dat said. "And for right now, the boys can milk our herd first, and then come over to do yours."

"I appreciate that, Victor." She got up and handed me her cup, and I smiled at her as I dunked it in the hot, soapy water. "But twenty years of imposing on you and your family will wear us all down, in the end."

"Carrie and her family could come and live here," I said, a little hesitantly. I liked Carrie. Having her living here would wipe the stain off this place, given enough years. Like the trees growing back where a forest fire had burned through.

"That's true." My aunt nodded. "But she hasn't been back here since she left to get married, even for Christmas. I don't think she likes the old place. Her husband farms his own land and his dad's too, so tearing him away would only hand my problem to them. No." She sighed again. "I'll probably just sell the place and go and live with her. Though that will mean not seeing you folks so often." She smiled at Mamm, who squeezed her hand.

"Sell it to whom?" my father asked.

"You, if you'll buy it."

Mamm and Dat exchanged one of those glances that bring old conversations to mind. "Victor, we don't have money for something like that."

"But Caleb is going to want his own place soon. And four or five years of running two farms will pass a lot more quickly than twenty."

"Has Caleb talked to you about being baptized?"

I think they'd forgotten I was there. Caleb had been running around for two or three years now, and if he was going to settle down and find himself a wife, he'd have to think about joining church soon. The problem was, he hadn't shown any signs that his thoughts were turning that way. Not to me, at least.

"No, but you know Caleb. Not exactly a talker about the important things."

I didn't know much about anything, but it seemed to me that the price of a farm was a lot to gamble on my brother choosing to join church. And how would he feel about that? Would it force him to make up his mind—or would the responsibility send him running for Council Bluffs, like Hannah?

"At least if I sell the place," my aunt went on, "I wouldn't have to be a burden on Carrie and her husband. I'd even have enough to maybe build a *daadi haus* next to theirs, so I wouldn't be living in their pockets but I could still help with the children and the cooking."

"They would never think you were a burden," Mamm said, patting her hand.

"Maybe not. But I'd still want to pull my weight."

Our whole family has this philosophy. Well, except for Jonah. And where were my brothers while the grownups in the family discussed their future? This was important. Quietly, I pulled the plug from the sink and dried my hands.

No one noticed me slip out the kitchen door; they were deep in a discussion of who owed what to whom and who was going to ask for more in order to buy the land. The yard lay dark and silent, and for the first time, that spring nip in the air was gone. It would be May tomorrow, and I could almost feel summer waiting on tiptoe on the far edges of the fields.

No sign of the boys. They'd probably be out in the barn, then, doing whatever boys did with their spare time and no doubt avoiding the place where ... well, avoiding what had been cleaned and bleached days ago. It wouldn't take me long to—

"Sophia."

My heart somersaulted in my chest. "Gabriel?" He stepped out of the shadow of the barn. "What on earth are you doing here? Are Caleb and Jonah with you?"

"I haven't seen them. I was waiting for you."

Joy trickled from my heart to my veins, and I felt myself flushing in the dark. "Were you?"

"Death is never easy for the ones left behind."

Something in his tone told me he didn't mean me, even as his warm hand clasped mine. Without saying another word, I abandoned my brothers to their own devices and Gabriel and I started walking toward the distant poplars on the ridge. "My family is in the kitchen right now, talking about what to do with the farm. My aunt wants to sell it and go live with her daughter. My dad wants to buy it for Caleb."

"Will he do that even though Caleb hasn't joined church?"

"I don't know. That's why I came out here. To find him and tell him he needs to stop goofing around and grow up."

Gabriel chuckled, a rich sound like a contented bumblebee in the flowers. "I have a feeling that's the sort of conclusion one comes to on one's own, not by being told by one's sister."

"If *one* had any sense, he would see how important it is to stop being selfish and disobedient, and start listening to the call of God."

"Now, that I agree with wholeheartedly."

Which took the indignant wind out of my sails. "It's so nice talking to you. You actually listen to what I say, instead of telling me to not be an idiot and mind my own business."

Still holding my hand, he let me precede him over the plank laid across the ditch as the night around us filled with the rush and gurgle of runoff. Hawthorn bushes fringed the ditch, their white blossoms like midnight lace. "I would never say something like that to you. You deserve to be protected and loved. And now you are."

What an odd way he had of putting things. "I suppose. Is that why we're walking instead of looking for Caleb?"

"We're walking because I needed to see you, and because Caleb and Jonah went to get ice cream with Katie and the Miller boys."

"Oh. Why didn't you tell me that five minutes ago?"

"Because not talking about Caleb is much more interesting to me."

I had to laugh, and in the last reaches of the yard light, I saw the flash of his answering smile before he handed me off the plank like a princess stepping down from a coach. Wherever he'd gone to school, they had given him much more than a classical education. Or perhaps his mother had taught him little graces like this. He would probably even know which fork to use if he were eating with more than one.

In companionable silence, we walked up the hill and through the poplar break into the hay field. But instead of stopping, as we'd done to watch the sun come up, he kept going up and to the left, setting a slow pace across the field toward the smudge of deeper darkness on the far side.

"Are we going into the woods?" Not that I cared. We could walk into Mitternacht and out the other side and I wouldn't care, as long as I got to be with him.

"Is that what you call that little copse there?"

"My great-grandparents never cut them down to plant seed. We just call them the woods. We used to play there a lot in the summer when we were kids, because it's cooler. And I like walking there in the winter. You can see the tracks of all the animals and birds in the snow."

"And see who's hunting whom?"

"Mm-hm."

"No one's hunting you now."

"No," I said before the words registered completely. "What? What did you say?"

"I was right, then."

I dropped his hand and stopped, so that he had to turn back if he wanted to talk to me. "What are you talking about? Right about what?"

We had reached the edge of the woods, and he leaned on the trunk of a maple. "That's the thing about birds, you know. There's safety in numbers. One little bird out on the snow by itself is going to be the one chosen by the predator, isn't it?"

"You are making no sense at all."

"When are you going to tell me about what your uncle did to you?"

"We've already been through this." How could he ruin our lovely, romantic walk? "And now he's dead and I don't have to worry about it anymore, and neither do you. So please stop bringing it up."

"But you don't mourn his death, do you? I've been here all day, same as everyone else. I saw how you didn't cry. How you kept yourself busy all day doing everything you could lay your hands to, just so you wouldn't have to think."

"There's nothing wrong with that." I couldn't help sounding defensive. "So did my aunt and all the women in our family."

"I wonder if she knew what kind of man her husband was?"

"Of course not."

"How do you know?"

"Because how do you live with someone, knowing something like that? I'm her own niece. She makes me shortbread at Christmas because she knows I love it. She reads her library books fast so that I can read them, too, before she takes them back. If she knew, she would have done something."

"Like you did something?"

I stopped. The defensive stream of words stopped. I think even the earth stopped in its slow revolution, just for a second.

Was that why my aunt couldn't cry for the death of the man she'd been married to for thirty years? Why she'd said "It's the will of God" with such throaty sincerity at least fifty times today? Why she would rather leave this farm she'd lived on for those thirty years and go twenty miles away instead?

Why my cousin Carrie had got married at seventeen and never come back?

Had my Aunt Sallie known what he was doing this whole time and done nothing to stop it?

Gabriel closed the distance between us and took me in his arms. It seemed the most natural thing in the world to turn my face into his chest, to absorb the heat of his body, and let him warm the chilled chunk of stone that I'd turned into.

"Why didn't she do anything?" I finally mourned, muffled in his shirt.

"Maybe she couldn't," he said gently. "If she exposed him, what would happen to her? To you? There would be police asking questions. Maybe she would have to leave. What would she have to live on? Who knows why people do—or don't do—what they do?"

The Gingrich place lay quiet in its fold of the hill, the barn blocking our view of the house. "I can't go back there. Not while she's still in the kitchen. I don't know if I could control myself."

"That's what I love about you, Sophia. You're so honest. Even when it hurts you."

"That's not true. I haven't been honest this whole time. Because ..." My voice trailed away as I realized the truth. Gabriel had been right. "Because I didn't speak up, either. Because I had as much to lose as she did. And it was easier to know and not say anything, to just go on hoping no one would ever find out."

"No one will find out. Not from me. I swear to you." He tightened his arms and I welcomed the strength of them. He meant what he said. His silence would protect me just as his loving hold would.

Silently, I begged forgiveness from Father *Gott* for my sudden flash of hatred toward my aunt. Because of course she would sell the farm and leave. I would do the same in her shoes. Compassion and love worked on my hard, fearful heart like two hands in a bowl of bread dough.

"I need to tell her," I said softly. "I want her to know that it wasn't her fault. That I understand."

He paused so long that far off in the distance I heard a dog howl. And then another. "Do you really want to do that? What if the only way she can get through the day is pretending it didn't happen? What would she do if you told her you understand? She has a façade to hold up, Sophia. If you say anything, the whole thing will come down and all her sacrifice of silence will be for nothing."

"I won't say anything to anyone else. Just her. She's the only one who needs to know."

"Does she need to know, or do you just need to tell her?" he asked softly into my *kapp*. "Think of the poor lady. Her husband has been disloyal to her in thought—with you."

And maybe others—maybe her own daughter. What kind of hell did my aunt live in? "In deed, too, Gabriel." My own voice felt rough in my throat.

"Even worse, then. He was wicked, and she had to lie next to him knowing that. Have a little mercy, *liewi*. Let her take her past away with her. It has nothing to do with you, now." He linked his hands loosely at the small of my back.

"Where did you learn to be so wise in the ways of the world?"

"My many years of experience," he said solemnly, and I laughed, feeling it wash away the anger and bitterness and leaving only the compassion behind.

His stillness made me lift my head, and I found him gazing down at me, waiting. Without a word, I lifted my chin and our lips met. After that, there was no room in my mind or heart for anyone but him.

I woke at the tap on my bedroom door. Dat pushed it open and shone the lamp inside, as usual, and continued on his way downstairs when he saw that I was awake.

I had no idea when or how I'd gotten back to my room.

I lay there for a stunned second, rolling through my memory in reverse. Meeting Gabriel. Kissing him. Walking through the woods, talking about my aunt. Kissing. Lying down. Feeling the crisp cotton of his Sunday shirt, which he'd worn to the funeral, under my cheek. Closing my eyes and wondering if married couples ever fell asleep under the trees.

And that was it. Nothing past that but a blank space. Had I fallen asleep? Or sleepwalked back here, through two doors, and up a set of stairs?

I looked down at myself.

Dressed. I was still in my Sunday dress and apron, both wrinkled beyond recognition and wadded up around my waist.

"Are you losing your mind?" I muttered.

With fumbling fingers that felt too thick, I unpinned my apron and stripped out of my dress, dropping both in the laundry basket. In fresh underwear and a regular work dress, I rebraided my hair into its bun and cast around for my *kapp*. Not on the bureau. Not on its peg. I pulled open the drawer, but only one sat inside—the frayed one with the stain on the brim that I used for heavy work days.

Where was my good Sunday kapp?

And how had I managed to lose it and not remember coming home last night? I couldn't turn up in a work covering with spots on it. There was no time to think any further. If I didn't get out to the barn, Dat would have me on hands and knees with a bucket of bleach solution, cleaning up after the cows.

It wasn't until the next day that I had fifteen minutes to call my own. I took off at a run over the creek and up the slope to the woods, where I found my *kapp* caught on a bramble tangle by its tied-together strings, about thirty feet from where Gabriel and I had lain, talking. The crisp organdy hadn't survived a heavy dewfall and the curiosity of birds very well.

Now I had two work *kapps*. I held it in both hands as if it would tell me by what weird chance it had landed there.

But it and the birds were silent.

Dear Hannah,

Thank you for your letter, typed or not. I hardly know what to write, so much has happened. Our brothers send their love, and Mamm does too—or at least, I'm sure she would if she knew I was going to send this today.

We are all fine. I don't know if you've heard, but we had a baptism recently. Five people joined church. One of them was Gabriel Langford, who is boarding with the Hodders. He is a very interesting person from England. I like to listen to him talk because he sounds like a book. I think you'd like him. I haven't heard if Malachi is seeing anybody ... I think he's working pretty hard at the RV factory.

I was hoping to see you at the funeral. Mamm and Dat were disappointed you didn't come. Did you have more exams? Aunt Sallie is probably going to sell up and go live with Carrie and Dan. Dat wants to buy the farm for Caleb but I don't think we have enough money. And I don't know who would work it—he and Caleb are out there from dawn until dark, and you know Jonah. He helps when he feels like it. Plus Caleb hasn't joined church. He keeps talking about hopping on the train and coming to see you. Has he written?

Joshua Hodder hires Gabriel out as a day-jobber, so I guess Dat could hire him.

How do you know when you meet the right one, Hannah?

I'll let this do for now. Hope to hear from you soon.

Your loving sister,
Sophia

9

Gabriel had meant what he said about taking me to the volleyball game at Cara Troyer's place the following Friday. And I had meant what I said about not going with one boy and coming home with another; it would make me look like a flirt and all the boys would think I was shallow—or desperate. We compromised by going back to Hodders' and collecting Rebecca, and then rounding out the foursome by picking up Katie, too.

Since Caleb had crammed several of his friends into his buggy and not even brought up the possibility of taking her, Katie was delighted to arrive in the company of the best-looking boy in the district—especially since I'd offered her the front seat next to him so that I could talk to Rebecca about having a stitching frolic to make a bunch of new *kapps*.

By the time we had our plans made, Gabriel was pulling the Hodder gelding to a stop in Troyers' yard.

"I hope they don't plan to have the game in the barn where that poor cow ..." Rebecca's voice trailed off at the sight of the net set up on the freshly mowed front lawn, with energetic spiking and blocking already in progress. "*Ah, gut.*"

Gabriel unhitched the horse and took it out to the pasture while we girls took our covered dishes into the kitchen. I'd made an apricot and coconut square on a shortbread cookie base that afternoon. I spotted the place at the end of the assortment of chips, dips, popcorn, and appetizers where people were putting their desserts, and set it down next to a plate holding a mountain of rice cereal squares.

"Those must be Cara's," Katie said, putting her raisin pie next to my square. "She makes them for everything because the boys like them."

"Nothing wrong with that," I said. "No leftovers."

"And we all know raisin pie is so *popular*," said a voice behind us. We both turned to see Cara standing in the doorway.

"Cale—" Katie flushed and glanced at me. "Lots of people like raisin pie. I put a bit of rum extract in mine to make it different."

"You just hope the boys will get drunk on it and ask you to take a walk."

I stepped between them. "Wow, somebody got up on the wrong side of the bed this morning."

But with three brothers, Katie didn't need my help defending herself. "If you don't want to host the game, we can move it to our place."

"And then Gabriel Langford can drive you back? Or were you just sitting up front in that buggy for no reason?"

Katie and I exchanged another glance. Cara Troyer was sweet on Gabriel? Now, why did that not surprise me? Probably every girl here was, with the possible exception of Rebecca. But I was the only girl in the crowd who knew the others' chances were exactly zero. And Cara was the only girl in the crowd who would make her preference so obvious.

"Gabriel was nice enough to give us all a ride," I said. "He wasn't *with* any of us."

"That's good," she retorted. "I'd hate for David to think you were two-timing him."

"David and I aren't ... like that." I sounded lame even to myself. "And it's none of your business anyway."

Cara's green eyes snapped, and the front of her crinkly blond hair seemed to crackle with energy before it was smothered by her white *kapp*. "I'm going to make Gabriel Langford my business," she said with so much pent-up emotion that her voice sounded hushed. "You just keep away from him."

"Oh ho, Miss Pride and Prejudice," Katie mocked. "You'd better make sure he feels the same way before you go around warning the rest of us off him."

What girl in her right mind would announce her intent to chase a boy like this? Cara must have a bottle hidden in her bureau drawer to make her do something so crazy. Because when she didn't get his attention, all the girls would make fun of her for her vanity.

"Pride goes before a fall," I reminded her. "Be careful you don't say things you might be sorry for."

Cara flushed and pushed her shoulder off the doorjamb. She marched right up to me and, practically nose to nose, said, "And what makes you so sure he won't go with me? Do you have some kind of special knowledge? Some claim on him? Maybe I should tell David to work a little harder at keeping your attention."

Okay, David didn't deserve this. He might not be much in the looks department, but he was a hard worker and an eldest son, which meant he'd have his dad's farm someday. I mean, not that that would mean anything to me, but David would make a good catch for someone else. And not only that—he had been my friend for most of my life.

Back to the point. Gabriel was none of her business. "Don't be mean, Cara," I said at last. "What's gotten into you?" She'd always been a little raucous, a little too slow to think about her words before they came out of her mouth, a little too quick to act before she thought ... but not like this. Once in a while the things she said would embarrass me, but she'd never meant to be mean. At least, I'd never thought so before.

Maybe I'd just never had a reason to notice before.

"Into me?" At least she backed away a little. I felt Katie move closer, as if she'd sensed that Cara's irritation wasn't directed at her so much as at me. I was grateful for the silent moral support. "Nothing's gotten into me. I'm just telling you not to set your *kapp* at him. You're taken and you've got no business chasing after him. Leave him for those of us who are free."

"Cara Troyer?"

His musical voice sounded from the doorway right behind her, and Cara spun so hard her skirts belled out around her. "Gabriel!" She flushed so deep a scarlet that it might have actually hurt. "What are you doing here?"

He held up a pan. "Rebecca forgot to bring this in. I saw it on the floor of the buggy when I went to put on my tennis shoes. Where do you want it?"

He must have heard her. There was no way he could not have heard her, with the tone of voice she'd been using. But now she was completely mute. She pointed in the general direction of the desserts and fled through the other door into the living room. The front door slammed behind her.

Gabriel put the pan down and raised an eyebrow in our direction. "Did I say something wrong?"

"It wasn't you," Katie said. "She's been running off at the mouth for five minutes straight."

"What about?"

"Nothing you'd be interested in," she told him firmly. "Come on. Let's see if we can get on a team sometime before midnight."

Gabriel and I were careful to get on opposite teams for the game, which went on until we could no longer see the white volleyball to bump or set it. At that point we all straggled into the house, laughing and hungry, to fall on the food like so many gabbling chickens.

Katie made a point of cutting her raisin pie when Caleb happened to be standing the closest to it, and handed him a plate with studied casualness. "Pass that on to anyone who wants it." She cut the next piece and slid it onto a plate.

"Is that raisin pie?" Caleb held the plate up against his chest, as though protecting it against all comers. "Not a chance."

"Others before yourself," she reminded him pertly, but her fair skin, which showed every emotion, turned pink with pleasure. It faded, however, when Caleb reached over with one long arm and snagged a rice square, stacking it on the pie to make room for two chocolate macaroons. If Katie was looking for a love message in his eating patterns, she'd have to keep looking.

When we'd demolished the food, Cara's father stuck his head around the kitchen door. "I rigged up some lights outside if you young folks wanted to have another game." Sure enough, a diesel generator muttered next to the house, and as we spilled out onto the porch, we saw he'd hung white Christmas lights all around the square of our makeshift court. It not only gave us enough light, but it looked festive, even though we were weeks on either side of a holiday.

While some of the kids had ten or more miles to drive home and had to leave, the rest of us split off into teams and waved farewell to the departing buggies in between dives for the ball. *"Umph!"* I grunted, landing on my knees in the grass with my hands clasped in front, digging under the ball and lofting it high enough for David in the back row to bump it over.

"Carrying!" Cara shouted. "Our ball."

"Was not. I bumped it. Ask David."

"I heard her hit it," he said mildly. "But you can have the ball if you want."

"Of course you'd agree with her." Cara grinned. "You'd have to, wouldn't you, or she might go home with Gabriel."

"Caraaaaaa," I moaned. She heard me, too, under the barrage of teasing.

Gabriel just smiled his charming smile and shrugged it off, but David could hardly raise his eyes from the ground, even when it was his turn to serve. I had moved into the front row again, opposite Cara, and flexed my fingers, ready to set. David served, skimming the ball over the net with an inch to spare. Cara leaped, whipped one arm down in a wicked spike, and sent the ball straight into my head.

"Ow!" I shrieked, stars dancing in front of my eyes. I stumbled and fell to one knee as Cara ducked under the net to help me up.

"Sophia, are you okay? I'm so sorry, I didn't mean to—"

"That hurt. Ow, no, don't touch it. Can someone re-place me?" I waved blindly to the line of players waiting to come on, and Adam loped in to fill my spot. I was go-ing to have a shiner tomorrow if I didn't do something quickly. "I need some ice."

"I'll get it." Katie dashed across the yard, heading for the kitchen and the coolers that had held the soda. When she came back with a dripping towel full of ice, Gabriel had left his place in the rear line on Cara's side.

"Here, I'll do that. I have some medical training." Gently, he elbowed Cara and Katie out of the way and pressed the makeshift bag of ice to my face. "Can you hold it there?" I put my hand on the bag and he pressed it with his, under cover of adjusting it. "Does anyone have a flashlight?"

"Oh come on, Gabriel," Adam called. "It was only a spike, not a broken bone."

"I want to see if she's concussed."

Adam had no more to say. One of the Miller boys brought Gabriel a flashlight, and the light blinded me as he shone it in my eyes.

"Dilation's normal," he reported, as solemnly as any doctor. "That's good. But keep the ice on it to keep the swelling down. With any luck, you won't have much of a souvenir in the morning."

"Thanks," I whispered. "Next time I'll move faster."

"Next time it probably won't be deliberate," he murmured back. "That was no accident."

"Oh, come on. Cara's aim isn't that good."

"If you say so." A little louder, he said, "Hold it there for a few minutes."

"You should be our team doctor," Katie said with admiration. "Where did you learn that?"

"I drove an ambulance for a while," Gabriel told her slowly, as if he didn't want to say too much. "You pick things up."

"You can drive?" Half the boys in the line waiting to join the game swung around, and Adam missed his serve altogether. The ball rolled under the net. "You have a driver's license?"

"Not any more. I um, I let it expire."

"Are you nuts?" Adam walked off the court to join the conversation. "My folks won't even let me take the test. They say it's stupid when I don't have a car. I'd still like to have it, though. I might buy one someday."

"Right," Caleb said. "And that fancy buggy of yours will gather cobwebs in the barn after all the work you put into it?"

Adam just shrugged. The boys got into a discussion of how a person would rig a string of flashing lights along the bottom of a buggy so that the light would chase itself all around the body of the carriage, and the volleyball game fell apart.

Fine with me. I wasn't going to be playing any more tonight, anyway.

"Sophia, are you ready to go?"

I peered around my towel full of melting ice to see David standing next to me. And I remembered what I'd promised. For about two seconds I considered asking him if I could go home in the ambulance with Gabriel, but I didn't think he'd get it. And besides, I might get another volleyball—in the back of the head this time—if Cara heard me. "Yes. Let me get my dish from the kitchen."

"I—I'll hitch up and meet you at the end of the drive."

So he did listen when I talked. That was something.

When I came out after dumping the ice in the sink and wringing out the towel, Cara stood in the glow of the twinkle lights in front of the Hodder gelding, stroking its nose. Gabriel had already hitched him up and brought the buggy around for Rebecca and Katie, so they must be leaving as well. Cara looked up through her sandy blond eyelashes and said something to him, but he only laughed and shook his head. Her forehead wrinkled into a frown that quickly smoothed out into the face of a gracious hostess when Rebecca came out and thanked her for a great time.

Then again, Rebecca hadn't had a volleyball in the face—on purpose or not. I was lucky not to have a broken nose.

As Katie climbed into the back, Cara skipped over to where Adam was adjusting his harness. She reached into the back of his buggy and suddenly a blast of *Englisch* music flooded the yard. Adam laughed and boosted her inside, jumped in next to her, and together they rolled up the lane, the music drowning out Cara's attempts at singing along.

I resisted the temptation to say good night to Gabriel with my eyes, and contented myself with a general goodbye to the whole group as I walked to the end of the lane. And once I had climbed in beside David, I didn't look back at the Hodder buggy even once, though I was sorely tempted. I'd had my gift for the evening—that stolen touch over the ice. For that, I was willing to trade a backward look. I owed David that much.

Even on 70th Avenue, which cut across the highway and paralleled Old Cooper Road, David and I could still hear odd bursts of Adam's radio as the road dipped and rose.

"Noise pollution," I said. "Isn't that what one of our teachers used to call it?"

David flapped the reins, which Roan ignored. "My dad does, too. Don't you like music?"

"Well, sure. I like some country. And bluegrass. And there was this harp CD that Lilian Borchardt had playing in the shop at Christmas—I liked that, too."

What did Gabriel like? And why didn't we talk about things like music when we were together? Because there were much deeper things to talk about—like betrayal and pain and family relationships. He was a deep, serious person. Not for the first time, I wondered what he saw in me. Certainly not depth and seriousness.

David nodded in the direction of the sound. It seemed to be fading. "That's more like somebody yelling at their dog."

I resigned myself to talking about the shallow and harmless. "Do you think Cara really likes it, or is she just pretending to?"

"I like bluegrass, too," he offered without answering me. Maybe he thought I was gossiping. "Who's your favorite?"

I didn't know enough about it to have a favorite. "Anyone who sounds like a real person playing and not too jazzy."

"Would you ever go to one of those band hops?"

Luckily it was too dark for him to see my surprise, even in the light of the buggy's side lamps. I never would have predicted David Fischer would even know what a band hop was. His family was even stricter than mine.

"Depends. If it was real bluegrass and not a bunch of boys goofing around on borrowed instruments, I might go and see. You won't catch me dancing, though."

He laughed, maybe at the very thought of either of us doing that. "Maybe we could go sometime."

Goodness. Shallow topics, maybe, but becoming more and more unexpected. "Do you know anyone who does? Because that's the only way we'd know where one was."

"No," he admitted. "Adam probably knows. He goes away on weekends a lot. Or your sister Hannah."

"Maybe. I don't know if she's into music, though." There was so much I didn't know about my sister's life at that college. Mostly because I was afraid to know. My letters gave her news from home, but didn't ask too many questions.

"Even if she isn't, she might know who to ask. Word travels pretty far, especially if you have a cell phone."

"Or even if you don't." Both of us smiled. It might be a joke that the Mennonite grapevine was faster than the Internet, but it was pretty close to the truth.

We crested the last hill, and the lights of home shone through the trees. Even as I looked at them, the ones on the upper floor winked out. "I think my parents know we're coming. Do you think they can hear Roan's hooves from here?"

"Probably."

I hoped he didn't think my family was hinting that we needed privacy. Even if they were. We turned into the lane. I'd never realized before how many potholes there seemed to be in what looked like neatly graded gravel. Maybe that wasn't so bad. If he had any ideas, the potholes gave me a way to head him off. "Can you slow down a bit? My brain feels like it's slapping the inside of my skull."

"Sorry." He crooned at the horse and we rolled slowly to a stop in the yard. This time, David hopped out and came around to help me down. "Will you be all right?"

"I think so." I pressed a hand to the side of my face. "I wish we had a freezer so I could get some more ice."

For a moment, he stood silently. What was he waiting for? How could he even think of asking a girl for a kiss when she had a bruise forming the size of a pie plate?

I made the decision for him. "This really hurts. I need to get a cold compress on it. Thanks for driving me home."

"You're welcome." He stepped back, and I breathed again. "I hope you feel better in the morning."

"Me, too. Good night."

I saw the white flash of a smile, and then the buggy creaked as he got in. He had barely got Roan moving when I ran up the kitchen steps and pulled the door shut behind me. Standing in our dark, warm kitchen that smelled faintly of cinnamon and bacon grease, I leaned on the closed door and breathed deeply.

Safe. Quiet. Familiar.

After a moment, I got a clean cloth out of the drawer, ran water over it at the sink, and climbed the stairs to my room, welcoming the cool relief.

It has been a long time since I've felt this protective toward a girl. Even in my previous worldly life, when my sister Charlotte married that blackguard Bellingham against all of our wishes, I wanted less to protect her than to call him out and make sure he ate grass for breakfast. What a hothead I was then.

But this is different. Every hurt Sophia suffers hurts me, too. Is this what it means to be in love? But how can that be when there is no marrying or giving in marriage in eternity? I am beginning to think that the words of Jesus have been mistranslated over the centuries, because if it is possible to buy land, it seems as though it would be equally possible to marry.

Were I given a choice, I would marry her in a heartbeat, just to be able to stay at her side and ward off the attacks of the wicked.

Perhaps I do have a choice.

I have my mission: to protect the lambs from the ravening wolf. Anyone who inflicts so much pain with so little care must be one of these predators, and not one of God's obedient sheep at all. Oh, how cleverly they disguise themselves, and choose their moments to rend and tear!

But all things come to pass in God's time. I must wait for His prompting.

10

Sophia.

I woke out of a dream of someone calling my name to see the light dancing on the wall, just as it had the day ... the day we'd found my uncle. The alarm clock told me I had an hour before my parents would wake up.

An hour with Gabriel.

I practically hugged myself with delight as I wrapped my shawl around me and picked up my shoes. Seconds later I was out in the yard and running toward the cherry tree, and a moment after that I fell against him, laughing as his arms closed around me.

He stopped my laughter with a kiss, but I couldn't help smiling under it. Lifting his head, he said, "You seem awfully cheery for an injured party."

"I'm glad to see you, all by yourself." I tugged on his hand. "Let's get away from the house."

"Are you in pain?"

"Not now." As we crossed the creek, hand in hand, and made our way up the familiar slope to the woods, I remembered the last time. "Gabriel, it's the strangest thing. I don't remember getting home the last time I was with you. You know, when we fell asleep up in the woods."

"That is because you're a very deep sleeper." He squeezed my hand and a smile broke out like the moon through a bank of clouds. "I carried you back."

I opened my mouth to speak, and surprise closed it again. I tried a second time. "What?"

"What's so surprising about that? Your father has probably done it a hundred times when you were small and fell asleep in his lap."

"If he did, I don't remember."

"Then at least you're consistent." He laughed, and the sound was so infectious I couldn't help joining in. The questions backed up in my throat. If he had been carrying me, how had he opened the back door? Or made it up the stairs? How had he known which room was mine?

The thought of Gabriel in my room, laying me on the bed the way a husband might ... my breath stopped. Had he lain next to me and I'd missed the sweetness of that moment?

"Next time," I said, "wake me. I'm perfectly capable of walking."

"I know you are. But it pleased me to do that for you."

"I lost my *kapp*, though. I found it on a bush a couple of days later. Ruined."

"I wish I had known. I'd have gone back for it." He was so sweet. I threaded my fingers through his and let the moment trickle through me like warm honey. "That must be why you arranged with Rebecca for a sewing party."

"Yes. And for another reason, too." I squeezed his hand. "She has a very heavy sewing machine. Can't move it, so we all have to come over there."

"How fortunate."

This time I felt as shiny as the moon, glowing at him. Then a thought struck me, and my smile faded. "Gabriel, I have to do something about David."

"What has he done?"

His tone changed, and I hastened to reassure him. "Oh, nothing. Except I think I'm leading him on. He's starting to talk about us doing weekend trips together. I need to tell him I can't do that—or even accept rides home with him anymore." I waited for him to say something, but he didn't. "It isn't right to let him think something might be possible between us when it isn't."

This would be the moment when he was supposed to say, *As soon as you do that, then we'll start appearing in public together.*

I waited. "Gabriel?"

"Weekend trips?" He sounded distracted, as if his mind was going a mile a minute.

Maybe I'd just shocked him by being so forward. Men liked to do the pursuing, didn't they? And he was pursuing me. It wasn't David out there under the cherry tree waiting, now, was it?

"He likes music, so he mentioned going to one of those band hops. Except there aren't any around here; they're closer to Council Bluffs. I'm supposed to ask my sister, but I don't think I'll bring it up. Not if—if you—"

"If I what?"

"If we, um, start courting. Publicly, I mean."

"There's no need for that, is there?"

A needle of hurt inserted itself between my ribs and pricked my heart. "Well, no ... not if you don't want to." Lots of couples kept their relationships a secret from their families. That's why the seating at weddings in the winter was so interesting to grownups. Parents with teenagers would crowd the door as the bride paired people off at the tables, because couples would have told her in advance whom they wanted to sit with. Sometimes that was a parent's first clue about who their prospective son or daughter-in-law might be.

But I hadn't realized Gabriel wanted to keep us under wraps. I had sort of hoped ...

You wanted to ride on the front seat of his borrowed buggy and sit opposite him at singings so everyone would know that painfully ordinary Sophia Brucker had landed the catch of the county. Didn't you?

No, of course not.

Uh-huh. Let's not add lying to your pride and vanity.

Be quiet.

Gabriel is right to do it his way. He knows your faults and he's helping you grow out of them.

Is now the moment? She is waiting for me to declare my-self. But ... but how do I know it is the will of God? Should I propose? Keep silent?

O Lord, show me what I should do!

I am assailed by this weakness. I have not sacrificed to the Lord in a week, and my immortal body betrays me. But I know whom the sacrifice must be. I hope God speaks very soon, so that I can regain my strength and set Sophia's mind at rest. She must know how deeply I care. After everything I have done—and continue to do—for her, she must surely know.

But marry? I cannot make such a decision now, with my mind spinning from lack of blood. I must keep silent.

For now.

I made it back to my room on my own two feet, with lots of time to spare before Dat poked his head in. I couldn't help it. Gabriel's unwillingness to be seen with me—even if it were only in front of the *Youngie*—hurt. The magic had evaporated slowly from the night, to the point where all I wanted to do was run back to my room, where I could cry in private.

Maybe he was coming down with something. He had seemed different tonight—listless, almost. Depressed? Oh, I hoped it was simpler than that—spring cold season was in full swing. He had seemed pale and not his usual smiling self last week, too, before ... before my uncle had died. The better I came to know him, the more I could see his ups and downs.

Or maybe I was fooling myself and he was simply having second thoughts about us. I mean, why shouldn't he? Who was I to keep the attention of someone like him? I wasn't as pretty as Rebecca Hodder, and my family didn't have as many acres as, say, Cara Troyer's. Not that these things were supposed to carry any weight with a plain man. But Gabriel hadn't been plain very long. Maybe, deep down, these things mattered more than magical nights and cherry trees and the ability to talk about the deepest of subjects.

While my hands tugged and squeezed the teats of the cow, my mind worked, chewing the same bitter cud over and over. Finally I looked over the boards at my dad's broad back in the next stall.

"Dat?"

"Hm?" Often he got into a meditative state when he milked. He said it was his prayer time—and I hesitated to break it. But I had an idea.

"Are Uncle Joseph and Aunt Irene leaving soon?"

"The van is coming for them on Monday, I think. Why? Are you in a hurry to see them go?"

"No, of course not. Do you think you could lend me enough money for a train ticket to Ontario?" If Gabriel didn't want me publicly, then maybe we'd see how he did without me privately. Wasn't it true that absence made the heart grow fonder?

The rush of milk into the pail paused for two seconds, then resumed again. "Have they invited you for a visit?"

"I have a standing invitation I've never taken them up on. I've never been to Ontario. It would be interesting. And I would help Aunt Irene out as much as I could, of course."

"She has three girls for that already, and your mother has only you." Oh, dear. There went my spontaneous plan. "She and Aunt Sallie will need you to help pack up the house."

What? "Has she decided to move? So fast?"

"We will discuss it at breakfast."

I knew better than to pester him with questions. He already sounded distracted, as if he were listening to me with one ear and God with the other.

Instead, I got down to business with the cow and tried to come to terms with the fact that I couldn't just run away from my problems or teach anybody a lesson. If Gabriel wasn't prepared to court me in front of others, then maybe I had read far too much into our few hours together. How did I know when a man really cared? All I'd ever known were friendships with people I'd grown up with. I mean, there were two men in my life, but look what I had to work with—on one hand, the man could barely get a conversation going. And on the other hand, the man knew my darkest secret.

My hands stilled. Had Gabriel kissed me and laid down with me because he knew I wasn't innocent of mind like the other girls my age? Did he think that my uncle had paved the way for him?

No, no. Nausea at the very thought made my stomach lurch and churn. I pulled on the cow's teats, and she shifted uneasily.

I might not know Gabriel that well, but I did know one thing. He wouldn't take advantage of a girl and use her that way. He respected me. He cared. I knew it.

But for some reason he wasn't willing for everyone else to know it.

Maybe God thought I needed lessons in acceptance and willingness. Maybe this was a test for my vanity. Maybe my prayers should go a little deeper than they had lately.

Lord, I know You hear me as I do the work that glorifies You. Help me to know what Your will is for me. If Gabriel isn't Your choice for me, help me accept that. I don't know what You have in mind for me, Lord. Walk with me, please, and guide me in the right direction. In the name of Jesus, amen.

Mamm handed me the covered bowl of biscuits, and dished up the bacon and onions out of the heavy cast-iron frying pan with the ease of long experience. With wifely intuition—or maybe just a finely tuned sense of timing—she always had a hot breakfast ready and on the point of serving when Dat and the boys and I came in from the barn and finished washing up. When everything was on the table, she and I took our places and Dat said grace.

Once everyone's plates were filled and we'd begun to eat, Dat glanced at her. "I told the children I'd tell them about their aunt."

"What's going on?" Caleb buttered a biscuit and stuffed half of it in his mouth while Jonah reached for another boiled egg to mash into the top of his biscuit.

"Your Aunt Sallie came over yesterday to give us some pretty astonishing news," Dat began slowly. "It has to do with you directly, Caleb."

"She's going to sell the farm to you for Caleb and go live with Carrie," I said. "She said as much before, didn't she?"

Caleb would have to settle down now. And from the frozen deer look on his face as he held the other half of his biscuit in front of his mouth without biting into it, that thought had just hit him, too.

"I had thought so, but apparently between the night of the funeral, when we talked about it, and sometime this week, word of her plans got out."

"But no one knew except the family," Mamm said. "And really, what should it matter to the church if she stays or goes? It's not as if she's moving to another district."

"Apparently it does become the church's business when its brand-new convert makes an offer for a valuable working farm right out of the blue."

I dropped my fork with a clatter.

No one noticed over the sound of Caleb shoving his chair back. He leaped to his feet. "Dat, what are you saying? New convert? You mean—"

"Sit down, son," Dat said with more gentleness than I would have expected. When Caleb did, he went on, "Apparently Gabriel Langford made Sallie a very generous offer for the farm yesterday."

"Gabriel ... Gabe ..." I got control of my mouth with difficulty. "But he doesn't have any money. He drives Joshua Hodder's buggy when he has to go somewhere, for goodness sake."

"Apparently, from what Sallie says, he would give her cash. No paper." Dat's mouth twisted wryly. "He seems to have a very happy relationship with his *Englisch* bank."

Gabriel had a bank account? But didn't he work all those long hours to pay Joshua Hodder his room and board? "You don't buy a farm on a day-jobber's wages," I said faintly. "Where did he get the money?"

"This is the question in Bishop Stolz's mind, as well."

My brain had turned into a howling wilderness. Gabriel had said his family was rich. Had he inherited it all? How could he, if everything was in England? And why had he never said one word about his plans to me?

Caleb made an impatient gesture. "The question in my mind is, will Aunt Sallie do the right thing by her family, or will she be tempted by the money to sell her farm to a stranger?"

"He's not a stranger." The words snapped from my mouth before I had time to think.

"What does that mean, Sophia?" Mamm eyed me with the focus of a hen on a worm.

Hastily, I backpedaled. "We all know him. He was baptized right here in our meetinghouse and he's worked for half the men in the district." I babbled the obvious while the truth settled on me with all its weight.

He is a stranger. You don't know him at all. And if you didn't know this, maybe you've completely misread how he feels about you, too.

The attention of both my parents had returned to Caleb. "Son, when you talk of 'the right thing,' does that mean you want Aunt Sallie to sell the farm to us so that you can have it some day? Does it mean you'd end your running around and join church?"

Caleb chewed the inside of his cheek and pushed at his onions as if he'd lost his appetite for them. "I—I don't want the farm to go to someone outside the family."

"That's not what I'm asking," Dat said.

"I know what you're asking. And I don't have an answer."

"When will you have one?"

"It had better be soon," Mamm put in. "Sallie told me that she can't wait too long. If she takes the cash, she can have a *daadi haus* built and move into it by fall, before the snow flies."

"There are more important things going on here than a *daadi haus*," Caleb muttered.

"Not to Aunt Sallie," I pointed out. "Well, Caleb? You're eighteen. Old enough to make up your mind."

"You haven't joined church yet, either," he reminded me.

"We're not talking about me," I said, devoutly grateful that was true. "And don't worry about not having a girlfriend. With a farm in your future, plenty of girls will like you."

He blushed as red as the geraniums coming into bloom on the front porch. "That's none of your business."

But the Gingrich farm was my business. The full importance of this news sank in with stunning clarity. If Gabriel did go through with this in the face of my family's opposition, he would no longer be a boarder. He would work the farm himself and hire other boys to help him. He would live right next door instead of two miles away.

Gabriel. Next door. Close enough to see every day. Or every night. Is that what he was planning? Was this about me?

No, that couldn't be right. That was pride and vanity, and I felt my cheeks burn with shame that I'd even harbored the thought.

But oh, it was so tempting to dream ...

11

The news that Gabriel had offered to buy the Gingrich farm for cash money flashed from one end of Mitternacht to the other in a matter of hours. As a result, it was the hot topic of conversation at the stitching frolic on Wednesday afternoon.

I kept my head down and my fingers busy—and listened with every cell in my body to everyone around me talking about him.

"Girls, you shouldn't look to me if you want to know about Gabriel," Rebecca finally said in exasperation. "He boards here, but he doesn't confide in me. I'm just as surprised as you."

"Has he given your dad notice?" Brenda Miller wanted to know.

Rebecca shook her head. "He's just made an offer. That doesn't mean Sallie will take it. After all ..." Her voice trailed away and she glanced at me as if I should finish the sentence.

"That farm should go to Caleb." I knew how Katie Hertzfeld felt about it. In her mind, this was what the *Englisch* called a no-brainer. "If Sallie doesn't want to keep it for Carrie's little boy, then Caleb is the next rightful person. Isn't that so, Sophia?"

They were both determined to drag me into this. "It's not for us to say," I said at last. "We've been through it all at home, but in the end it's up to my aunt to decide."

"Gabriel's getting ready to settle down." Cara Troyer had the air of one who knows. "First he's baptized, then he offers on a farm. Next he'll be buying a courting buggy, you watch."

"If he buys a farm, he won't have any money left for a buggy, never mind a horse to hitch it to," Rebecca pointed out.

I bit down on the urge to disagree. I had to stay out of this. Someone got up from the sewing machine, so I gathered up my half-dozen brim bands and seated myself behind it. With my foot moving up and down on the treadle, I sewed pleats to brims as if I had nothing more important in the world to think about.

"What I want to know is, where does all this money come from? Is it true he's going to pay in cash?" Brenda wanted to know.

"That's what we're saying," Cara said. "You can tell by the sound of his voice that he's rich."

"But he doesn't show it," Rebecca said. "There's no pride in that boy. He did right to keep it quiet. And you should know better than to talk about someone's money, Cara Troyer."

"Actions are better than words, anyway," Cara said mysteriously. None of us would satisfy her by asking what she meant, except for Brenda, who took everyone literally and couldn't spot an undercurrent if she was standing in it. "You'll see. But not till after tomorrow night."

Katie rolled her eyes. "Oh, that's right. You two are courting. Or hasn't that worked out for you yet?"

"You're just jealous," Cara said with airy certainty. "You wish Caleb Brucker would talk to you the way Gabriel talks to me."

"I didn't notice Gabriel talking to you at the volley-ball game." Katie's retort came whip-quick. "The one time he did, you turned beet red and ran out of the room."

"Boys like to tease," Cara said stubbornly. "It's how they show a girl they're interested. Not that you would know."

"Cara ..." Rebecca said in a warning tone.

"When they're ten years old, maybe," Katie said. "They get past that once they're out of the schoolroom. But maybe the boys you pick aren't very mature."

"All right, you two, that's enough." Rebecca looked from one to the other with exactly the same expression Mamm used when Caleb and Jonah used to fight at the table. "You're not being very kind."

Katie bit back something she obviously wanted to say. Instead, she held out a hand to Cara. "Do you want me to do the pleats on that covering for you? Mine are finished."

With a glance at Rebecca, Cara nodded and passed the half-finished *kapp* across the table. We made our prayer coverings in the shape of a flour scoop, with a row of pleats that you could make wider or thinner depending on how long or thick your hair was. I guess we could be glad the *Ordnung* didn't specify the number or how deep they had to be, as I'd heard was common in some other districts. "Denki. And I'll edge-stitch your ribbons for you, if Sophia is done at the sewing machine yet."

Rebecca sat back with her work, satisfied, and the conversation turned to who planned to visit where after meeting on Sunday.

Cara brought a handful of *kapp* strings over and stood waiting while I finished my last seam. "You're awfully quiet," she said after we'd exchanged places.

I shrugged. "I'm not the best *Näherin* in the world. It's hard to make your hands work the fabric and your feet work the treadle at the same time. If I don't concentrate, my seams go all over the place."

Cara eyed me, then returned her attention to starting a ribbon running under the needle. "I think it's more than that. I think you know more than the rest of us do. You're just not saying."

"I promise you, Cara, I don't. It was as much of a surprise to me as you."

"There's something going on between the two of you, though, isn't there?"

How had she known? I hesitated, the past couple of weeks flashing past the eye of my memory, like the scenery when you ride in a car. No. We had never even been seen in public except for the four of us arriving at the volleyball game. Then how ... ?

"What's the matter, Sophia? Cat got your tongue?"

"No."

"No, the cat hasn't got your tongue, or no, you're not seeing him?"

What could I say? I couldn't lie. And I couldn't tell the truth. Gabriel did not want us to be public, for reasons I couldn't fathom. And even if he did, Cara Troyer and I were not exactly the kind of friends who exchanged confidences about boys—or anything else.

"Just ... no," I said at last.

Cara's eyes narrowed with dislike. "You are such a hypocrite." My cheeks turned cold, then flushed hot. "After your uncle's funeral my mother and I got in a mix-up about our tablecloth and dishes, so I walked back to get them." When I still didn't say anything, she went on, "Why don't you ask me what I saw then? Or are you too ashamed?"

With every word, her voice rose. I don't even think she was aware of it. But I was. I wanted to drop through the floor—sink into the wall—anything but turn to face the sudden silence at the table.

"Ashamed of what?" Brenda Miller asked. "Did someone catch Sophia and David Fischer doing something naughty?"

"Oh, no. David's not enough of a challenge for her," Cara said. "She'd rather steal a boy from someone else."

"Sophia?" Brenda sounded amazed. "Steal who?"

"Gabriel Langford, that's who." Cara sat behind the sewing machine in triumph as the whole table promptly went into a tizzy fit.

"Sophia, are you and Gabriel courting?"

"How could you keep a secret like that?"

"That can't be true. I heard he was courting a girl in Myerling."

"I heard he was courting you, Rebecca."

"But Cara says he's courting her."

"Maybe he's courting all three at once. You just can't trust those good-looking ones."

"Sophia, tell us! Which is it?"

Standing there against the china cabinet with my hands full of white organdy, I felt like that animal that had been trapped in the milking pen by my uncle. I had thought that with his death, I would never feel like this again. Sick. On fire. Desperate to escape.

Trapped between the truth and a lie, and unable to speak either aloud.

"You'll have to ask Cara," I finally mumbled. "She seems to know much more about it than I do." I pushed past Rebecca's chair and began to gather up my sewing things, shoving them blindly into the plastic shopping bag I'd brought.

Surely she wouldn't say it in front of all our friends. Surely, for the sake of her own self-respect, she'd keep her mouth shut.

"I caught them holding hands on the night of her uncle's funeral." The attention of everyone at the table swung back to her. "And they ran off behind the barn together. I hope someone plans to tell poor David, because I don't have the heart."

You don't have a heart, period. How could we be friends after this? We shared the same bunch of friends, for goodness sake. We saw each other practically every day. Didn't she know how this show of meanness and spite was going to divide our little group? And for what? Some dream she had that could never come true? It wasn't my fault Gabriel had chosen me and not her.

Rebecca looked a little shocked. "You and Gabriel were carrying on at your uncle's funeral?"

"We weren't carrying on." I could barely speak, and my face burned. "I'm going to go now. Thanks for hosting, Rebecca."

"Aren't you staying for *kaffee?*"

I shook my head and would have offered some excuse, but Cara got up from the sewing machine with her finished *kapps*. "You don't have to run away just because you've been found out."

"Leave her alone, Cara," Katie snapped, pushing out from behind the dining table. "You're just mad because Gabriel isn't interested in you."

"Is that so, Katie Hertzfeld? Then I'd like to know why he walked me to the phone box this morning and spent ten minutes talking with me."

"Because he's polite?"

Cara implored heaven for patience with such a *maedel*. "You say things like that because you've never had a boyfriend."

"What were you doing at the phone box?" Brenda wanted to know.

"That's my business. Maybe I had to make an appointment."

"With somebody who's *Englisch*?"

Lots of people had telephones on their farms, but they were out in the barn or in a box at the end of the drive. It was pretty hard to just call someone and expect they'd be standing there right when you wanted them. Mostly the phone was for calling *Englisch* folks or for emergencies. So chances were Brenda was right.

"Maybe I'm going on a trip and needed to know the bus schedule. Don't be so nosy. The point is, Gabriel was coming along the road and he walked me there." A dreamy look crossed her face, at odds with her pale eyelashes and snub nose. "He's so easy to talk to. And I could listen to that British accent all day. And all night."

I barely restrained myself from jerking around to stare at her, and took advantage of the fact that everyone else was doing just that to grab my shopping bag and purse and slip out the kitchen door. How did she know what kind of accent he had? He'd had to tell me. As I began the two-mile walk home, for the millionth time I wondered what he saw in me when even Cara Troyer knew more about the world than I did.

Even when Katie caught up to me ten minutes later and walked the rest of the way fuming out loud about Cara's behavior and what she thought that was going to get her, I couldn't find any comfort in it.

The law of the hunt is the same for humans as it is for the lower orders of creatures. If you set up an expectation in the mind of the prey, it will behave according to that expectation, no matter what evidence you later give it. It will believe in what it expects right up until the moment when you prove it to be incontrovertibly, fatally wrong.

This had been Paul Gingrich's mistake. He expected to find me whitewashing in his milking pen. He expected me to behave with the respect a younger man shows an elder. Both these expectations gave me the freedom to get close to him, and when he realized what was about to happen, it was far too late to escape.

I know that Cara Troyer harbors what we used to call a *tendre* for me. In any circumstances but these, I would feel pity for her. If I could not return her affections, it would simply be a matter of turning her attention to someone who could. But I do not feel pity—on the contrary, my knowledge of what she is has firmed my resolve, even if I have had to be rather more forward than an Old Order man in Mitternacht would ever be.

She is delighted. And by it shows her immodesty. God has shown me the truth. She is no lamb, and what is more, she endangers the other lambs. Her bad spirit will infect them all, with lies and unkindnesses multiplying daily. She must be stopped.

Yesterday morning she chattered for a full ten minutes as we walked along the road. All I needed to do was to look meaningfully into her eyes once or twice, and she was mine. She has agreed to meet me by the phone box tonight after her family is asleep. So, here I stand in the shadows, shivering with a cold that comes from this infernal weakness deep inside rather than from the breeze that rustles the copse of wild plums. I believe my teeth are actually chattering. To distract myself, I try humming a hymn, then singing to keep my jaws moving.

"Gabriel?"

In the night, her whisper sounds like fingertips on sandpaper. "I'm here." I step out from under the trees.

"I thought you might not come," she says, and to reassure her I take her hand in both of mine. "My goodness, your hands are cold."

"Cold hands, warm heart. Where shall we go?"

"That depends on what you have in mind." She sounds like a woman of the demimonde, not a plain girl of sixteen.

"I just want to be alone with you." I lead her under the trees and she gasps. "Whose car is this?"

"It's mine."

"But you said you don't have a license!" She is already in the old Sun Valley, running her hands over the upholstery. I am its original owner and keep it in good condition, both inside and under the hood. That God provides a reliable way of escape is not only scriptural, it's necessary in the most practical sense.

"I don't." I get in and turn the key. I haven't had a license since the middle of the last century. Too easy to trace. "But I don't need one to own a car. I keep it in an *Englisch* man's barn over in Furniss. For emergencies." I researched the bus routes and chose that location because the bus stops a hundred feet away. With all the abrupt departures I have had to make over the years, I've learned to have transportation at hand. And I wouldn't be without the old Mercury for hunting, because I often range far afield.

Cara is clearly shocked. "Gabriel, if Bishop Stolz finds out, he'll make you give it up. You can't be baptized and still own a car."

"I know. I'll sell it this summer." And buy one that is less likely to cause comment. I love the old girl, though. She has served me well. "Since this might be your last ride, shall we make it a good one? Would you like to go to Omaha?"

She squeals and bounces up and down on the seat. "I would love to! Oh, I wish you'd told me. I'd have brought my real clothes."

"That would have made your family ask questions. Your parents—do they know you're with me?"

She snorted. "Adam Hertzfeld came over earlier and took me for a ride in his silly souped-up buggy. They think I'm still out with him."

As we drive, she fiddles with her seat belt, as though she would like to slide over to the middle, where there is none. She is looking for encouragement from me. Direction. I am clearly not behaving like Adam Hertzfeld.

The Mercury's V8 engine is powerful and it doesn't take long before the lights of Omaha glow on the horizon, then all around us. I have hunted here before, and know the territory. Wehrspann Lake will suit my purposes admirably, and she treats it as an adventure as we park the car and she chooses a tree-shaded path. In a romantic spot not far from the lake's edge, I take a step closer and run one finger over her hand.

"Your skin is like apricots." This is true, though the only lights are some distance away in the parking lot.

I feel the heat of her blush as the lovely blood fills every capillary on her cheeks and forehead. I can practically smell it. It takes every ounce of my control not to fall upon her. I have one thing to say first.

"Do you really like me?" she whispers. "Because Sophia Brucker thinks you're courting her."

I will not have the name of my beloved on this girl's lips. I lean down and breathe deeply of the scent of young, rich life racing through her veins. It makes her breath speed up and her temperature rise, and her eyes close. She tilts her head to receive my kiss, a she-wolf acknowledging the strength of a power greater than hers.

Against her fragile skin I whisper, "Into God's hands I commend your spirit."

Her body stills in confusion as expectation crashes rudely into reality, and in that moment, I strike.

The hot, delicious fountain curves into my mouth and I nearly forget the holiness of my mission as I drink deeply, endlessly, joyously. The life and vigor pours from her veins into mine, the racing pleasure like a storm front barreling into my body and setting every cell and nerve to tingling, right out to my fingertips.

When the heart ceases its work and the flood slows, I lower her to the grass under the trees and fold her skirts out of the way. In contrast to the bright spouting of the carotid, the femoral artery yields with a flow as slow and strong as the *Moonlight Sonata*, all downbeats and inevitability.

I drink and drink, feeling the strength return to my limbs and the function to my brain. At last God's will is satisfied, and my eternal body is ready for whatever my Lord will ask of me.

Before I leave, I turn her skirts back down, covering her bare legs so that she is not found in an immodest pose. Her face under her *kapp* is still. White. At peace.

She did not even open her eyes.

12

When word went out that the Friday night volleyball game would be at Troyers' again, I almost didn't go.

"I just can't take any more of Cara's bad temper." I sliced at the weeds between the young rows of vegetables while Katie worked behind me, carrying the piles to the compost heap. "Why should I let myself in for more of the same?"

"Because I need someone to talk to, that's why," Katie said firmly. "Besides, Caleb might drive us."

"I'm certainly not going with Gabriel two weeks in a row. That's all the grapevine needs."

I hadn't seen him since the stitching frolic two days ago—not that a brief exchange of glances and a friendly wave as he unhitched the Hodders' horse from the seeder counted as "seeing" him. Not when I craved the heat of his chest under my hands, or his soft lips slanting over mine as we fell together into the dark well of a kiss.

"Don't let Cara Troyer get to you." Katie's voice was steady as she shook the soil off the roots of the weeds. "She has the attention span of a mosquito. Next week she'll decide she likes Adam better, and the week after that she'll be chasing one of the Miller boys."

"She's as bloodthirsty and annoying as a mosquito, that's for sure. I feel sorry for Adam. I hear they went to a band hop somewhere up near Council Bluffs." Maybe I should let David know that Adam was the right person to ask about things like that. Then he could ask another girl to go with him.

"Really?" Katie sat back on her heels. "I thought he only took her driving last night."

"Maybe they kept going."

She shook her head. "He and Dat had to go to Furniss to the auction today. One of the blades broke off the old discer again and they were going to bid on a new one. So if she went, she didn't go with him."

"Maybe I will go to the game, then, if she's not there." I needed to stop hiding. Wasn't that what I always did? Hid from other people? I would be as welcome as anyone at that game. And if Gabriel didn't want us to go together, I would hold up my head, enjoy myself, and make him regret it.

"If Caleb drives, will you let me sit in the front? I saw him looking when we arrived with Gabriel last week."

"You know I will. Now, let's get back to work. And don't let me forget to put the roast in at three o'clock. My aunt is coming for supper."

This wasn't unusual, but I suspected there would be more to it than a simple family dinner. I was sure she'd made up her mind about the farm and was going to tell us. Anxiety spritzed into my stomach. I wanted Gabriel to have that farm, no matter how strange and wonderful his buying it might be. If Aunt Sallie sold it to my father, what would Gabriel do? Farms in this district rarely came up for sale. Everyone thought like my parents and kept property in their families. The only difference here was Gabriel's inexplicable possession of that much money. If you threw money into any mix, it changed things.

Two hours later, I put the roast in, and Mamm came home from a trip to town in time to scrub potatoes and cut up the vegetables to go with it while I made a dried-apple pie. Aunt Sallie seemed quite chatty during dinner, which was becoming normal lately. She'd never been much of a talker while Uncle Paul was alive, but since his death she seemed to have opened up. Had she always been like that, and no one ever noticed? Or was she just finding her voice now that she didn't have to answer to anyone?

Over the pie and the ice cream Katie and I had made, my father finally cleared his throat and plunged in. "So, Sallie, are you tired yet of having the whole district tromping around in your business?"

She snorted and speared a piece of pie with her fork. "If one day went by without someone coming over to ask me about it, I'd wonder what was wrong. I had to do some baking on Wednesday, just to keep people in cookies while they got around to what they wanted to know."

"And what did you tell them?" Mamm asked.

"Nothing. There are only two interested parties, and it's none of anyone else's business."

"Have you made a decision?" It wasn't Dat's way to beat around the bush, either.

Sallie nodded. "I am going to accept young Gabriel's offer."

The ladder back of my chair was practically all that kept me upright as I let out a long breath. Dat and Mamm stared at her. Caleb got up and left the kitchen. Jonah, true to form, ignored us all and helped himself to another piece of pie.

After a minute, Dat found his voice. "Is there nothing we can do? No counsel we can give you?"

Sallie shook her head, her dark eyes pleading with him to understand. "I have prayed long and hard about this, Victor, and the counsel I get from lieber Gott is to let go."

"Let go?" Mamm repeated. "That could mean anything."

"I don't think so. I think our Father wants me where I can be useful, and that's on Carrie's place, watching her children grow and helping to teach them to serve Him."

"You could do that here." But even Mamm didn't sound convinced, and Sallie heard it.

"We helped each other in the early days, Irene, and I'm glad we could fill that place for each other. But now Carrie needs me. So I'm going to build myself a little house and spend the rest of my days watching my grandchildren run through my tulip beds."

Put like that, you could hardly wish anything else for her. I tried hard to see it from Dat's point of view, but honestly? Caleb, a farmer? He just didn't, as my *Grossdaadi* Brucker used to say, have dirt under his fingernails. He worked the fields because as the eldest son, he was expected to, but in his heart I thought he'd be happier making cabinets in town.

"Gabriel Langford is no farmer," Dat said in a low tone, as if he'd read my mind. "I hope you don't regret your decision, for the sake of the land the Gingriches have farmed for a hundred years."

"I'm not responsible to the land, but to God's will," Sallie said crisply. "Paul and I were good stewards of what we were given. Now that task passes to young Gabriel. He knows what he's getting into. I hope you'll do the right thing and give him good advice if he needs it. He seems a teachable young man."

"Of course," Dat said gruffly. "Well, as long as you've made up your mind, we'll help you. When do you think you'll move?"

"Carrie's husband has already organized a construction crew. They'll be ready to pour the foundation of my little house on the first of June."

Mamm set her coffee cup down. "So soon? That's only two or three weeks away."

"There's nothing to keep me here longer," Sallie told her. "I can stay with Carrie until the house is built. And Gabriel will want to move in and have a look about him before the hay comes off. We've agreed it will be official on the first of July, but I'll be putting the keys in his hand before I leave."

The calendar over the stove said there were nearly three weeks to go before June first. Twenty days until I could walk up the hill and see the lights of Gabriel's home shining through the trees. My imagination could hardly hold the beauty of that picture.

And then my practical side added depth and scope, rounding out the picture to a possible future. He would need help inside the house. Paint colors, linoleum, new carpets. Would Sallie take the icebox and propane stove, or leave them and buy new? Curtains, trim, shelving. Furniture. Beds. Bedding. Quilts.

A girl started putting those last things away in her hope chest years before she started courting. Katie had a complete set of pots and pans in hers, wrapped up in quilts she and her mother and aunts had made. But boys? They didn't usually accumulate household goods until they got married, and wedding gifts began to flow in.

As far as I knew, Gabriel owned only the clothes he stood up in, and possibly a few books. Did his bank account have enough in it to furnish a home? And more important, would he ask me to help him make decisions about such things, which were usually a woman's business? What kind of statement would that make to the grapevine? If I started choosing paint colors, they'd say I was imposing my taste on his house because I expected to be mistress of it.

Not that I would deny myself that joy just because of the grapevine. Oh, no. If he asked me, I would say yes.

Um ... to helping him fit out the house, I mean.

When Gabriel didn't bring Rebecca to the volleyball game that evening, but merely dropped her off at the end of the drive, flapped the reins over the horse's back, and went on down the road, the grapevine practically tied itself in knots with speculation until Rebecca put it out of its misery.

"Komm runter, alles." She set the volleyball again and again with her fingertips—*thup, thup, thup*—as we gathered around her. "He bought the Gingrich farm and he's on his way over there now to talk with Sallie about what will stay when she goes."

A noisy storm of questions and editorial comments and general amazement ensued. Through it all, Rebecca just smiled in her quiet way. "You won't get anything else out of me because that's all I know. You'll have to wait until he comes." She bumped the ball over the net. No one went to get it.

"Is he coming over when he's done?" I asked.

"He said that depended on how long it took, but I'm sure he will." Was it my imagination, or did her gaze add a deeper meaning? One or two of the girls nudged each other.

Right, then. Not my imagination.

Unlike Cara Troyer, who could build an entire relationship in her imagination. She might be all talk, but at least some of the girls saw past the surface to the emptiness and indecision underneath. Cara didn't know which world she wanted, and it showed.

As for me, all I knew was that Gabriel wanted me, but he didn't want to be seen in public with me. That was taking discretion to the point of humiliation, and I wasn't sure I had the constitution for it. Was it so wrong to want to walk beside someone openly? Did other couples make such a big deal about who was going to ride in whose buggy, and whether it was open or closed? I wanted to ask Rebecca Hodder, who out of all of us had the most experience, but I was afraid she'd laugh at me.

Maybe I would write to Hannah again—a longer letter this time, and with more specifics. At least if she laughed, she'd be far enough away that I wouldn't know about it.

I could barely concentrate on the game. We were two miles from Aunt Sallie's place, but all the same, the road drew my gaze so often that my teammates figured it out.

"What's the matter, Sophia? You expecting someone?"

"Hey, is that a horse I hear? Oops, no, it's only a cow."

"Watch and pray, watch and pray—" somebody sang.

"—He will come and bring the day," the rest of the group chorused.

I'd never been so glad to hear someone call game point in my life. When the final ball dropped through Adam's hands and hit the ground, I practically ran under the net toward the house.

"Sophia, where are you going?" Katie panted as she ran after me. "Wait up."

I paused on the wide front verandah, half hidden in the shadows of the wisteria vine that twined up one of the posts. "Maybe *Fraa* Troyer can use a hand in the kitchen."

"Don't let them bother you. Everyone wants to talk about Gabriel. Nobody really believes what Cara said the other day. About you and him at the funeral. I mean, I was there the whole time."

"Not the whole time," I heard myself saying. I had never kept anything from Katie except—well, except for the business with my uncle. But everything else, the details of our daily lives, was like clear water between us— transparent and constantly moving. What else were friends for if not to talk about everything?

"I knew it!" she exclaimed, then hushed her voice. "It all started that day in Mitternacht. Does his buying the farm have something to do with you?"

"I don't know," I said honestly. "I haven't talked about it with him."

"You're kidding. But you're really courting?"

"I—I think so."

"You think so?" She moved closer, the leaves of the wisteria brushing against her *kapp*. "If I were seeing Gabriel Langford, I think I'd know it. Though that will never happen."

"I do know it. It's just that he doesn't want it to be public."

"Why not?"

"Katie, if I knew, I wouldn't be standing here. I'd be over at the farm helping him choose things."

She stood silently for a moment, turning this over in her mind. "Lots of people see each other without telling the whole district about it. Sometimes even their parents don't know."

Meine Busenfreunde. She thought everyone saw the world in light and dark, the way she did. I wished it could be that easy.

"Parents are one thing. But being together when we're with the young folk is different. I would have thought ..." My voice trailed away.

"Well, since you're not sure, can I ask you something?" When I nodded, she went on, "You know how sometimes I get these ... feelings about people? Like when I knew it started with you and Gabriel?"

"*Ja.* So?"

"Sometimes it goes a little deeper than that. Sometimes ... Sophia, are you sure about him?"

I couldn't be sure of anything unless I was with him. "How do you mean?"

"I don't know. It's just a feeling. Like when the sun goes behind a cloud."

Katie and I hardly ever got tempery with each other, but at this moment I felt a twist of annoyance. "You're not making any sense."

She waved her hands, as if this would clarify things. "There's something about him that—"

Fraa Troyer pushed open the door with her hip. "Sophia, Katie, could you give me a hand?" As we followed her in, she said, "I don't know what's come over Cara these days." She handed me a bowl and a couple of econo-bags of chips. Her hair had escaped the confines of her *kapp* and a strand waggled down on either side of her center part. "One minute she's driving with Adam, the next—who knows? I didn't think she was going to Council Bluffs, but she must have gone with him last night after all."

Katie and I exchanged an uneasy look. Didn't she know Adam was right outside in the yard? I supposed she'd find out as soon as everyone came in. And it wasn't like we knew the details of Cara's social life. Half of them were made up, anyway. Maybe she had gone to Council Bluffs. She'd told us she had to use the phone to make an appointment, hadn't she? Maybe that had been some *Englisch* boy, and she'd gone away for the weekend with him.

"Can one of you watch this caramel sauce? Keep stirring it until it thickens. I'm just going to run down to the root cellar and get some more apples. I thought I'd counted right, but I think we'll need more for dipping."

She dried her hands, while at the front of the house the noise level rose with more and more of the young folk coming in looking for snacks. I'd filled the big bowl with chips, put it on the dining table, and was just coming into the kitchen to take a peek at the caramel sauce when I heard the crunch of gravel outside in the drive. And not the kind that came with the clop and scrape of hooves, either. The kind rubber tires made.

"Who could that be?" Apples forgotten, *Fraa* Troyer hustled to the front door, half the crowd on her heels. By craning my neck, I could see out the front window over the jungle of houseplants she had there.

It was the sheriff's big car.

My heart stuttered, then resumed its normal beat as Deputy Palermo, his face lit on one side by the porch light, got out and spoke to Cara's father, who had met him in the yard. Both men turned to Cara's mother as she joined them, and after a few more sentences, she clapped her hands to her mouth, shaking her head violently from side to side. Her husband tried to take her in his arms, but she shook him off and backed away, hands still clamped to her mouth.

Even through her fingers and the window glass, I could hear her screaming.

"Gabriel, come in." Sallie Gingrich opens the door wide and I step into her spotless kitchen. "Would you like coffee?"

"Thank you." She pours me a mug from the pot on the stove and fills a plate with cookies. When she sits across from me, her smile is hesitant, tremulous. "I went to the bank today," I say, thinking to reassure her. "The transfer came through. Once we agree on the things you don't plan to take, I'll bring you the money."

"I never thought it would be so easy." She looks past me, her gaze taking in stove, woodbox, glass cupboards with their white dishes, pictures on the walls. "Any of it. I don't understand why I don't feel more." She shakes her head.

Can it be because this is her husband's home? Because she hated her husband for his ongoing humiliation of her? Because she has more compassion for Sophia than forgiveness for herself? But these are questions I cannot ask a woman I barely know.

"Have you decided on what you're taking and what you will leave?" It's best to get on with what I came for.

She nods. "I'll leave the icebox and stove. Carrie says I don't have to cook with wood ever again—the new propane stoves are easy to maintain and less expensive than I would have thought. Besides, I haven't had new appliances ever. Those ones were already there when I came to this house as a bride." She glances up. "I hope you know how to cook on a wood stove."

Her skepticism makes me smile. "I do. I may not be able to bake a perfect pie, but I can get my own dinner if I have to." Two hundred years of eternal life has taught me to speak the truth whenever possible. I can get up a reasonable meal. She does not need to know it is not necessary. This eternal body needs its blood cells restored from time to time, but I do not need to eat for the same reasons others do. I eat for show, when I cannot escape it.

When I am living here with Sophia as my wife, I suppose I will need to get used to eating regularly. It is her needs and preferences that I should be consulting tonight, but I cannot do that until I make my intentions known to her.

I will go to her in a few hours. Until then, there are a few decisions I can make.

"I won't need a washing machine, because I can use Carrie's," Sallie continues. "And I'll use her clothesline, too. As for furniture, I'll be taking the guest bed and dresser. You can have the bed in the front bedroom, or move it to whatever room you like."

Her marriage bed. She is leaving it behind. I will be buying a new one, then—for I shall not burden Sophia's heart with the knowledge that she must sleep in Paul Gingrich's bed. Ours shall be as clean and new as our marriage itself, and belong only to us.

"There is a big wardrobe in the front bedroom, too, that Paul and Irene's father made. He was a skilled carpenter. Would you like to see it?"

I follow her upstairs, noting the sturdiness of the farmhouse's construction. It has weathered almost as many winters as I have. This thought pleases me.

The armoire fills nearly half the wall, and is carved with figures of trees and birds. "Are you sure you would not like to take this with you?" I ask her. "It's a wonderful piece."

"There isn't a man in the district who could get that down the stairs," she says. "It was built right in this room. You're welcome to it if you like it."

I picture Sophia hanging her dresses inside, and my shirts, and putting the extra sheets for the bed on its shelves. I see her quiet smile in my mind and feel certain she will be pleased to live with her grandfather's handiwork. "I'd like it very much. Thank you."

The Gingriches are not collectors of modern things, it is clear. A basin and ewer such as I might have used long ago in England stands on the dresser, though I note modern plumbing in the bathroom as we pass. Of all the technological advances I have seen since I left Langford Hall, the flush toilet stands at the forefront, in my opinion. I can leave most of the rest—television, radio, the Internet, the combustion engine. They were made to make life easier, but as far as I can see, all they do is steal time. That is why living with the Mennonites suits me. It is what I am used to.

Sallie Gingrich pauses in the hall. "Do you want to go out to the barn and look it over? I'm afraid I don't know as much about what Paul had out there as I do what's in the house."

"No, that's all right. I have a good idea from working for him off and on."

She nods. Hesitates. Then, "I hope you'll be happy here, Gabriel. Happy and useful for God's work."

"I believe I will. And I know your daughter will appreciate having you at their place."

Again, she looks around her, as if she has already said good-bye and is merely standing on the platform, waiting for the train. "I started packing. I'll be leaving at the end of next week. I told Victor and Irene I would give you the keys on June first, so you'll have time to settle in before you have to take the hay off. Is that all right?"

The hay will not be ready to cut for some weeks yet. If I propose to Sophia tonight, then we will have two weeks to paint and buy furniture she likes before I come here to live permanently. We can speak to the bishop about being married in November, and spend our first Christmas here together.

The thought takes my breath away.

"Gabriel?" Sallie is looking at me as I stand there woolgathering. "I said, is that all right?"

June first. Keys. "*Ja*," I assure her. "I couldn't have planned it better myself."

She sees me to the door, and stands watching as I light the buggy lamps, back the horse, and set off down the lane. When I turn onto the highway, she is still standing there, a small, wiry figure in a white *kapp*, silhouetted in the light from the kitchen.

The moon has not yet risen, which means that the game at Troyers' may not have ended yet. The horse senses my anticipation, and breaks into a trot. I do not rein it in. I am filled with a sense of urgency to see Sophia, to speak with her, to lay my heart open to her. She feels rebuffed by me, and I must rectify that as soon as I can.

I see the odd rhythm of light coming from the Troyer farm as soon as I turn the corner onto 70th. At first I cannot place it—an unnatural flash of red, then blue. Flashing, flashing. Then I see. The sheriff's car is parked in the yard.

Even as I slow the horse, headlights and a powerful engine roar up and then pass me—another one, with Police and Omaha emblazoned on the side. It dives into the Troyers' driveway and as it cuts its engine I realize the buggy has come to a stop and I am sitting with the reins limp on the horse's back.

They have found Cara Troyer.

13

It took a long time before Cara's parents recovered enough to speak to anyone, including the police. It took even longer for the sheriff's deputies to decide who among the *Youngie* knew what, and then take down their names and addresses so that they could talk to us all separately, some that night and some later. Finally, at midnight, Caleb and I walked home, where I spent most of the night watching the shadows waver on the ceiling.

Someone who had been close enough to hear the police talking had passed on the fact that she had been dead at least twenty-four hours, lying somewhere in a city miles away while everyone thought she was in Council Bluffs having a good time. *Fraa* Troyer had been hysterical, until finally one of her sons had produced a little white tablet that had calmed her down and put her to sleep.

I didn't ask where he got it.

After breakfast the next morning, I went out to the barn with the intention of topping up the chickens' feed, but wound up playing with the gangly adolescent chicks. They were so cute at this stage, all feet and untidy pin-feathers and curiosity about the world. They would run up my arm and perch on my shoulder, then flap and flap as they tried to fly up on my head. Since I didn't want peeper prints on my new *kapp*, I lifted them down into my lap, where they settled happily, panting with exertion.

Nothing calms a disturbed mind like chickens. They're so unaware of the cruelty of the world outside the barn that you just have to be happy for them.

The sound of an engine coming down the driveway and the crunch of gravel under its tires signaled the end of my quiet half hour with them. The sheriff's deputy hadn't wasted any time getting to the B's on his list. I stepped out into the sunlight as he got out of the car.

"Hello, there." Deputy Palermo lifted a hand in greeting. "We meet again."

"Yes." Unfortunately.

"Are your parents home?"

"My mother is in the kitchen. Dat is out in the field."

"I'd like to talk to you with an adult present, if you don't mind."

I didn't contradict him with the fact that Mamm considered me an adult, even if the *Englisch* law didn't. Mamm didn't contradict him, either. She simply got him a cup of coffee and settled next to me at the table while he pulled out his ever-present notebook.

"You're probably wondering why I wanted your mother here, when I spoke to you alone last time," he said. His brown eyes were so dark they looked black.

I shook my head. It had never occurred to me to question the reasons why the police did the things they did.

"I'll tell you anyway. It's because we treated the previous case as an animal attack. We're treating this one differently."

"Differently how?" Mamm asked.

"Because it seems pretty clear that the young lady didn't get to that park in Omaha on her own, and an animal of the four-footed variety certainly didn't follow her there."

"There aren't animals in the park?" I had no idea. I could count on the fingers of one hand the times I'd been to the big city. Council Bluffs was enough confusion for me.

"There was other evidence at the scene that points to a human attacker," he said, but wouldn't say what. "So, Miss Brucker, when was the last time you saw Cara?"

"On Wednesday. We were at a stitching frolic at Rebecca Hodder's."

"Was she still there when you left?"

"Yes. I left a bit early because I was—" I stopped. Stupid. Now you'll have to come out with the one thing you don't want to say.

"Because?" The ballpoint pen hovered over the notepad.

"Because I was upset."

"And why were you upset?"

"Because Cara was saying things."

"What kind of things, Sophia?" Mamm asked gently. "You didn't tell me this."

I let out a long breath. "She was being mean because she wants—wanted—Gabriel to court her, but he's courting me."

Mamm had taken a sip of coffee, and it went down the wrong way. She coughed and spluttered while the deputy reached out to thump her on the back, then hesitated, as if he wasn't sure whether it would offend her. She got control of herself and reached for a napkin. "This is a fine way to hear such a thing," she said when she could speak.

"It's—it's not really public," I said miserably. "Half the time I don't even know if it's true myself."

"Getting back to the point," Deputy Palermo said in a level tone, "what exactly did you mean when you said she was being mean?"

"Sarcastic. You know, things like I was cheating on David Fischer and someone ought to tell him. And she spiked a volleyball into my face last week, but that was an accident."

"So there was some conflict between the two of you."

"It was mostly in her head. She thought she was going to see Gabriel the next night, but it was all her imagination." If he hadn't been with me Thursday night, he wouldn't have been with anyone else. "Cara and I are in the same group of friends, but we don't—didn't—really pal around. We're too different."

"Where were you Thursday night?"

"Right here," Mamm said.

His gaze didn't move from mine until I answered. "I was here, sewing."

"All evening?"

"Yes."

"And after that?"

"She was in bed, of course," Mamm said.

"All night?"

Denkes, mein Gott, that Gabriel stayed away Thursday night. "I didn't wake up once."

"We get up at four-thirty for milking, and she was sound asleep," Mamm added. "Why are you asking her this? Sophia didn't take a bus up to Omaha and do away with poor Cara Troyer."

"Just trying to get a picture of everyone's whereabouts, that's all," he answered mildly, scratching notes on his pad.

But my mother's words triggered an image in my head. "Deputy, was she killed in the same way as my uncle?"

He glanced up at me while he finished his note. The last words—4:30 a.m. wakeup—wandered between the lines. "We're not in the habit of giving out details of crime scenes. But since you're a witness in the previous case, I'll say only that the cause of death was identical."

What had I been thinking? Now I would have two sets of dreadful images in my mind.

The deputy went on, "Which makes me think your uncle—excuse me, Mrs. Brucker, your brother—wasn't killed in an animal attack at all."

"But that's crazy," I burst out. "What possible reason could someone have to kill Uncle Paul and Cara?"

"That's part of what we're trying to find out. So, you last saw her on Wednesday at the stitching, er, frolic. You didn't see her at all on Thursday?"

I shook my head. "No, but my friend Katie Hertzfeld said she went for a ride with Adam—that's Katie's brother—that night, and they were thinking of going to a band hop up by Council Bluffs. But she didn't go with him because he had to go to the auction with his dad yesterday. When she didn't show up at the volleyball game, we just thought she went with someone else."

"What made you think that?"

"Because at Rebecca's she was talking about having to make a phone call. I thought it might have been an *Englisch* boy, and they went to the band hop after all." I paused. "I guess not."

"What time was this call?"

"Sometime Wednesday morning. You could ask Gabriel Langford. She said she talked to him for ten minutes at the phone box."

"I'll do that."

"Gabriel is buying my brother's farm," Mamm said. Then she gave me a long look, as if the real significance of that had just hit her. "You'll find him at Joshua Hodder's or over there."

"Thank you. And you say this boy Adam was with the vic—er, with Cara Thursday night?"

"Yes. I don't know what time, though." Adam could have been one of the last people to see her. What a strange thing—to be someone's last memory.

Deputy Palermo frowned and flipped back several pages in his notebook. "The last time we talked, you said that Adam Hertzfeld was the person who came and got your father after he discovered your uncle's body."

"Yes." Poor Adam. Not a sight either of us was likely to forget, ever.

"And he saw Cara on Thursday night." Both Mamm and I sat silently, waiting for him to go on. "For an Old Order boy, he seems to get around a lot."

"What are you saying, Deputy?" Mamm's voice was unusually measured.

But he didn't answer, only scratched another note in his book. When he was finished, he closed it. "Is there anything else you can think of to tell me, Miss Brucker?"

My mind had gone completely blank while I tried to figure out what my mother seemed to know. He took my silence as an answer.

"If you think of anything, you have my card?"

Oops. "It went through the wash. I'm sorry."

He pulled another one out of his chest pocket and gave it to me. "Give me a call if you think of anything at all, or if you remember the name of the person Cara might have called."

"She never said."

"Or anything else." He crossed the kitchen while my mother was still halfway out of her chair. "Don't get up. I'll see myself out."

Mamm sat again, a little more heavily than usual. When I heard the gravel crunch and the car accelerate down the highway, I said, "What did he mean about

Adam getting around a lot? Of course he's around. We're all around, all the time."

Her hands curled around her mug, as though she were trying to keep them warm. "I think he thinks that Adam may have done it."

All policemen seem to share certain similarities. Perhaps it is the deliberate way they walk, with their shoulders squared, or the level gaze that barely hides their suspicion that you have committed a crime. I knew a Bow Street runner once who believed himself the equal of a gentleman when he was in pursuit of his duties—and even when he was not. This sheriff's deputy climbing out of the black-and-white police car is just like that long-dead man, filled with assurance that he is in the right, and the world needs sorting.

I confess I am surprised to see him. He and the Bow Street man have not been the only policemen in two hundred years to approach me, but it has been thirty years or more since the last one died.

He sees me oiling tack in the open door of the barn. "Hello. I'm looking for Gabriel Langford."

I put down the tack and wipe my hands with a rag. "I am he."

"Deputy Palermo, Stinson County Sheriff's Department. Do you live here?" He looks around at Joshua Hodder's spotless yard and freshly painted barns.

"I'm a boarder at the moment, but I'm in the process of buying my own place."

Hands on hips, he regards me. "The Gingrich farm, right? I was just talking to Mrs. Brucker and her daughter."

He'd better not have frightened Sophia with his assured poses. "Yes. What can I do for you?"

"I need to ask a few questions. I'm going around to all the folks who were at Troyers' last night."

"I wasn't, I'm afraid. I was with Mrs. Gingrich. We had some decisions to make about the furnishings."

"Ah. Thank you for volunteering that." He leans on a wagon and pulls a notebook out of his jacket pocket. "I understand there was some bad blood between the victim and Miss Brucker because of her relationship with you."

I stare at him. What nonsense is this? "I'm sorry, I don't understand. Bad blood?"

He smiles, watching me. "Maybe bad blood is too strong a term. The victim believed that you and she were courting. Is that correct?"

This is a strange piece of misinformation. I hope it does not get back to Sophia. "I don't know what she believed, but we certainly were not. My intentions are toward Sophia Brucker."

"You're not from around these parts, are you? 'Intentions.' Haven't heard that word in a while."

I make a conscious effort to speak in the casual way Americans do. "I'm from England originally."

"Don't get too many Brits converting to Mennonite ways, especially the Old Order." When I do not dignify this comment with a reply, he consults his notebook. "I'm told you spoke with the victim at the phone box on

Wednesday morning. Do you remember what time that was?"

"Around nine. I was on my way to the bank in Mitternacht, and it opens at nine thirty."

He makes a note. "And what did you talk about?"

I have no idea. Cara chattered and I made agreeable noises, while I thought about what I needed to do for the wire transfer and then what I needed to do about her. "This and that. She was quite the talker. I don't really remember."

"Nothing about who she was calling or why?"

I shake my head. "She was making some kind of appointment. I got the impression it was about travel."

"Not a call to an English boy?"

This surprises me, but I school my expression to thoughtfulness. Here is an opportunity. "I suppose it could have been. If he were *Englisch*—" I pronounce it the way the Mennonites do. "—she would have to travel to see him."

He clicks his pen. "Was that the last time you saw her?"

I cannot lie, for I worship the God of truth. But at the same time, I cannot answer his question. "On my way back from town, I thought I saw her in the yard at her place, but I can't be sure. I was on the highway in the buggy."

He accepts this trivial truth as an answer, and consults his notebook. "Miss Brucker said that the victim mentioned something about seeing you after that. 'The next night,' her words were. Care to tell me about that?"

I am all puzzlement. "I don't know what she could have meant. Unless ... wasn't she to have gone somewhere with Adam Hertzfeld? Maybe that was what her phone call was about. Traveling to Council Bluffs."

"I doubt it. Miss Brucker says that Adam had to go somewhere with his dad Friday morning, so he couldn't have left for the weekend."

"Ah." I shake my head in regret. "Then I don't know what else I can tell you."

"You didn't see the deceased on Thursday night?"

I choose carefully from among several truths. "Cara Troyer and I weren't seeing each other. Not then, not ever."

"Not now, that's for sure." His gaze is steady on me and he waits, as if I will behave like a guilty man and rush to fill the silence. But I am skilled at waiting, as any hunter learns to be. "Anything else?"

"No." Then I add, "I hope you find the person who did this."

"Oh, I plan to," he says, and turns away.

As he drives out of the yard, I see him watching me in his rear view mirror.

14

I know it's wrong to pray for worldly things.

On my knees next to my bed, I prayed for Cara's family. I prayed for Aunt Sallie. I prayed that God would give me the strength to do His will, and that He would make me willing for every task He asked me to do.

But when I'd climbed into bed and lay there, once again staring at the ceiling, I couldn't help the plaintive little voice in the back of my head. *Please let him come. Please let him think of me, and know I'm thinking of him.*

He had told me that if I ever needed him, I should call. Well, I couldn't very well lean out the window and shout his name, so I did the next best thing.

Gabriel. *Gabriel.*

I fell asleep with his name ringing in my head like a bell, and when I woke suddenly, hours later, it was to see the flashlight beam dancing like a happy will o' the wisp on the ceiling.

Thank you. Oh, thank you.

I didn't know whom I was breathing gratitude to as I dressed and crept down the stairs—God or Gabriel himself. One or both had heard me and answered, and that was everything I could ask for.

I felt the difference in him as soon as he wrapped his arms around me, tightly enough that I could feel my own heartbeat bumping against his chest. "What is it?" I whispered against his open collar.

"I missed you. And with Cara—" He cut himself off and kissed me, his face hot, the way mine gets when I'm about to cry. "I won't let anything happen to you."

Any doubts I'd had about his feelings wavered and evaporated. He feared for me. He cared so much he could barely speak. Joy bubbled up in my heart like spring water, and the rush of it washed the dregs of my insecurity away. I kissed him with a confidence I'd never felt before—as if I had a right to. I think he felt it as well, because when we broke the kiss, he said, "Come on. Let's walk up to the woods. I have something to say to you."

Anticipation prickled under my skin. We crossed the creek single file, holding hands, and all the while my mind raced. He was going to tell me the real reason he'd bought my aunt's place. No, that was vanity.

He was simply going to caution me about going anywhere alone because he was afraid whoever had killed my uncle and Cara was still close enough to do harm. No, he wouldn't have walked two miles in the middle of the night to say what my father had already said half a dozen times today.

He would ask me what my favorite color was, so he could paint the walls of his new home. No, he needed advice on something else.

By the time we reached the woods, the possibilities were all gabbling in my head at once like a barn full of turkeys, drowning out the stillness of the night. His voice, quiet and serious, was almost a surprise.

"Let's sit here." He folded himself onto a patch of grass just at the edge of the trees, then pulled me down to sit between his knees, so we could both look out over the fields. They lay quietly, as if they knew they wouldn't be harried by anyone in these early hours of the Lord's day. I leaned back against his chest and he let me wrap his arms around myself like my favorite shawl.

"It seems so strange to think that Cara won't be in meeting later this morning," I said softly. "Or at volleyball, or anything."

"It does." He was silent a moment. "But you and she were not close, were you?"

I shook my head, the back of my braid brushing his shoulder. I'd forgotten to put on my *kapp*. "Still. She was a part of all of our lives. We were in school together, in the same group together. I'm praying for her family. Somehow they must find peace in God's will, even if none of us can see what that is yet."

"It *was* God's will. The harvest can come for any of us when it is His time." His voice was firm with the kind of faith I envied.

"How do you know?"

He moved a little, and I leaned forward in case he wasn't as comfortable as I was. He pulled me back. "Everything that happens is God's will."

"Even someone killing Cara? And my uncle?"

"Even so. As you say, we may not be able to see it yet, but God will show us eventually. Perhaps not until eternity, but He will."

"You sound so sure," I said wistfully. "I wish I was half so sure of things."

"But you have faith," he said. "I know you do. You wouldn't have chosen to be with His people if you didn't."

"His people are all I know," I pointed out. "I didn't really choose to be Mennonite, I just ... grew into it. Not like you. You had a whole life before you came here."

"You could always begin *Rumspringa*." I heard the smile in his voice and gave him a gentle elbow in the stomach.

"Sure I could. I could put on a pair of jeans and frighten you into the next county."

He chuckled. "I cannot even imagine you in a pair of jeans. Or in any worldly clothes. You're perfect just as you are."

"But I'm not, Gabriel." I twisted a little so I could see his face. "I said just as many mean things to poor Cara as she said to me. I lead David on when I don't mean it. I try and I pray, but it doesn't seem to do any good. I'm afraid of my shadow half the time, which means I must not have enough faith." I could go on, but that was enough to shame anybody. "I'm the last person you could call perfect."

"But love covers all that."

"I suppose. At least, I hope that when I get to Heaven, God will let me in." I didn't really know for sure that He would, though. All a person could do was strive after perfection, follow the Bible, and hope it was enough.

"I wasn't talking about God's love, though it does, too. I was talking of my own. For you."

He had been speaking close to my ear, but at this I twisted around again, and rolled to my knees so that I could face him. Even in the faint light of the stars, the most I could make out was the outline of his nose and the wells of his eyes. I peered at him. "What?"

He pushed himself to his knees, too, and took both my hands in his. "Sophia Brucker, will you marry me?"

My mind went completely blank with shock. Even the air seemed to stop moving.

Then I felt my heart bump, as if it had kicked into motion, and my brain began to function again. A moment before, all I would have asked was for him to be willing to be out in public with me. That's all. Simply to be acknowledged as a courting couple, for everyone to see.

I had never dreamed of this. I mean, not really. People got engaged when they were twenty-one, not sixteen.

He was waiting.

"Are you serious?" I finally managed.

"Completely."

"Marry me. *Me*."

"Who else?" His voice was warm with humor. "I haven't exactly been staying up at night to meet other girls."

"But—but *why?*"

At this, he laughed and pulled me closer, so that we both sat on the ground again, arms around each other. "I suppose 'Because I love you' isn't good enough for you?"

There was no possible answer I could make to that, because it was absolutely true. How could he say "I love you" when we had only been seeing each other less than a month? How did a person know the right one, the one they would spend their life with? The one God had chosen for them? Love at first sight was an expression, not what people actually did.

Wasn't it?

"I—I don't know what to say."

He nuzzled my neck. "'Yes' would be a good place to start."

"Gabriel, be serious."

He lifted his head and in his stillness I read what he was going to say before he said it. "I told you, I am. Utterly. You are the one I want. You will heal me with your compassion and make me perfect in the eyes of God. I will protect you from anyone who dares to hurt you. You are the one who lives in my heart now, and I want you in my home, too." His tone lightened, teasing and tempting. "In my kitchen. In my sitting room." And in a whisper, "And in my bedroom."

"Gabriel!"

"That's part of marriage, *liewi.*" The Dutch sounded completely different on his tongue than it had on ... anyone else's. He healed the word simply by speaking it. "But not all of it. I want to work next to you, pray next to you, sleep next to you. No more rambling about in damp fields. We should be sleeping comfortably in our own bed, which I plan to buy next week."

Had any girl ever had such lovely things said to her? Could I doubt him when every word held complete sincerity?

The only person I doubted here was myself, and that was nothing new.

Maybe it's time to start something new. A life with Gabriel. Can you imagine anything more wonderful?

I couldn't. The boundaries of my imagination had been laid right here, right in front of me. And with Gabriel, it wouldn't be imagination anyway. It would be real. Life with him would be real. How could anyone be afraid?

"Yes," I blurted.

"Yes, you'll come with me to buy the bed?"

"That, too. But I meant yes, I'll marry you. And help you choose your paint colors, and buy furniture." I wound my arms even more tightly around his waist. "But I'll tell you right now, that cookstove in the kitchen has to go. Nobody cooks with wood anymore."

"Your wish is my command, wife-to-be."

And he kissed me so deeply I forgot to breathe. Or think.

When Dat opened my door to wake me for milking, it was all I could do to keep Gabriel's proposal to myself. There was a time and a place for everything. I would let Mamm know he was coming for dinner, and we would tell my family then, together.

This day could not go fast enough for me, especially in the meetinghouse where Gabriel and I could actually be in the same room together, connected by the invisible cord of love. As we sang the hymns and then listened to the preaching, I hugged my sweet secret to myself. By this time next week, my whole family would know, but it would go no further. Gabriel had pointed out last night that it would be cruel and selfish of us to announce our happy news when the Troyers were grieving Cara. Her funeral was scheduled for Tuesday, and once that was behind them, it would be more appropriate for the life of the community to begin moving again.

In the meantime, we would keep it in the family, and if we were seen together, well, after the stitching frolic it was no secret that he was courting me.

Everything I wanted was coming true. As Bishop Stolz announced the final hymn, I realized that not once in the last several years could I remember being this happy. I had been entertained by our vacation out at the coast. I had laughed with Katie. But I had never experienced this soul-deep happiness before.

He loves me. Gabriel Langford loves me.

Fraa Langford. Sophia Langford.

Oh, my. Didn't that sound wonderful? Like music. As though Mamm had named me Sophia for that very purpose. Imagine if she'd named me Ursula, after my grand-mother. That would have sounded awful.

With a start, I realized people were getting up all around me and filing out. I gathered up my shawl and handed the hymnbook to Laura's youngest brother at the door, whose duty it was to collect them and put them back in their box. Then I was free to look for him. I didn't need to speak. Simply knowing where he was was enough for me. And then I would need to catch Mamm after the first rush of visiting was done, to tell her about that extra place for dinner.

Some people left after the service, but many went for lunch at someone's home, followed by an afternoon of visiting. Summer had stopped her flirting with us and settled over the county in earnest. After lunch, I found my mother visiting with *Fraa* Hertzfeld, so while I waited for them to finish talking, I took baby Miriam from her and entertained myself making silly faces at her.

Eventually, a chummy laugh between them made a good time to get her attention. "Mamm, I need to talk to you."

Katie's mother smiled as she moved away. "Every-thing is urgent when you're sixteen. We'll see you around five, then."

Mamm gave me the once-over, as if expecting to see a muddy apron or a hole in my black stockings. "What is it?"

I hitched Miriam higher on my shoulder, where she babbled at the people walking in little groups behind me, talking and drinking iced tea. "What did Katie's *mamm* mean? Are we having supper at their place?"

"They've invited us. Her brother and his family are visiting, so they want us to come over and see them."

"But we can't!"

"Why not? Calm down, Sophia. It's nothing to get all het up about. I thought you'd be glad. Here, give me the baby before you jiggle her to death."

I handed Miriam over. "But I invited Gabriel to our place tonight."

My mother can say a lot with one raised eyebrow. "And you're just telling me this now? Why would he be coming?"

"He ... we ... there's a reason. A good reason."

"That can't wait until tomorrow?"

"Yes."

"And this reason would be ...?" She patted Miriam's back in a soothing rhythm.

I looked around a little desperately, as if the sight of Gabriel would give me courage. But I couldn't see him anywhere in the big side yard. He was probably with the other men in their circle of chairs in the sun in front of the barn doors, talking about seed and stock and not paying attention to how much I needed him right now. "We all need to be together," I said at last.

"I see," Mamm said in a tone that told me she didn't see at all. "Then let me ask your fa—"

"Irene!" Aunt Sallie hustled up behind me and when I turned, she didn't even acknowledge that I was there. "Irene, where is Victor? I need to speak with him."

"I imagine he's with the men. Sallie, what is it? Goodness. Here's a hankie."

My aunt dabbed furiously at her face. "I've tried to calm myself. I spent the whole service on my knees in prayer. But I still don't know what to do. Blast that man."

I'd never heard Aunt Sallie even approach a swear word, much less use one. "What man?"

She wasted barely a glance on me. "That sheriff. He was over to the house last night. Spoiled my entire evening when I was trying to get ready to meet with the Lord today. I could hardly sleep a wink."

"What did he want?" Mamm sounded as mystified as I did. She switched the baby to the other shoulder, patting her automatically.

"Why, he wants to dig poor Paul up, that's what! He says there's some kind of evidence they need and he wants me to sign a form giving my permission."

"Dig. Paul. Up." My mother repeated the words in horror. She clutched Miriam to her chest as if the baby herself was being threatened. "How can they do that?"

"I have no idea. With a backhoe. Who knows?" my aunt said impatiently. "Will you come with me to get Victor? I need a man's advice."

"We'll get Victor, and Bishop Stolz, too." Mamm's lips had thinned in the way they used to before someone got a spanking. The two women marched away around the side of the house, heading back toward the barn.

Dig up Uncle Paul. My face and hands had gone cold, though the breeze that fanned my cheeks was warm.

It's all right. He's dead. Nothing will bring him back. He'll never hurt you or shame you again.

I tried to reassure myself, and somehow I heard the words in my head in Gabriel's musical voice. *I will protect you from anyone who dares to hurt you.* He'd promised me.

But how could a mere man keep such a promise? Even Dat had been unable to protect me from his own brother-in-law. I began to walk slowly across the lawn, directionless, hardly noticing anything but the grass under my feet, starred with shaggy yellow dandelions. Only God protected us from the wiles of Satan. It still mystified me that He could have allowed my uncle to do what he did. And if the police thought his death was not an animal attack, but an attack by a person—*call it what it is, Sophia, a murder*—then was the murderer doing God's will? How could that be, when the Sixth Commandment said, *Thou shalt not kill?*

I felt so stupid. I obviously needed to spend more time reading my Bible, because a person could get tripped up in their faith thinking this way.

15

Like wasps buzzing around the entrance to their nest, my thoughts flew hither and yon, up and down, in and out. It wasn't until I realized someone had called my name twice that I looked up and saw Katie jogging after me.

"Are you deaf?" she called. "Wait up."

I'd reached the flower border against the fence dividing the lawn from a hay field. Katie joined me, a little out of breath. "I used to be able to run. Time to cut out the bread. What are you doing down here by yourself?"

"Just walking. Thinking."

"That's some pretty deep thinking. Want some company? I haven't seen you since ..."

Since the volleyball game.

Neither of us needed to say it. Instead, I said, "Did that policeman come and talk to you, too?"

"Yes." She pushed open the gate and we walked out into the field. "He asked Adam about a zillion questions, most of them over and over. I felt sorry for my brother. He took Schatzi out bareback afterward and rode for two hours. My dad never said a thing, just asked him to curry him good when he put him away."

"That deputy doesn't think Adam did it, does he? You should have heard him at our place. I told him Cara had gone riding with Adam that night, because you told me. And he already knew Adam found Uncle Paul. He sure seemed to wonder why Adam turned up in both places." I closed my mouth on the urge to tell her what Mamm thought. No need to hurt her any more.

"Dat was so mad he asked him straight out what he was thinking. The deputy said maybe Cara had gone to Omaha on the bus with Adam, and he killed Uncle Paul and then came running to your house saying an animal did it." Katie's cheeks reddened and her lips began to tremble.

"But that's stupid," I protested. Drat that deputy for making my best friend cry. "Why would he kill either of them? He's known them all his life, and he's got nothing against Cara. He must have liked her, to ask her to go riding and risk all the teasing and gossip." This was Katie's own brother. It was impossible. Period.

She pulled in a long, shaky breath. "I don't know if he liked her that way, or if he just wanted company to go rumspringing with. All I know is, he didn't have anything to do with it. It was someone else."

"But who? Why choose my uncle to kill? And then Cara? Did some guy just go walking down the road and decide to turn into the next lane and kill someone?"

"We're talking about somebody insane," Katie pointed out. "That's all the reason an insane person would need. Maybe Cara came out of the house at the wrong time, and that was that."

"But even Cara wouldn't go to the city with an *Englisch*."

Katie snorted. "No, but she'd go with a Mennonite."

Then we looked at each other, and I felt the blood draining out of my face.

Katie looked stricken, her eyes huge. "I didn't mean that," she whispered. "I didn't mean it could be one of our men."

"I know." My voice sounded strange in my own throat. "But don't you think it would have to be someone she knew? Not even boy-crazy Cara would be crazy enough to go so far away with someone she didn't know."

"Sophia." Now Katie's face had turned white.

"What? What are you thinking?"

"At the stitching frolic. Didn't she hint that she was going to be seeing Gabriel Thursday night?"

"She may have been tossing out hints, but it was just talk. She didn't see him. It was that *Englisch* boy."

"What *Englisch* boy?"

"The one she called from the phone box."

"I thought she was calling the bus station for a sched-ule. That's what I told that deputy, anyway."

Now I was having trouble remembering who had said what, and what had been hints and gossip versus actual fact. With Cara, sometimes it was easy to get confused. "Oh."

"Don't you remember? She said something about how we'd all see after Thursday night. And how she could listen to Gabriel's voice all night. I'm sure she meant that she was going to be seeing him."

"Impossible." This much I could be sure of.

"Because you two are courting?"

"No, because ... " I looked around us, but there was nothing but alfalfa for fifty yards. "Because we're engaged."

Katie's jaw sagged and I thought her eyes would fall completely out. She grabbed me by both arms. "Engaged? Gabriel asked you to marry him?"

I couldn't keep the grin from spreading over my face, warm and alive. "Last night. We're telling my family tonight at supper, so you have to get your mother to un-invite us to your place."

"You. And Gabriel. Getting married." She hadn't let go of me yet.

"Yes. Isn't it wonderful?"

"Sophia, you're only sixteen."

"I know. But he's the one, Katie. There's no one like him in the whole world, and he picked me."

"Do you love him?"

What kind of a question was that? "Of course I love him. And he loves me. Why are you looking at me like that? You're supposed to be happy for me."

At last she released the death grip on my arms. "I am happy ... if you are. Congratulations."

So much for squeals of delight and jumping up and down in the daisies. I'd told her ahead of my own family and this was the reaction I got?

Katie seemed to realize I'd been hoping for a little more joy from her. She pasted on a smile and hugged me. "I mean it, Sophia. Congratulations. It's just the surprise, you know ... I wasn't expecting to be saying that for five years yet." Her smile wavered. "But then, you're always ahead of me. Arithmetic or boys, there you are, already out in front."

"Arithmetic, maybe, but not boys. Gabriel is it for me. First and last." David didn't really count.

"Has he kissed you?"

"Of course."

"Well, see? No one has ever kissed me, not even in fun or as part of one of those stupid parlor games." She tried to make a joke of it, but I knew my friend. I could see the hurt hovering in the corners of her mouth.

"Your time will come." If I couldn't find her a boy-friend, at least I could give her encouragement. "And when it does, he will be so wonderful you'll be wanting to brim over and tell me, just like I've told you. Just you wait."

"You'll have to get him to notice me, first. Well. I can hardly believe it. How can one man be so handsome and come with a farm, too?" Unsaid between us was the fact that a minute ago she had practically accused him of murdering Cara—and that the other day she had compared him to a dark cloud. "But are you absolutely sure he's the right one for you? I mean, from what you said before, the first time you ever really talked with him was the day we had lunch in town. And that wasn't even a month ago."

I wanted her to get over thinking that way. "Of course I'm sure. We talk for hours. I know him better than anyone."

"But what about his family? Are they going to be at the wedding?"

"His parents are dead."

"Does he have brothers and sisters? They might like to come."

I hated to confess I didn't know. "Iowa is a long way from England."

"They live in England?"

"That's where he's from. Don't you hear his accent?"

Evading a straight answer to save my pride was skirting way too close to a lie. I needed to find out right away if we should be sending invitations to his family, because he must have some. Maybe someday we could travel to England to visit—surely we could get there without having to go in a plane, which was forbidden—and I could see a little of the world he had grown up in. He could take me to see that boarding school, even, and help me understand a family who would send their children away from home simply for the sake of an education.

As our conversation drifted into fixing up my future home and the best date for a wedding—because of course Katie would stand up with me—the questions stayed fixed in the back of my mind, wiggling and buzzing like flies on sticky paper. I just wanted to swat them.

I wanted to be happy. Loyalty to Gabriel demanded that my happiness have no flaws, no horrid questions lurking where they shouldn't. But with him, what I didn't know seemed to outweigh what I did. I mean, how could a person get engaged and not know if she was going to have a sister-in-law? Such a person might want to be involved in the wedding, which would be a bit difficult. *Englisch* family members did come to our weddings, but only as guests, not as part of the wedding party. If Gabriel had a sister, would she expect to wear a long dress and hold flowers and see all the trappings of a worldly wedding? I wouldn't even wear a ring, because that was worldly, too, though Gabriel would grow a beard as a sign that he was a married man with a man's responsibilities.

And speaking of responsibilities, his first was to me. If people were going to be talking about this mysterious Thursday night meeting, I needed to know about it. Cara could no longer tell me what she'd meant. But Gabriel could. I'd see to it he did, right after we told my parents.

It is surprisingly difficult to keep our secret to myself.

I find myself wanting to collar Joshua Hodder and tell him I am engaged and his unspoken hopes for Rebecca are in vain. But I must be patient. It is only right that Sophia's family know first, though finding them all together without distractions has taken several days. On Sunday it would not have been right to take their focus from the Lord. On Monday many of the neighbors, including myself, felt obliged to go to Troyers' to help them get ready for Cara's funeral the next day, and when we parted, it didn't seem fitting to share our news when Mrs. Troyer's paper-white face and dead eyes haunted us all.

I do regret her sorrow. Of course I am glad that Cara is resting safely in heaven, having done the will of God. But as Sophia told me quietly, "She's been her mother's companion—thoughtless and wild, sure, but still, the only girl in a family of boys. The poor woman. She's going to have a hard time of it."

My darling is the soul of compassion. Whether human, animal, or bird, her heart is soft for those who suffer.

So it has taken until now, Wednesday night, days after she accepted me, that we can finally tell her parents. "Should I speak with your father privately first?" I whisper as Sophia shows me into the front room. I have only done this once before, and customs have changed since I entered eternity.

She looks at me strangely, as if I had proposed having the ceremony in the Baptist church in Mitternacht. "What for?"

"To convey my intentions and ask for your hand."

She giggles, the most charming sound in the world. "Goodness. Now you really sound like a book. No, you don't have to ask for me, as if I were a horse or something. We'll just tell them at dessert. And then afterward I want to talk to you."

"Of course." I want to lean in and kiss that smiling, rosy mouth, but her younger brother Jonah comes clattering down the stairs and I step back.

After a dinner of lamb and braised greens and potatoes, which I remember to show every evidence of enjoying, Sophia clears the table and her mother brings in a cake that is furry with shredded coconut. As her mother slices me a piece, Sophia catches my eye.

"Mamm, Dat ... Gabriel and I would like to tell you something."

"Is this the thing that couldn't wait on Sunday?" her mother asks.

"Yes. We'd like to—"

"Dat?" Jonah takes a piece of cake and turns to his father as if his sister has not spoken. "Is Aunt Sallie really going to let the sheriff dig up Uncle Paul?"

"Jonah!" Mrs. Brucker snaps, echoing my own dismay. "Now is not the time. Your sister was telling us something important."

Jonah's face is rather blank. "It was just a question."

I get my reactions under regulation and attempt to speak. "One I would like to hear the answer to. If you don't mind," I add hastily. Sophia is staring at me in dismay. "I mean, surely your aunt will not allow it?"

"This is a funny time to bring this up," Victor Brucker says, frowning at his younger son. Any other time I would agree, but I am so shocked that my thinking has become disordered. I hang on his pause as though I am at the theater. "But no, Bishop Stolz has told them it's against our custom." I release a long, quiet breath. "That being said, the deputy—Palermo, his name is—has told Bishop Stolz that he will be getting a warrant. But we need have no fear. God will not allow such terrible disrespect to one who was His faithful servant."

Palermo. Whether God allows his warrant or not, he is a wolf of the world—a danger to the house of God. My resolution firms. He must be stopped.

"Can we talk about the living now, please?" Sophia glares at her brother, and her voice shakes me back into the room and the matter at hand. "Gabriel and I have something to say."

I cannot help but feel the atmosphere of happy anticipation has dissipated somewhat, but that could be more the result of my own agitated feelings than theirs. I rise, pull Sophia to her feet, and smile into those lovely eyes, as gray as a rainstorm bringing life to a parched land.

"Victor, Irene, Caleb, Jonah ... I have asked Sophia to marry me and she has made me the happiest man in the world by saying yes." Her smile is like the sun breaking through the clouds. I am dizzy with her happiness.

Dizzy. The weakness.

No. I shall not allow it to spoil this moment. It's merely the news of the warrant that has upset me, nothing more.

Her family sits as though turned to stone. No one speaks. Jonah seizes the opportunity to help himself to a second piece of cake.

"I—I will be moving to the farm on the first of June, and we'll ... be setting a date ..." I stumble to a stop. Why is no one speaking? Leaping to their feet to offer us congratulations?

Irene Brucker's eyes are so wide that I finally notice they are cornflower blue. Victor clears his throat. "Ma ... married?"

"*Ja.*" Sophia's brow creases. "Mamm? Dat? What's the matter?"

"We thought you were going to tell us you were courting," her mother finally whispers. "Not getting married."

"Well, I'm sorry, but things have gone a little beyond that," Sophia says.

Her mother's skin pales. "Are you ... expecting, *meine kleine Schnecke?*"

Sophia flinches as if her mother has run her fork into her. She grips my hand so tightly my bones grind together. "Of course not." Her eyes fill with tears. "What is the matter with you all? You're supposed to be happy for us."

Caleb pushes his chair back. "I'm happy. Now I can have your room instead of sharing with Jonah." He pecks her on the cheek, then offers his hand to me. "Congratulations." He strides to the door. "I'm going out with Adam. Welcome to the family, Gabriel."

He lopes out the kitchen door. With a glance at his wife, Victor rises, too. His face is somber. "I'm glad our girl has made you happy, Gabriel. But I cannot give my blessing. Sophia is too young."

My beloved stares at him in complete dismay. I must confess that neither of us had foreseen this eventuality. "Dat." Her voice trembles. "You don't mean it."

"But I do," he says gruffly. "You're only sixteen. No daughter of mine will be married before she's eighteen, and especially not to a man not born in our community, whom we have only known for six months."

"But Dat—"

"Your father is right." In Irene's face, shock is softening into compassion. It is clear I have an ally here. "If you really love each other, then you'll be willing to wait. Two years is nothing. That's barely enough time to get the farm running."

"It's already running," I point out. "I'm just stepping in where Paul Gingrich left off."

"Every farmer has a different way of managing," Victor says. "But this isn't about the farm. It's about Sophia being too young to make such serious decisions about her future."

"I am not," she protests. "I know how to cook and clean and look after babies."

"Of course you do," Irene says. "But there's more to choosing a life partner than that. Have you listened for what *Gott* has to say about this decision? Are you certain in your heart it's His will for you?"

Sophia is silent.

I take a deep breath, striving for calm. "I do. I have spent many hours in prayer seeking His will, and I am convinced that He means Sophia and me for each other."

"If that's the case, then two years of waiting will not change anything," Victor says firmly. "God's holy will is going to be just as true then as now, and you will know each other that much better."

"But—" Sophia tries again.

Her father holds up a hand to stop the words. "I've said my say, and that's that. You'll not announce an engagement until one year from now. Sophia's eighteenth birthday will be the October after that, and you can be married that November if you still feel the same way."

"We will," Sophia says with grim determination.

I am not so sure. I am not accustomed to others planning my life for me, down to the very month. My disappointment is almost a living entity inside. If this were

God's will, would her parents not agree with joy and let us work out our plans as we saw fit?

But in eternity there is no marrying or giving in marriage.

For the first time, I wonder if I have made a mistake.

16

I finished my cake out of respect for the work Mamm had put into making it, but it could have been wallpaper paste for all I enjoyed it. For one of the few times in my life, I was so angry at Dat I couldn't even look at him, and when Gabriel suggested going for a walk after the dishes were done, I grabbed his hand and was out the door before Dat could take a breath to say no.

"I apologize for my parents," I told Gabriel as I balanced on the plank bridge over the creek. He stood on the bank and gazed at me. "Aren't you coming?"

"Not without your hand in mine." The sun was an hour above the horizon, and in the long gold rays of it, his face seemed to glow.

My breath backed up in my throat. Had any man ever been so beautiful? How did I ever get so lucky?

How could my parents do this to us?

I backtracked and took his hand, and single file, we crossed over into our country, heading for the copse as though we had one mind.

"Do not blame your parents." Gabriel paced beside me, our linked hands swinging. "They're just doing what they believe to be best for you."

For a moment I thought he was reading my mind again, but then I realized I was walking as though I was punishing the grass. I tried to rein in my temper. "I'm old enough to make up my own mind about what's best for me." In spite of my efforts, I sounded stubborn and mulish and ungrateful.

"As am I, but then, I am a couple of years older than you."

"It may as well be a couple of hundred in experience." I gave a swift kick to a stone, knocking it out of its place and making it roll down the gentle slope.

Gabriel looked at me a little oddly. "What do you mean?"

"Oh, just ... speaking Latin and buying farms and knowing how to drive." I waved my other hand as if encompassing him and the whole district. "Sometimes I wonder what you see in me when you know so much and have the whole world to choose from." Yes, I felt sorry for myself. Otherwise I would never have said such a self-serving thing, as though I were asking for reassurance.

Well, then. Maybe I was. Anyone would, under the circumstances.

He captured my aimless, flapping hand and squeezed both of them, pulling me closer. "Would you like me to tell you what I see in you?"

"Yes." Half flirtatious, half serious, he could take that however he liked.

"I see eyes like rain and a mouth like a harvest of berries," he said quietly. "I see compassion and utter honesty, and the ability to see under the surface no matter how prickly that is. I see a wounded bird that I just want to pick up and protect until she heals and I can set her free again."

A lump formed in my throat, and I forced my deepest fear past it.

"You still love me, even after what my uncle did to me? You don't think I'm stained and used?"

"Oh, *liewi*." He folded me against his chest. "We all have hurts inside. In time you will discover mine, heal me, and I will be free as well. We can give this gift to each other."

"You have hurts?" Who had hurt him? When? Had it been another girl, long before me?

"Oh, yes. Things that will demand all you have of forgiveness and love."

He sounded so serious. His voice ... it almost frightened me. "What things?"

With a squeeze, he released me, and the moment fled. "We have two years to make discoveries about each other. And a lifetime after that."

With difficulty, I dragged my imagination away from the "after that." Because, if past experience was anything to go by, the more I hoped for something, the less I'd be likely to get it. And I wasn't about to take any more risks with my future with this man.

As we strolled under the eaves of the copse, I saw the thorny tangle where my *kapp* had got caught that night. It seemed so long ago now. The plant had budded out and I saw it was no bramble, but a wild climbing rose, heaped up over a decaying stump. A few buds were already blushing pink. For some reason it reminded me of Cara, and I remembered what I had been going to talk to Gabriel about.

"Gabriel, I'm a bit worried about that policeman. Deputy Palermo."

"Him again?" He dropped my hand and bent to pick a bluebell, but it was past its prime and he left it. "Don't worry about him. Let's talk about something more interesting, like our future home."

"Thanks to my parents, we have two years to talk about that. No, I mean this whole thing with Cara last Thursday night. She said she was going to be meeting you that night." He bent again, and pulled a stalk of grass from its sheath with a squeak like that of a mouse. "I'm worried that the deputy will find out."

"Find out what?"

"Well, if you were with her, he might think you ... Did you meet her or not?"

With a sigh, he slung an arm around my shoulders and walked slowly beside me. His fingers were cold on my upper arm, but the rest of him was comfortingly warm. "Cara had a lively imagination where the men were concerned. Don't you think she was just trying to get a rise out of you and using me because I was convenient?"

"She wouldn't have said she was seeing you that night if she wasn't. It's too easy to catch a person in a lie like that."

"And my fiancée is too honest. Not everyone is like you, darling."

Darling. I refused to be distracted, even by the sweetness of the *Englisch* word. "So you didn't see her?" What was the matter with me? It was so ridiculous to pester him. Was it just because I had imagined some other girl who could have hurt him, and now anyone who spoke to him on the side of the road was a potential threat to the man I loved?

Cara isn't a threat anymore. Not to you. But she could be to him. Even dead.

I tried to stifle the ugliness of my own thoughts.

"As I told the dedicated Deputy Palermo, I saw her in the yard on my way home from the bank."

"But Cara didn't mean later that morning. She was throwing hints all over the place that she was seeing you Thursday night. You have to tell me, Gabriel, because if that policeman comes back—"

"You have nothing to fear from him."

"You keep saying that, and I don't know why."

"God will deal with him."

"Maybe. But maybe not in time for him to stop asking questions." He kept changing the subject. What was so hard about a simple yes or no?

"You let me deal with his questions."

"But I want to know if—"

"Sophia, enough. I do not want to talk about Cara Troyer. This is between me and Palermo. It has nothing to do with you."

"*What* is between you? That means there's something. I need to know."

He stopped walking and turned to face me. The sun had sunk low, the bottom of the burning red disk blurred by the hills in the distance. It was enough to make me squint, especially when he stood with his back to it.

"Don't you trust me?" The pain in his voice broke my heart. "Is that what all these questions are about? You don't trust me, after all I've done for you?"

I flung myself against his chest, wrapping my arms as tightly as I could around his waist. "I'm sorry," I wailed, hiding my shame in his shirt. "Of course I trust you. Forgive me. I'm so sorry."

At last his rigid body relaxed, and he folded me in his arms. Murmuring endearments, he patted my back until I got my emotions under control. I never wanted to hear that dreadful, hurt note in his voice again. To prove it, I was only too happy to talk about paint colors and curtains until the sun went down and the stars pricked out in the night sky above us.

After he had gone and I went upstairs to bed, I couldn't get to sleep. But it wasn't visions of renovating together that kept me turning over, punching my pillow, and finally lying there watching the shadows of the tree branches moving on the ceiling.

No.

As the downstairs clock struck the first hour of the new morning, I gave up and let my mind go where it had been wanting to go ever since I had tried to look into the sun and been unable to face it.

Gabriel had not told me yes or no. I wanted to hear him say, "Sophia, I didn't see Cara that night. She was just throwing darts intended to prick you and make you jealous. I love only you and I would never want to be alone with another girl, day or night."

But he hadn't said it. Instead, he had changed the subject, and when I'd persisted, he'd accused me of not trusting him. Jonah used the exact same strategy when he wanted to get out of the spanking he knew he deserved, and didn't want to add a lie to the list of his crimes. A lie wouldn't just get him the wooden spoon—it would get him a whipping from Dat, and he wouldn't risk that.

Gabriel had not lied to me. But he had not told me the truth, either. So why risk being caught out in an evasion? What kind of whipping was he trying to avoid?

He doesn't want Deputy Palermo to find out. He won't tell me in case the deputy comes back, and he knows I'm incapable of getting away with a lie.

We had all innocently told the deputy that Adam Hertzfeld had taken Cara driving that night. She had to have come home afterward. What if Gabriel had seen her then, but was willing to let the deputy think Adam had been the last one to do so?

Why let poor Adam take the blame?

No. No. I couldn't think that. Not of the man I loved.

There had to be some other explanation. Of course Gabriel had told the truth. He hadn't seen her. He had been nowhere near the place.

Can you prove that?

No, I couldn't. And if he were chasing after Adam, Deputy Palermo wouldn't be able to, either.

What had Gabriel told him?

I would never know. Short of asking the deputy, and bringing his questions back to the man I had promised to marry, there was no way for me to find out.

Because Gabriel refused to answer you. What is he hiding?

My mind shuddered away. *Don't think it. It's wicked and untrue and how could you be so evil as to think such a thing?*

If idle hands were the Devil's playground, an idle mind was an entire amusement park. There I lay, trapped in sleeplessness, unable to make the noise in my head stop. Thoughts surfaced from the depths like mud churned up from the bottom of the pond when you waded in it. Mud, and old weed, and dead things that should have been decently buried.

A long black bag on a gurney, being taken away in a silent ambulance. Wounds to her throat and thigh, just like my uncle. Gabriel whitewashing my uncle's milking pen, only to have fans of bright blood splashed on his good work.

Adam and Gabriel. Both had been with my uncle. Maybe both had been with Cara. But Adam had not gone away with her. She'd gone to Omaha with someone she knew.

"She'd go with a Mennonite," Katie's voice said in my memory.

She'd go with Gabriel. Any of the girls would.

I would.

"You don't trust me, after all I've done for you?" Now it was Gabriel's voice in my head. What had he done for me? Why did he keep saying that? He must mean buying the farm. Or looking after my head injury at the volleyball game. But those weren't the kinds of things you made lifelong vows for.

What do Uncle Paul and Cara have in common besides their injuries?

I clapped my hands to my ears in the darkness and willed my screaming head to be silent. Tears leaked from my eyes—tears of frustration and grief and shame.

Somehow, some way, long hours later I managed to fall asleep.

And when I woke in the clear gray dawn, I knew.

After the breakfast dishes were done and the men had gone out to the fields, I collected as much change as I could find and walked to the pay phone. Here Cara and Gabriel had talked on the last day of her life. I fed coins into the slot and gazed down the road as if it might tell me what they had really said.

The call rang through and I nearly hung up. Was I well and truly crazy? How could I do this? Maybe I should just—

"Yo," a male voice said.

Male? "I—I think I must have the wrong number." I recited the number I knew by heart. "I thought I was calling my sis—"

"Yup, that's us. Hannah!"

I held the phone away from my ear as my sister's name blasted out of it. In a moment, someone took the phone. "This is Hannah."

"*Guder mariye, ischt mir.* Who was that?"

"Oh, that's just Gordo. He has the manners of Jabba the Hutt." This last seemed to be hollered in the direction of Gordo, whom I could hear laughing in the background. Certainly not me. I tried to spell the strange words in my head, but could make no sense of them.

"Are you living with someone?" My voice sounded faint, but I couldn't help it. Mamm would absolutely die of shame, and my hasty plan suddenly looked not just hasty but impossible.

"Sophia, this is a co-ed college. Gordo and Rennie are my roommates. I told you I had two roommates, didn't I?"

"I don't think you mentioned what sex they were."

"That could be. Anyway. Now you know. What's up?"

This was never going to work. It had been difficult enough imagining talking things over with my sister at all, even if her roommates were female. But speaking my horror out loud with men around? Impossible.

"I, um ... how are you?"

"I'm fine, as you can tell. Come on. Spit it out—Chemistry starts in twenty minutes and I haven't had anything to eat yet."

I lost my courage. "It's okay. I'll call back another time."

A second of silence ticked past. "It doesn't sound okay to me. Are you crying?"

I gulped and tried to speak. "*Ja.*"

Her voice lost its breezy impatience. "*Liewi*, what is it? Deep breath. One more. Okay, *gut*. What's going on that's brought you out to the phone box on baking day?"

The fact that she even remembered what day it was triggered a spasm of fresh tears, but Chemistry was getting closer and the simple fact that I couldn't hear her voice without crying told me I needed to do this.

"Can I come and see you this weekend?"

"Of course. Tomorrow night? I'll meet the bus in Council Bluffs and we'll have an early supper."

"You don't have other plans?"

"Sure, but I'll cancel them. Rennie and I were just going to see a movie, but we can do that anytime."

"If you're sure you don't mind."

"I'd dump Jensen Ackles for my little sister, who never comes to see me and hardly ever writes."

"Is he your boyfriend?"

She laughed. "Never mind. Tomorrow night, you and me. And I'll flog Gordo into moving his stuff off the fourth bed. We lost our other X chromosome at the beginning of January, so you won't have to sleep on the floor."

"*Denkes*, Hannah."

"Whatever it is, we'll work it out. Gotta go, 'kay?"

"Okay. Bye."

As I hung up the receiver, a shape moved in the opening of the phone box, and my heart kicked my ribs in sudden fright. "Who's that?"

I stepped out to see David Fischer, looking unsure of where to put his hands or feet. "Sorry," he said. "I didn't know there was anyone in there."

My breathing settled into something like normal. "You scared me." Which was also crazy. What was there to be afraid of on a sunny May morning?

"I didn't mean to." He prodded a stone with the toe of his work boot. "How are you? Haven't seen you in a while."

How was I? I couldn't even begin to answer that. "I'm fine," I said at last, and he gave me a look from under his straw hat, as if he was wondering why I had to think about it.

"Are you still interested in going to one of those band hops? I did some asking around, and there's one up by Council Bluffs on Saturday night. Adam was going to ask someone, but he ..."

Adam? "But he what?"

David chewed on his lip, and then came to a decision. "I don't know if I'm supposed to say anything, but that sheriff guy asked him not to leave and go anywhere."

"Why?" But I already knew. "Because of Cara?"

Clearly uncomfortable, David nodded, his shoulders hunched. "I think they're barking up the wrong tree. His whole family told the deputy he took Cara driving, took her home, and came back and went to bed, but he still seems to think Adam had something to do with it."

"Do they think he has something to do with my uncle's death, too?"

David shrugged. "Maybe. He and Gabriel were both whitewashing over there. The deputy was going to ask Gabriel if he saw anything."

I'll take care of the deputy, Gabriel had said. What did that mean? That he'd tell him the truth? Or that he'd ... do something?

"When is he going to talk to him, do you know?" I tried to keep the urgency out of my voice, to sound casual, as if it didn't really matter.

Again, David shrugged. "Are you wanting to talk to Gabriel yourself?" He half smiled, as if he was making a joke, but his eyes were wary. Did he expect me to say yes and get his feelings hurt? How much damage had my careless behavior done?

"No," I said. "That was my sister I was just talking to. I'm going up there for a visit tomorrow. If you're taking the bus, maybe we could ride together."

His smile widening, he straightened up. "I'd like that. Maybe Hannah might want to come to the band hop."

"I'll ask her. Who are you going to stay with?"

"My cousin married outside, but he's a nice guy. They invited me. I'll bring the address and phone number, and if Hannah wants to go, maybe you could call me."

"I'll do that." Maybe by then, she'd have talked some sense into me and I'd be glad of a little diversion before coming back to what used to be a normal life. "I'll tell Jonah we'll ride into Mitternacht with him. Want us to pick you up?"

I'd never seen David Fischer smile like that before—with the dimple creasing his cheek. He didn't seem to have as many freckles as he had when he was a kid. How long was it going to take the girls in this district to realize what a nice boy he was?

"Sure," he said. "That would be real nice of you. I'll be ready."

I fluttered my hand in a wave before I began the half-mile walk back to our place. When on a whim I turned to look back, he wasn't talking on the phone. Instead, he was leaning on the box, watching me go.

17

Like a trumpet announcing a charge, a car horn blared behind me. I whirled in sudden fright, certain I was about to be run down. David must have thought the same thing—he grabbed my arm and pulled me to one side, making my backpack slide off my shoulder.

"Sophia!" Hannah leaned out the car's window, waving. "Here we are—sorry we're late."

The car was long and black with an engine that sounded like an angry animal. The back door swung open with a creak, and David and I climbed in. "*Denkes*," I said a little breathlessly, hauling my backpack into my lap. "I didn't know you'd be driving."

"I'm lucky one of my roommates owns this magnificent vehicle." She made a gesture with both hands as if handing the driver something on a tray. "Gordo, my sister Sophia, and David Fischer, one of the guys from home. Sophia, this is Gordon Dunleavy the Third, but don't ever call him that. He gets cranky."

"I won't. Hi, Gordo. Thank you for picking us up."

"Anything for Hannah, queen of light. I am her servant in all ways."

Through the gap in the seats, I raised my eyebrows at her.

"He's just ripped because I totally beat him at *Demon Peril.* Ignore anything he says. He's just driving."

I'd been expecting her to be different—but not *this* different. From the jeans to the language *(Demon Peril?)* to the—oh, my, Mamm was going to have a tizzy fit—

"Hannah, when did you cut your hair?"

"A couple of months ago." She sounded completely unconcerned. "Do you like it?"

She had always worn her blond hair braided into a fat bun at the nape of her neck. Now it just brushed her shoulders, and with all that weight removed, it had softened into a wavy mass that even had a bit of curl at the ends.

"I do," I said at last. "I shouldn't, but I do."

"*Should* is a fantasy," Gordo intoned from behind the wheel without taking his eyes off the busy downtown street. "*Should* is what we try to impose on reality instead of accepting it."

David and I exchanged a glance. The man was a philosopher.

"Nice car, Gordo." I could always depend on David to keep things down to earth. "Big."

"Gordo's car rules," Hannah told him, settling into her seat.

"It's a 1967 Impala Super Sport with a rebuilt 427." Gordo wheeled the car around the corner with one hand, and from the muscles working in his arm, I figured this took more effort than he was willing to let on. "Where to, folks?"

"I have no idea what he just said," I told David.

"Me neither, but I think it means this thing is fast." He grinned, and in the front, Gordo grinned too.

"Right you are, my Mennonite friend. Hannah tells me you're staying with relatives?"

David gave him the address, and the engine snarled as Gordo tromped on the accelerator pedal. When we dropped him off at a little house on a street of identical little houses, David handed me a slip of paper. "Phone me here if you still want to go tomorrow night. Have fun. See you, Hannah. Thanks for the ride, Gordo."

"Any time," Gordo said. David loped up the walk and Gordo pulled away. "What's up tomorrow night?"

"There's a band hop somewhere south of here." The backseat felt like a huge black vinyl cave without David's comforting presence filling up the other side. "We were talking about going, but it was just an idea. Nothing definite."

Gordo leaned Hannah's way. "And a band hop is ... ?"

"An orgy of dancing, drinking, and loud music, Mennonite style."

"Meaning a can of soda and a transistor radio?"

"Sometimes," Hannah allowed. "Mostly it's a couple of hundred kids, a band who may or may not be able to play their instruments, and a few kegs of beer."

"Ah." Gordo sat upright again and took off from the light. "That might tempt even me."

"You'd be welcome to come," I said. "Everybody brings their friends."

"How were you planning to get there?" Hannah wanted to know. "Walk?"

I shook my head. "I think David's cousin would have taken us. But you probably have more exciting things to do."

"Don't be so sure," Gordo said. "Like *should*, my social life is often a fantasy I impose on reality as a survival mechanism."

I appealed to my sister. "What did he say?"

"He said he doesn't have a date."

"Neither do we." I sat back and realized we had left Council Bluffs behind and were blasting along the highway at—no, I would not lean over the seat and look at the speedometer. Gordo might think I was being critical. We crossed a river and turned into a wide driveway with the college sign. I hadn't realized the school was so far out in the country. "Do you live here?"

Gordo wheeled the car around a curve, passing thick clusters of trees with groups of students talking and reading under them. The campus was very hilly. He pulled into a parking lot on the side of a wide expanse of lawn, facing what looked like apartment buildings with their roofs built at all angles, as if the carpenters had flipped a coin every time they started one.

"Welcome to the aptly named Riever Suites," he said. "Let me take your pack."

"You don't have to. There's not much inside it."

"Still. I am the bearer of burdens until my queen decides to release me."

"Let him carry it." Hannah led us into the nearest stairwell. "He's a sore loser, but he usually gets over it by dinnertime."

I could think of one or two sore losers back home, and they didn't get over it by carrying things for people. After the third evening of playing the same unending game of Monopoly, Caleb used to go out to the woodpile behind the barn and split kindling until pieces flew. Finally he quit playing altogether. He said it was too frustrating.

Hannah's dorm room was not, as I had feared, a single room with two bunk beds in it. Instead, there were four separate bedrooms all opening into a common room in the middle, plus a bathroom and shower. The bedrooms were small—half the size of mine at home—but each one held a bed, a wardrobe, and a desk. And each had a door. That was the important part.

On the far side, a tousled head poked out of one of the bedrooms. A forefinger pushed a pair of glasses higher on a beaky nose. "You're back."

"We are. Sophia, meet Rennie, master of the obvious. Rennie, this is my sister. Do not hit on her. She's underage."

The heat of embarrassment singed my cheeks as he came all the way out of his room and offered his hand. The rest of him was as beaky as his nose. If Gordo was thick and *schwartz*, Rennie was his complete opposite.

But his smile was wide and changed the shape of his face into something charming.

"It's nice to meet you, Rennie." I willed my blush back to where it had come from.

"Likewise. She's kidding, you know. The last time I hit on a girl with any success was in kindergarten." He looked wistfully into the distance for a moment. "Sally Baumann. I've been ruined for tall blondes ever since."

I had to laugh. How strange. I couldn't remember the last time I'd really laughed. What did that tell me?

"What's on the menu over at the cafeteria?" Gordo closed the door of a little refrigerator in the corner. "I'm pretty hungry, what with all the chauffeuring and servitude."

"It's Friday. What do you think?"

"I can't face another tuna melt." Hannah made a face. "Let's try that new Thai place back in town. Sophia, you'll love Thai food. It's one of my favorite *Englisch* things."

"Technically, I don't think it's English," Rennie said in a thoughtful tone.

"Don't do that." She gave him a push that detached him from the doorframe he was leaning on. "Stop splitting hairs. You know it drives me nuts."

"I can't help it. I'm a literal person."

"OCD, you mean." But she smiled at him in a way that told me maybe OCD wasn't so bad. They had been going to see a movie before I'd called and changed their plans. I looked from her to Rennie with new interest. Were they courting?

I had been to Council Bluffs once or twice before, but always with my family, and under the close watch of Dat's eye. Going to town with my sister and "the boys" was like riding a hurricane unleashed on an unsuspecting world.

Was her life like this all the time? With the windows down, the wind blew through the car with deafening force, helped along by the radio turned up and people having to holler at each other to be heard. Even pinned in three places, my *kapp* blew off twice before I finally resorted to holding it on with one hand.

"I'll have to lend you a pair of jeans and a T-shirt," Hannah shouted, holding onto the headrest as Gordo sailed around a corner. "We'll disguise you as a freshman in Rievers colors."

"No, thanks," I shouted back, holding on for dear life. "No one's going to survive this trip anyway."

If riding in Gordo's car was like going to a foreign country, the restaurant was even more exotic. There was a gold Buddha ("You don't have to look away, Sophia, he's not going to hurt you") and beaded curtains and napkins folded up to look like flowers. I wondered what Mamm would say if I tried something like that at home, but when I unfolded the napkin, I couldn't figure out how it was done. And the food! Hannah and I hadn't grown up liking many of the same things except for ice cream, but I had to agree with her there. Thai food was wonderful, and I ate two helpings of everything.

After another hair-raising ride back to campus, we went for a walk on the grounds and stopped to listen to a student concert. They were some kind of rock band, I think. David would have said they were just shouting at their dog, but Gordo seemed to like it. Or maybe it was the girl playing the guitar that he liked.

It was after eleven by the time we finally got back to the dorm. "Oops." Gordo went into the fourth bedroom and began throwing things on the floor. "I forgot to clear this off for you." When he started carrying boxes of books out into the common room, I stopped him.

"You don't need to do that. I'm just glad I don't have to sleep on these cement floors. Your things are fine in there."

Hannah picked up my backpack and swung it onto the end of the bed. "But you're not going to bed yet. Come on. Gordo smuggled a bottle of wine in yesterday that he thinks I didn't see. Or the house monitor."

"You drink?" I tried to keep the surprise and—*ja*—the judgment out of my tone, but Hannah's face told me I hadn't tried hard enough.

"There's no sin in a glass of wine, Sophia. Paul told Timothy to have some once in a while for his stomach's sake."

"There's nothing wrong with your stomach."

"There is with mine," Rennie groaned, flopping onto the navy blue couch. "Never let me eat green papaya again."

"Then you can have my share," I told him. "The green papaya is sitting just fine with me."

Hannah got the wine and some plastic glasses, and before long she was curled up next to Rennie on the couch, while I took the block-shaped armchair and Gordo reclined on the floor. Luckily, he was well padded.

It looked as though they were settling in for a long talk. And I wanted to talk. The problem was, I needed to be alone with my sister to do it. I either had to find a way to get her by herself, or wait until tomorrow—and goodness knows what the boys would come up with then.

"All right, Sophia, spill." Hannah's clear blue eyes weren't the least bit affected by the half glass of wine she'd already swallowed. "I know you've got something to tell me by the way you're fidgeting all over that chair."

"Stress," Rennie said, as though diagnosing my problem. "She hasn't kept still all night. Are you ADHD?"

"I don't know what that is."

"Here." Hannah pressed her plastic glass into my hand. "Down the hatch."

"No."

"It'll settle your nerves."

"There's nothing wrong with my nerves." I slid out of the chair and away from the smell of red wine, which wasn't a bit like grape juice.

"Then what is wrong?" When I didn't answer, Hannah waved at the boys as if she expected them to vanish in a puff of smoke. "Don't mind these guys. I tell them everything."

"I don't—"

"We might not be Mennonite, but I'm a foster kid and Gordo's a disappointment to his parents," Rennie said.

"What's that got to do with anything?" What strange boys these were.

"Nothing," Gordo said. "It just means we're not a threat to you. And nothing really surprises us."

"I bet that's not true." If they only knew.

"Yeah?" Gordo sat up and patted the chair. "Come on, Hannah's sister. Try us."

He looked so complacent—what can the little Mennonite girl say? Oh, look, the corn grew a whole inch. Look, I sewed a dress. He had no idea. None at all.

"All right, then." I flopped into the chair and looked my sister in the eye. "I'm engaged."

For a second nobody moved. Hannah looked as though she were translating the English back to *Deitsch* in her head.

"Engaged to do what?" Gordo finally asked.

"Engaged." I flapped my hands. "To be married."

"What?" Hannah leaped off the couch, dislodging Rennie, whose feet hit the floor with a *thunk*. "What did you say?"

"I'm engaged." There. And they'd thought nothing could surprise them. But this was nothing. Wait till they heard the rest. At least this was the real part.

"To whom?" Hannah's voice spiraled upward in disbelief.

"Gabriel Langford."

She grabbed me by both shoulders and shook me. "Sophia, stop playing with me. Are you serious? Who in the world is Gabriel Langford? Not the day-jobber you were talking about in your letter? The one boarding at Hodders'?"

"That's the one."

She released me and stepped back. "Dat will never let you." Her voice held absolute certainty, and I wilted a little under the cold dash of truth.

"No. He said we had to wait two years, until I was eighteen. But Gabriel isn't a day-jobber anymore. He bought Aunt Sallie's farm."

This time her eyes practically bugged out of her head. "Aunt Sallie sold the farm to an outsider? What about Caleb?"

"Caleb's no farmer, and Gabriel had cash money. He gets the keys on June first. And he's not an outsider. He's been living at Hodders' since November."

"Looks like she got you, Hannah," Gordo observed from the floor. "You done been surprised."

Hannah looked from him to me, mouth opening and closing. Finally she got out, "Congratulations. I think." Her eyes narrowed. "Sophia, this is not why you came all the way up here to see me. This face does not exactly say *happy bride*. He joined church, right?"

With a sigh, I folded into the chair, and Hannah sat on the edge of the couch, which was all Rennie had left her, having stretched out his legs over the rest of it. "I told you he was baptized a couple of weeks ago."

"Then why ... ?"

"*Romeo and Juliet*," Rennie said. "His family is a bunch of New York stockbrokers and don't want him to be plain."

"Naw, it's more like *Witness*. He's hiding from a mob hit." Gordo sounded equally sure.

"Stop it, you guys, this is serious." Hannah turned back to me. "What's the real trouble, *Liewi*?"

She hadn't called me *darling* in years. I firmed up my trembling lips and began at the beginning. I told them all of it—about David and Cara and Gabriel and Adam.

About Uncle Paul. When I got to the part about the police wanting to dig him up, I saw that her face had paled to the color of the papers stacked on the coffee table. I stumbled to a stop.

Rennie pulled his legs in and slid an arm around her shoulders. "You okay, girl?"

She shook her head. "I'm glad, is what I am. Glad he's in the ground. They'd better not dig him up."

Our gazes locked, and I saw in her eyes the same look that had so often been in mine. The one that said *I must endure and keep quiet. I must put peace first.*

Sound seemed to fade. My vision narrowed as my entire being focused on what couldn't possibly be true. "You're not rumspringing at all," I whispered. "You moved up here to—to—"

"To get away from him." She took a shaky breath. "How did you know?"

Mein Gott, help me now. I was not alone—though I'd have given years off my life if I could have spared her this. "Because I couldn't get away."

Whatever color had crept back into her face abruptly fell out of it. "Are you saying—?" I nodded. "*Ach, liewi.*" She slid off the couch, knelt on the floor, and threw her arms around my waist. "He didn't. Not you, too?"

"*Ja,*" I croaked. Could I just die of shame now? How had this dreadful thing suddenly leaped into the room, right in front of two men who were the next thing to strangers to me? "Hannah, I can't talk about it. Not in front of them."

"Yes, you can." She lifted her tear-streaked face. "I have. They know all about it. These guys are the only reason I don't scream and run every time a middle-aged man stops to ask me for directions. How long, Sophia?"

"Since I was nine."

"Me, too." She hugged me fiercely. I wrapped my arms around her shoulders and bent over her, my own tears dripping onto her T-shirt. Grieving the years and the innocence we had both lost.

I don't know how long we clung together, grieving with each other. Strengthening each other. Finally she croaked, "I used to imagine all the ways I wanted him to die, and then have to pray for forgiveness for every single one. When I heard that animal got him, I was glad. Bless coyotes, wherever they are."

"It wasn't a coyote," I got out. "It was a person. The same person who killed Cara."

She pulled back and sat on the floor, her back against Rennie's knees. He was sensitive enough not to move or offer comfort. Her blunt honesty in front of both boys made me feel as if I could, indeed, say what I had come all this way to say.

"A person?" she repeated, prompting me.

"There's a policeman, a Deputy Palermo, who's been driving all over the district asking questions and trying to find out who." My stomach rolled, and not because of the strange, exotic food. "But I think I know. There's only one person who knew what Uncle Paul did to me ... us. One person who saw the way Cara treated me. One person who thinks he's my avenging angel, meant to protect me from anyone hurting me, ever again."

"Who?" Hannah's eyes were huge, her lashes still spiky with tears.

"Oh, no," Gordo murmured. "Train wreck alert."

"I think it's Gabriel." I could hardly hear myself. Why should I? Why should anyone else? My heart squeezed with loathing. Who wanted to listen to the ravings of someone who could suspect her fiancé of such a thing?

18

I am angry at Sophia for deserting me at a time like this, but enough self-control remains for me to take my anger outside and use it profitably. It is full spring and the Hodders do not need kindling, but I set block after block of dry pine on the stump and split them until the pile has grown as high as my knee.

Anger helps fuel a body that is becoming weaker by the day. I must find sustenance soon. Even Rebecca's chickens look toothsome as they peck and wander in the yard, but I know that if even one goes missing, she will set up a hue and cry, and when it is not found, she will grieve. I do not wish the needs of this eternal body to bring grief to anyone. Only the foolish hunter kills in his own yard, anyway.

As if my thoughts have summoned her, Rebecca steps into the barn. "Gabriel, supper's almost ready. Can you let Dat know?"

"I will." I straighten, and attempt a smile. I wish ordinary food would satisfy this body. It would make the untold ages of eternity much easier to contemplate.

I pass the message on to her father, who is putting a new wheel on the market wagon in his shop, and when he goes in to wash, I pick up the fresh kindling and stack it in the metal holder he has made for it next to the pile of cut logs. A flash of light blinds me for a moment, until I realize it's not Rebecca, come to summon me a second time, but the low rays of the sun striking the windshield of a car.

"Gabriel." Deputy Palermo strolls over to the woodpile, the implements of his trade—gun, stick, pouches—hanging from his belt, where he has hooked his thumbs in a casual pose. "Got a minute?"

I straighten, wishing the sun would set more quickly. I am always more at home in the dark than the earthbound, and I am in no shape to bandy words with this man. "I'm about to go in to dinner."

"This won't take long."

I can't protest again for fear of being rude, and rudeness will make him think I have something to hide. "I hope so. Splitting wood is hungry work, and I don't like to keep the family waiting."

"Only two more weeks until you'll have to do for yourself."

This is a familiarity I'm not prepared to respond to. He clears his throat. My silence has embarrassed him. Good.

"I've been asking around, and I understand you and Adam Hertzfeld were both hired by Paul Gingrich to whitewash the interior of his barn. Is that true?"

"Yes." The news Rebecca passed on at lunch about Adam had made me feel safer, but not entirely secure. "If you've come by to tell me not to leave the district as well, you can rest assured I won't. I have nowhere else I'd rather be."

"I'm glad to hear it, but if you're offering yourself up as a suspect, you're jumping the gun."

"I wasn't, of course. I was just assuring you that I am not a ... what do you call it? A flight risk."

"Interesting you'd know that term." His eyes are the color of mud, and rest on me like those of a minor predator, unsure whether it has the skill to strike. "Been around the courts much?"

I shake my head, and a wave of dizziness rolls over me. I must keep my head clear. Even an uncertain hunter is a danger to me. I must not let him see any physical vulnerability. I am the stronger, not he.

"You all right?"

"Yes, of course. Just hungry."

"I'll make this fast, then. So you and Adam were whitewashing the victim's barn. How was your relationship with Mr. Gingrich?"

"My ... relationship?"

"Your working relationship. Because any family ties developed after his death, didn't they?"

I will not discuss Sophia with this man, though he insists on bringing her into every conversation. "I suppose so. It was fine."

"No fights? Arguments?"

"Not that I can remember. He was a man who liked things just so, and he would correct me if I didn't do things the way he liked them. That was his right, though. It was his property."

Then. Now it is mine. No one will tell me what to do, ever again. My allegiance is to God, and none other.

"What about his relationship with your fiancée?"

My temper begins to simmer, giving me inner strength. "I don't see what that has to do with your investigation, Deputy."

"You'd be surprised. Connections among people often tell me a lot."

"Then you must ask Sophia when she returns."

"Oh, is she gone?"

"She's visiting her sister in Council Bluffs."

"I didn't know she had a sister there. Is she in church?"

"I don't believe so. But she and Sophia are quite close."

"Ah. Well, since she isn't here to ask, how about you give me your opinion?"

"Of what?"

"Of her relationship with her uncle," he says slowly, as if to a child.

The lid on my temper begins to rattle. How dare he patronize me—someone who, had we been at Langford Hall, would get no further than the servants' entrance. But I am not at Langford Hall, and never will be again.

"As far as I know, their relationship was normal."

"Define normal."

"I don't know." I am feeling nettled, and do my best not to show it. "He was her mother's brother. They had Sunday lunch with other families. They had dinner at each other's houses. Normal." I will not divulge the true nature of their relationship. Sophia has given me her confidence, and I will never break it.

"All right. So any ideas about what Adam was doing in the barn at four in the morning on the day of the murder?"

I clamp down on my anger, welcoming this return to proper topics with relief. "I imagine he was reporting for work. Paul Gingrich needed help with the milking, and then we'd get down to business with the paint once the cows had been turned out."

"We? Were you there with him?"

"It was a long job. Paul divided it between the two of us. Sometimes we alternated days, depending on what Adam's father and Joshua Hodder needed."

"Were you there the day before, or Adam?"

He can check this too easily. "I think I was."

"So when was the last time you saw the victim?"

The spurt of the blood of a healthy man before I captured it in my mouth, spattering on the wall I had painted just the day before. My knees go weak at the memory.

"Are you sure you're okay, Gabriel? You look like you're about to pass out."

"I'm fine. I must have seen him the day before, when I went over to work. I can't really remember."

"We've established that. I'm looking for a time."

I must have blood. Mine has lost its life, and if I do not replenish it soon, I will collapse. Or worse, betray myself by saying something stupid, and then this clumsy wolf, this minor predator, will stop his cowardly circling and move in to pounce.

Because, sad though he is, he is still a wolf and he is endangering the flock I am sworn to protect. If he discovers my mission and behaves as foolishly as that Bow Street Runner, then how will I serve God? The will of the Lord must come before everything.

To conceal my thoughts, I furrow my brow as if trying to recall a memory. It is a memory. It just did not happen on the day we are discussing. "Wait. I did see him. It was just before sunset, I think, up at the copse. He was walking slowly, as if he was looking for something."

"What copse?"

"The one at the top of the hill that's between his farm and the Bruckers'. He had his head down, as if he'd lost something, or was looking for something."

The deputy regards me steadily. I wish he would blink. I lock eyes with him, and suddenly his fill with challenge. "Why don't you show me? Is it far?"

I shake my head, and inside, a glow of anticipation begins to build. My mission is clear. Yet another wolf must die so that the people of God may be left in peace, and not be troubled by his continued questions and visits.

"No," I say. "It's not far at all. In fact, there's an access road up there, if you want to take the car."

If I'd hoped it would take as much time to convince Hannah and the boys as it had taken to even whisper the possibility to myself, I soon learned otherwise.

"It makes sense," Rennie said after I'd finished the story—as much of it as I knew, anyway. "This guy Gabriel is the only thing outside of your religion that connects your uncle and the other girl."

"Cara." Hannah's voice still hadn't recovered its vibrancy. "Her name was Cara."

"But how can it be true?" Having brought up the awful possibility, now I wanted to make it go away. "He can't be a murderer. He loves me."

"There's your answer, sad to say." Gordo really was a philosopher. "But you're missing something. People don't just jump into murder. They work up to it. What we need to do here is a little research. See if there's anything on record about the guy."

"How are you going to do that?" Was this something you could just make a phone call about?

"You're talking to the master of the interwebs," Rennie said to me, as if this was an answer. "Watch and be amazed."

From under the pile of papers on the table, Gordo unearthed a sleek, silvery case. He opened the computer and swung it around to face Hannah and me, tapping away on the keys. "Ever been on the net?"

"Of course," I said. "I learned to use it at the library when I was a scholar."

"They let you do that?" He glanced at me, as if Mennonite standards were on a downhill slide thanks to me.

"No. I got into an argument about something with my best friend Katie, and the only way to prove she was wrong was to ask the lady at the public library. She showed me." I paused. "It's not that hard."

"That depends on what you're looking for. What did you say his name was?" I told him, and he began to type. A few seconds later, a list of names came up. "Is he any of these?"

"No. He's from England."

"Ah." Tap-tap-tap. "Hm." This list was much shorter. In fact, it had more to do with—

"Langford Hall." I pointed. "That's his family home." A strange feeling prickled over my shoulders. Relief? At least he had not lied to me about this.

A few more clicks, and Gordo and I both frowned at the same time. "I don't understand. That doesn't look right."

"Langford Hall in Surrey was deeded to the National Trust in 1971," Gordo read. "Prior to that it had been in the hands of the Bellingham family, but on the death of Annemarie Bellingham, the last surviving member, the terms of her will made it a gift to the government."

"He told me that was his home," I said. "Do they let people live in museums?"

Gordo tapped again. "Prior to 1820, the Hall was the home of the Langford family. In 1820 Gabriel Langford became the sole heir following the death of pneumonia of his parents Richard and Anne Langford. He disappeared at the age of nineteen and is generally supposed to have been pressed into the Navy while on a trip to London. He was not heard from again. Upon having him declared legally dead ten years later, his sister Charlotte Maria Langford Bellingham inherited the property."

I shifted. This floor was hard. "That's not the right Gabriel anyway. Maybe it was his ancestor and he was named after him. Try some of the listings on the previous page."

Tap-tap-tap. "Here's the diary of a lady in 1861. Says she was 'accosted by a highwayman' who looked exactly like the boy she was supposed to marry when she was young."

"Let me guess," Rennie said. "Gabriel Langford."

"Maybe he came back," Hannah said. "Maybe he got out of the Navy and retired and came back to warm up cold soup."

"I have to print this." Gordo pressed a button, and a minute later there was a wheezing sound from the bedroom. He came back in a moment carrying a copy of the diary page. "There. Look at that."

He pointed, and obediently I tried to make out the curly, old-fashioned script. "'I called his name—Gabriel—for it was he, to the life, still the handsome boy I had loved at seventeen. You are mistaken, madam, he said, and it was his very voice. It does not signify whether he was or was not, for my husband shot him.'"

"Good heavens." I sat sideways on the floor.

"I thought highwaymen were pretty much stamped out before the 1860s," Rennie said. "Interesting that he hadn't changed."

"Obviously it was his son or grandson," Hannah said. "How could someone remember her old boyfriend forty years later?"

"My mom does," Rennie told her. "Every time my dad screws up, she throws the guy in his face. But that's only twenty years."

"We're getting off track. Can you look some more, Gordo?" This was all very interesting, but dead heirs and highwaymen didn't have anything to do with my Gabriel.

Gordo was thorough, I had to give him that. He followed trails I couldn't even see, but all he turned up was a stockbroker in New York in the forties and a name on a list of volunteers during World War I. "Looks like he drove an ambulance."

A goose walked over my grave. "Really?" I leaned in to look. "That's an ambulance? It looks like a tractor."

"Maybe, but here's the name of the driver posing for the picture. Gabriel Langford."

Wunnerlich. "Maybe things like that run in the family. Gabriel said he drove an ambulance for a while. Adam was all excited that he could drive, but he said he'd let his license lapse."

Gordo opened another window on the screen. "Let me see if I can blow up this photo a bit." He swung the screen toward himself. Tappity-tap-tap-tap. Then he turned it so I could see. "Look like this guy could be from the same family as your guy?"

My blood seemed to stop in my veins.

Dressed in a stained duster, his hand resting on the fender of the ambulance as if he and it were partners, my Gabriel smiled out at me, his face sepia-colored with the passage of a century.

"No," I breathed. How could this be possible?

"No, there's no family resemblance?" Gordo studied the picture, doing things with buttons to make it larger and smaller.

My stomach rolled again, and I measured the distance to the bathroom from where I sat. "No, it's impossible." I cleared my throat. "It looks exactly like him."

"That's what the highwayman's girlfriend said, too," Rennie pointed out.

"This is weird." Hannah swung the computer out from under Gordo's fingers. "Is this him?"

"It's Gabriel. I don't know how or why, but that's him. Or his dad or grandfather or something."

"Or something." Gordo and Rennie exchanged a look. Then Gordo said, "Pretty odd to have such an exact resemblance passed on over a hundred years. Like extra genetic material didn't even get added into the mix."

"Yeah." Rennie's voice sounded muted as he got up. "Odd. Only one or two impossible explanations for that, if you ask me."

"Those would not be explanations," Gordo told him. "Those would be myth."

"I did say impossible."

"You guys are babbling," Hannah said in the exact tone she used to use when she babysat us *Kinner* long ago.

"Wait." I couldn't take my eyes from the image still on the screen. "He said his parents died of pneumonia. That the winter before was really cold and they never recovered."

By now Rennie had returned with his own computer. "Interesting. That tallies with the National Trust blurb. One second." Clickety-click. "Yup, here it is. The National Weather Service in the U.K. is tracking global warming and has weather reports going back for two centuries." Click. "When did Gabriel say his folks died?"

"Three years ago."

"So subtract three from 1820 and you get ... uh-huh. Average daily temperatures in the south of England were near zero for four weeks straight during the winter of

1817. If you don't have central heating and you're relying on leeches for a cure, the chance of your surviving pneumonia are—"

"Zero," Gordo finished. "We're talking about the Little Ice Age still, dude."

"Will you stick to the facts?" Hannah said impatiently. "Why do you care if it was cold in 1817? Gabriel's parents died in 2009."

Again that exchange of glances. "Did they?" Gordo said.

"Of course they did."

Clickety-click. "Except that the winter of 2009 was one of the wettest on record in Britain. We're talking floods and rain—not a lot of freezing."

"You can get pneumonia from being wet. Anybody knows that."

"Okay." Rennie wasn't making sense. One minute he said a thing, and the next he agreed that it wasn't true. What did my sister see in this man? "Sophia, do you know anything else about your fiancé?"

I tried to riffle back through my memory. Oh, wait. How could I have forgotten? "He went to boarding school when he was eight. It was—" What was the name of it? Something about a bird. "Robin Hill? No, wait. Sparrow Hill. His parents sent him miles away from home when he was so little. I felt so sorry for him."

Clickety-click. Rennie's eyebrows lifted, and then he looked over the lid of his computer at me. "You're not going to like this."

"Why?"

"Because Sparrow Hill Academy burned to the ground in 1887. There's nothing left but the ruins of the old chapel, it says here."

I didn't even bother to look. I felt sick. "I don't understand. Is everything he told me about himself a lie?"

"Not if it's 1820," Rennie said.

"Or he didn't die," Gordo added.

"Okay, I'm getting a little tired of this," Hannah snapped. "Stop playing around and do something to help."

"We're not playing around," Gordo said. "If we start on the assumption that Gabriel isn't lying to her, then everything he's told her about himself checks out. Sophia, do you think he was telling the truth?"

As Pilate once asked, "What is truth?" How was I to know? I used to think God had given me a gift for discernment. Was this His way of knocking me off my proud pedestal? "I thought so," I said finally, sounding weak even to myself.

"The best way to live a lie is to tell as much of the truth as you can." I didn't even bother to ask Rennie if he'd learned this from personal experience. "So if you've been living for two hundred years, you'd have to stick pretty close to the truth or you'd get massively mixed up trying to remember which story went with which decade."

Words were coming out of his mouth, but my brain was not making sense of them.

"Added to that, you've got the whole murder angle," Gordo put in. "The uh, attacks to the throat and all. I'm putting two and two together and getting ... weirdness."

Rennie nodded. "Immortality plus a need for blood equals ... the impossibly possible?"

Hannah and I just stared at him. The screen on Gordo's computer abruptly went dark.

"Sophia, you're going to think I'm crazy, but all the evidence fits." Gently, Rennie closed his own computer. "I don't see any other explanation."

I didn't see anything. "What?"

"I'm sorry to tell you this, but ... I think you're engaged ... to a vampire."

The sum of what I knew about vampires amounted to the cartoon pictures Lilian Borchardt and the other shop owners put up in their little square at Hallowe'en. It took nearly an hour for the boys to tell us everything they knew or imagined about them, and that not only could vampires exist, but they could also be walking around in broad daylight in Mitternacht, Iowa. I very quickly became acquainted with a man called Bram Stoker and realized there was an entire population who believed in beings that I had not known anything about.

Which was not surprising. The elders always said that ignorance of the world was a protection from it. But now I was seeing that ignorance was no protection from anything. Cara had not known anything of such evil, either, but it had not kept her from being killed. If anything, her ignorance had made it easier.

The boys tossed a grubby Reivers sweatshirt over my head and bundled me off to the college library at one in

the morning. "Google has its place, but for serious research you need Skype and the university databases,"
Rennie told me as he swiped a plastic card through a slot
at the door. Even at this time of night, there were scholars huddled over their books, hunched behind their
opened computers typing away.

"Midterms," Hannah whispered.

The boys commandeered a computer in its own niche
and went to work. Screens flashed and scrolled, and now
and again Gordo would whisper, "Yes!" under his breath
as he made the printer in the next room wheeze. Many of
these references and pictures were for Gabriel Langfords
who looked nothing like my Gabriel, or who lived in
places like South Africa or Scotland. In every case where
the face was a familiar one, he was nineteen.

Nineteen for two hundred years.

All this evidence piled up like branches in a creek,
barely allowing the water of thought to seep through. I
couldn't take it in. Couldn't believe. Until Rennie dialed
up some students he knew in Britain over a microphone
in the computer.

"Hey Izzy, I'm doing some research for a history paper. Any chance you can get me into the databases at
Somerset House?"

"Easy as wink," the voice replied from across the
ocean. I stared, amazed. The depth of the things I didn't
know staggered me. "What d'you need?"

"Anything you can find on a guy named Gabriel Langford, of Langford Hall in Surrey. Born around 1801."

Even from where I sat, I could hear the tapping of the
British girl's computer. "Coming online now. Langford,

you said? Hm. Not much here with that birthdate. What is he, some obscure poet or something?"

"Genealogy project for Bio," Gordo put in from where he hung over Rennie's shoulder.

"Ah." Izzy typed some more. "Nothing much about him—poor blighter, didn't last long, did he? Oh, wait. Here's something. Guy had his portrait painted after he inherited this property. That's all I've got, though. D'you want the image?"

Rennie turned around and raised his eyebrows at me. "Yes," I whispered.

"Send it over, Izzy. And thanks."

"D'you want me to dig around a bit more?"

"If you can. I'm interested in whether he was a suspect in any murders. We're, uh, tracking whether a predilection for murder is passed down in a family. We can't find much in the databases over here because he's—er, was a British citizen."

"Gloomy lot, you are. All right, I'll see what I can find."

"Thanks, Izzy. I owe you a black-and-tan when I'm over there the next time."

"You owe me more than that. Cheers."

Within seconds, Gordo had opened up his mail account and found the image. "Wow. Look at this. It's the same guy, without a doubt."

In an oil painting set in a heavy, ornate frame, brown-and-white spaniels lay at the feet of a young man in buff-colored breeches and a cutaway coat. He held a whip and the reins of a horse that looked over his shoulder, and in the distance was a large house with pillars across the front.

Gabriel gazed straight out at me, his chin lifted in that proud way he sometimes had—that after all this time, he still couldn't help.

The lord of the manor. The lord of the Gingrich farm.

I covered my face with my apron and began to cry.

19

Stinson County Register

DEPUTY ASSAULTED, CLINGS TO LIFE

The Stinson County Sheriff's Department confirmed today that Deputy Carl Palermo, a four-year veteran of the force currently assigned to crimes against persons, was the victim of aggravated assault causing gross bodily harm late Friday night.

When the officer did not respond to repeated hails on his police radio, the GPS function of his cell phone was activated. Rescuers found him lying in a wooded area some two miles west of the town of Mitternacht. He was unconscious and bleeding profusely from wounds to the neck and leg.

Deputy Palermo has been investigating a series of murders in the local Mennonite community, and was in the process of interviewing witnesses when he was attacked. Sources in the department say that this investigation may have a larger reach than Stinson County. The national crime database holds records of at least three similar unsolved murders in New York and Connecticut.

"Deputy Palermo's vehicle is missing and we ask the plain community's help in locating the person or persons who might be responsible. Any sightings of the vehicle, which bears call code Bravo 17 (B-17), should be reported to this department as soon as possible," said Sheriff Wayne Aiken.

Deputy Palermo is currently in ICU at County Memorial, and has not regained consciousness. The district attorney's office has indicated the possibility that charges of attempted murder will be filed when the perpetrator(s) are found.

"Of course they're crazy." Hannah jumped down from the campus shuttle and waited for me to join her on the sidewalk outside the bus station. "Those two will be lucky if I speak to them ever again. I can't believe they sat up all night geeking out over this foolishness."

"*Loss uns geh.*" I didn't want to talk about it. The dam in my mind had broken and washed away all sense, and I didn't want to think anymore. I just wanted to go home. "Can you see David?" I hurried into the station, backpack bouncing on my spine, forcing Hannah to jog a little to keep up.

"There he is, by the ticket window." I made a beeline for him. Luckily the place wasn't very busy.

"Sophia, would you slow down? You're only going to have to wait half an hour."

I didn't care. A ticket in my hand would mean I was really getting out of here. Somehow even the smallest reassurances meant much—and since the discoveries of last night had completely destroyed my ability to sleep, I was hanging onto small, sane things with an iron grip this morning.

If I didn't do that, I'd lose my way. My hold on what was right and good. Maybe even my mind.

David's smile of greeting faded as his gaze searched my face. I could not meet his eyes. "I'm sorry about this. Are you sure you don't mind cutting your weekend short? You don't have to go back with me, you know."

"I know. We can go to a band hop another time. And my relatives had things to do today, so they don't feel offended that I was such a fly-by-night."

"I just—I had to—"

"You can tell me all about it when we get on the bus."

How could I explain what I was having a hard time believing myself? It would be such a relief to be able to lie and say I didn't get along with Hannah's roommates or we were all sharing one bedroom and I couldn't stay there. Something.

Anything but the truth.

When the bus driver opened the door and people began to climb on, Hannah gave me a hard hug. "Will you be all right?"

"I don't know. I suppose so. I'm just so *verhuddelt*."

"Not half as confused as I am. I mean, I know they're geeks and spend way too much time playing video games and watching monster movies on their computers, but who could believe that this is real? If I'm having problems with it, I can't imagine how you must feel."

"It was nice of them to do all that work for me." That was an understatement. "And for Rennie to give up his time with you."

"Rennie." Hannah snorted. "So much for me going to meet his parents this summer. Not that I wanted to anyway."

"Don't let this come between the two of you." Tears scalded my eyes, as raw as my emotions.

"Don't you worry about me." Hannah hugged me again and then reached into her pocket. "Look, I want you to have this."

I took the little cell phone. It fit into my palm like a good skipping stone. "Where did you get this?"

"Went without lunch for a month and bought it. It should have about twenty-five minutes still on it—more than enough for you to use."

"For what?"

Her gaze met mine, intense with concern. "I don't like this. Even taking out the weirdness, I don't. I want you to have some way to—" She stopped. "If you need it, you have it, okay? And if you don't need it, you can give it back to me next time." She showed me which buttons did what and moved aside to include David in the conversation. "David, you take care of her. She's had a bad night."

"I will." She hugged him, too. I wondered where she'd begun doing that. It wasn't something we did outside the family.

I slipped the phone into my backpack and followed David onto the bus. I found a seat next to the window, with his comforting presence between me and the people edging down the aisle and fussing with their luggage. He let the bus pull out and put twenty miles of Iowa farmland between us and Council Bluffs before he spoke, his voice quiet and diffident.

"Did something happen there at your sister's place?"

"Yes. But I can't explain it. And I don't want to talk about it."

He turned his attention to the scenery whipping past on the other side. Fifteen miles later, he said, "Wasn't anything to do with that Gordo she lives with, was it?"

I sighed. "Not the way you think. He didn't do anything, he just—said things. It's all right, David. The darts of the wicked don't do us any harm. I'll be fine once I'm home again."

And then I sent up a prayer for forgiveness. What kind of life was I living when even the offer of such simple comfort was an evasion?

When the bus reached Mitternacht, we had to walk home because no one was expecting us until tomorrow night, and it being Saturday, Jonah wasn't working at the cabinet shop. But I didn't mind. Five miles of country road was nothing, and it was a bright day, warm and smelling of the good green things bursting out of the roadside soil, and of leaves mature enough on the trees that they could offer us some shade.

Good things. Normal, familiar things.

When we reached the gravel driveway of the Fischer place, which was closest to town, David let his bag slide to the ground. "I could hitch up the horse and give you a ride the rest of the way."

"No. *Denki*, but I like to walk. It helps me think."

Hands on his hips, he nudged his bag with the toe of his boot. Finally he lifted his head. "If you ever want to talk, you know where I am."

I wish I could. The thought whisked through my head, surprising me. For the first time all day, I looked directly into his eyes. "David, are you so quiet because you have nothing to say, or because you're letting me think?"

His eyes crinkled. "Oh, I have plenty to say. But you're a girl who doesn't like to hear a lot."

"What does that mean? That I'm too fond of my own opinion?"

"More like you make up your mind that a thing is so, and then it's hard to change it. You made up your mind that Gabriel Langford was the one for you, and after that there wasn't much use for talking."

I hadn't had any sleep. My emotions had been curried with a hard brush and I'd lost what patience I had back at the bus station. "I'm engaged to him, you know."

He rocked back a little, then settled into place. "Then there's really nothing for me to say, is there?"

"What would you say, if you could?" What was I doing, picking a fight, when all he'd done was be completely kind to me?

"I can't, so there isn't much point."

"But if you could?"

The silence between us was so complete I could hear a bee bumbling in the rambling rose growing up the gate-post.

Wild roses. Something strange. How did Gabriel get you back in the house that night? Was it like Rennie said—because vampires can move up walls and stairs in a way ordinary people can't?

I really was losing my mind.

I felt almost grateful when David said, "If I could, I'd say maybe you should look a little closer to home, that's all. What you see might not be so handsome, but it might wear better in the wash."

"You don't think Gabriel will wear well in the wash?"

"I'm just saying we hardly know him. Where'd he get all that money of his? Why was he making time with Cara when he's engaged to you? A person might ask herself these questions."

"He wasn't making time with Cara."

"No? Then I'd wonder what he was doing out on the road with her so late the night she died." I stared at him, willing him to go on. "One of our cows calved that night, and my dad sent me over to get Cara's father. He knows a bit about animals. I saw her up on the road by the pay phone and he was waiting for her."

"You couldn't have seen that far in the dark."

"I wouldn't have seen him at all if he hadn't been singing while he waited."

"Singing?"

David shifted his shoulders, as if a weight had fallen off them. "The one about the reapers. The one Rebecca always says we sing too fast."

"Reapers." In my mind, I saw Gabriel making his way to me over the fields after Cara's death. Singing about reapers. He'd talked about God harvesting her on the very next day, when he'd come to me so alive, so joyous and vital—when he'd proposed. "Have you told Deputy Palermo about this?"

"I would if he asked me. Haven't seen him around much lately, though. Not since he told Adam to stay put."

I turned and left him there, and he didn't stop me. Like a horse finding its way home without a rider, I walked the familiar roads, made turns I had been making all my life, and saw none of it.

God had not harvested Cara. Or Uncle Paul.

Gabriel had. Because he believed they had harmed me.

This was my fault. I had to make it right. I had to do something.

I had left here yesterday running away from this awful, unbelievable truth. But it was still here, waiting for me, and it only seemed to have become more true. I could not run any more.

You make up your mind that a thing is so, and then it's hard to change it.

So if I could believe that Gabriel could do such a thing, then why not stretch my belief a little farther, to what Gordo and Rennie had spent all that time discovering for me? The largest veins in the victims' bodies had been opened—Gordo said that vampires did this. That they needed to drink blood in order to stay alive. Was this why Gabriel had seemed so sickly before each death, and so alive afterward?

Oh, what a dreadful sense it made!

"They can't cross over running water," Rennie had told me, "and this stuff about garlic and stakes and burning up in the sun is nonsense. You have to go back to the original documents. The original Drakul could go out in the daytime. He was just stronger at night."

Gabriel only came to see me at night. And he never crossed the ditch at the back of our yard unless we were holding hands.

If you believed one unbelievable thing, was another so difficult?

I crested the hill and saw the roof of our barn over the trees. I had not had many homecomings, but for the first time in my life, facing my family seemed the next thing to impossible. Instead of turning into the driveway, I kept going the few yards to the creek bottom.

Concealed by the trees from the view of anyone on the road or in our yard, I swung my backpack to the ground and pulled out Hannah's cell phone.

STINSON COUNTY
SHERIFF'S DEPARTMENT
13:01:04 2014-MAY-18

OPERATOR: Stinson County Sheriff. How can I help you?

U/F: I need to speak to Deputy Palermo, *bidde*—um, please.

OPERATOR: I'm sorry, Deputy Palermo is on sick leave.

U/F: He's sick?

OPERATOR: He was assaulted on Friday night, miss. He's in the hospital.

U/F: [Gasps.] Is he all right?

OPERATOR: We don't know yet.

U/F: Assaulted how?

OPERATOR: It's hard to say. I was over to visit yesterday and he has big bandages on his neck and leg. He needed big-time blood transfusions.

U/F: Neck and ... Was he bitten?

OPERATOR: Didn't I just say he had bandages there? I can't see through them. Are you a friend or relative?

U/F: I'm a ... he came to ask me questions about Cara Troyer's death. There's something he needs to know.

OPERATOR: You'll have to talk to someone else in the office, then. Carl's not in any shape, that's for sure. Let me transfer you.

[Call disconnected.]

The phone snapped shut and I closed my hand around it in a fist. I couldn't breathe. My legs trembled and finally gave out, and I sank onto a rock beside the creek.

In hospital. With wounds to the neck and leg.

The creek chortled past, a sound that usually cheered me up. This time I was only thankful for one thing—that it covered up the keening sounds rasping in my throat.

Lieber Gott in Himmel, help me. I know not what I do, Lord. But I believe now. Two might be a coincidence, but three people? It must be true. He is a vampire. But why have You brought him into my life if his only purpose is to kill everyone around me?

The tips of my fingers felt as cold as if I had dipped them in the creek, but it wasn't nearly as cold as I felt inside—numb, terrified, frozen in my inability to do anything. I may as well be dead, for all the use I was.

Uncle Paul, I would not have wished such a death on you. I'm sorry for the vengeance in my heart. I'm sorry your soul was so broken you felt you had to force yourself on young girls who couldn't protect themselves. I hope God is healing you now.

Cara, I may have been impatient with you, but I never hated you. Your death was my fault, and I hope both you and God will forgive me for it.

O Lord, please be with poor Deputy Palermo. He was only doing his job, and he didn't deserve this. Thank You for sparing his life. Give him strength, and good doctors who will take care of him.

The rushing of the water could almost be the sound of wings, bearing me up to God. I sat on my rock and just emptied my soul to Him, until all the noise and grief and indecision had gone, leaving me still.

Over my head, a trio of yellow finches trilled at each other, and I came back to myself.

I knew three things. Gabriel had killed two people and tried to kill another. I was the only person in Stinson County who knew what he was. The police would not believe he was a vampire, but they were all I had.

There were things in heaven and earth that we did not know, and vampires appeared to be one of them. I could just see the reaction in the sheriff's department if an Old Order girl called and told them the man they wanted was a demon, and the officers should bring wooden stakes and an axe along to arrest him. They would laugh, and it would bring shame and derision on my church. If I asked David or my brother Caleb, they would probably laugh, too—right before they were killed.

My head acknowledged the evidence. But my heart demanded that I ask Gabriel himself if all this was true. Only when I heard it from his own lips would I completely believe ... and then what? Would he try to kill me? What would I do then—I who had been schooled to be humble and a peacemaker all my life?

No. If he had killed Paul and Cara out of love for me, then I was in no danger. But Deputy Palermo had not harmed me. Had Gabriel attacked him because he had come too close to the truth?

I had no choice. I had to find out. I might not have physical proof to make the sheriff believe he was a vampire, but David had evidence that might help prove he should be locked up. I could not hurt him or even physically stop him. But others could. If I could convince him he was breaking God's laws, maybe he would stop walking this dreadful path long enough for the police to step in.

The finches flittered away to another tree, and I got to my feet. I had to think carefully. First, I needed to talk to David and get him to tell the sheriff's office what he knew. I could not approach Gabriel now—if he had drunk the deputy's blood, he would be strong. A few days needed to pass before we met, so he would be in that weak, pale state. I could lift a bale of hay and put it on the wagon without help, so maybe I'd have a chance to defend myself if he—

My mind shuddered away. Surely he wouldn't hurt me. Not the woman he loved. His love might have meant the death of others, but maybe it would save me.

That hope was all I had.

When the screen door slammed behind me, Mamm looked up from the stove in surprise. "Sophia! We didn't expect you back until tomorrow. Was everything all right? Did you find your sister well?"

"She's very well. She sends her love, and says she'll come down for a visit after exams are over." *To make sure you're all right* was what she'd really said, but I hoped God would forgive another tiny evasion.

"Did you not like it up there?" Mamm's face still held her astonishment.

"It wasn't that. I started feeling sick last night, and by this morning all I could think of was coming home." No need for lies there. It was the absolute truth. "I'm just going to go upstairs, then."

"Do you want some soup? I made some this morning."

"*Neh, denki.* Maybe at supper."

I escaped up the stairs before she could ask me anything more.

It was easy enough to avoid him the next day—a Sunday. Mamm had invited quite a number to lunch, and as I sat on the bench I kept my head bowed over my food, even though he was not expecting me to be there and would not be looking for me. When I finally did see him, standing outside and talking easily in a circle of the young married men, as though he were already one of them, it felt as though a hand had reached inside my ribs and squeezed my heart.

So beautiful, he was. That smile, that easy stance. That slender, strong body that still stood as if he were wearing riding boots and a cutaway coat.

How was it possible that he could be—as Rennie had so cruelly put it—the undead? And two hundred years undead at that. He had not felt dead when I had kissed him, but that was not saying much. It had been my first kiss, and I had nothing to compare it to.

Do not think of kissing him.

If I did, the howling grief and horror inside me would break its seal and I would begin that awful keening again. Which would go over badly as I passed a pitcher of water down the table.

During the afternoon, I got David's attention and took him aside, much to the amusement of his buddies. Under the noise of their whistling and pointed comments, I kept my tone low and serious. "David, you must tell the sheriff's office what you told me. About Gabriel meeting Cara on the road that night. You must do it right away. You could even use Hannah's cell phone."

"Is that deputy coming?"

"No. But there are others who will want to know. Promise me you'll call and tell them."

"It will cause a fuss. And what if I was wrong? Seeing them on the road doesn't mean anything when they found her in Omaha."

I barely kept myself from putting both hands on his arm and shaking it to make my point. "You weren't wrong. I believe you. Even if we don't know how she got there, it's still important."

His eyes held confusion and doubt. "But he's your man, Sophia. Do you know what you're saying?"

"I know. Believe me, no one knows better than me. But you have to tell the truth. Promise."

I waited in silent agony while he thought it over. Though his face still held confusion, he finally said, "All right. I'll call there tomorrow."

"Thank you." Now it was in God's hands. "Some day I'll tell you why it matters."

On Monday I didn't hear from him, and I couldn't get out of the house to watch the pay phone. I could only hope he had kept his promise. On Tuesday a note came for me in beautiful copperplate script.

My dear one,

Caleb tells me you are not feeling well, though from a distance yesterday you looked as pretty as ever. I hope I can see you soon. Look for me tonight.

All my love,
Gabriel

20

I woke with a start a few minutes after two to see the flashlight beam dancing on the ceiling like a firefly. I lay there, frozen into immobility by indecision.

It felt so normal, as though I should fly down the stairs to find him just the way he had always been, smiling and strong and loving me. But then the vision of Uncle Paul's body and the endless blood splashed on the walls intruded, imposing fear on love and strangling it.

I could barely breathe. Ten agonizing minutes passed before the light bobbed to the side and went out.

Sophia.

Had he spoken it or could I just hear him in my head? "Vampires communicate with their thralls through telepathy," Rennie had read from one of the many websites he'd found on the subject. "The blood bond produces a mental and emotional connection that makes communication possible, even over long distances."

"Sophia, are you awake?"

My window was open a crack. Not in my head, then. There was no blood bond. I was not a "thrall."

Enthralled. Oh yes, I had been that once. But not anymore. I did not move, though my breath sounded as loud as the wind in the grass.

"Sophia?"

I don't know how much time crept past. It seemed like an hour. But at length I heard gravel crunch softly out in the drive, and my breath whooshed out of my lungs. I threw the covers back and looked out the window to see nothing but the moonless night. Even so, I stayed there, watching, until the horizon lightened over the roof of the barn and creaks and rustles from Dat and Mamm's room told me they were up.

The next night I slept in Miriam's room, on the spare twin bed Mamm sometimes used when the baby was sick. It faced out on the weaning pen, not the orchard, and if he came I didn't hear him. By Thursday I knew I couldn't put it off any longer. He would know something was wrong, and that might make him suspicious or even angry. I'd never seen Gabriel angry, and I didn't want to.

"Goodness, Sophia, you're fidgety," Mamm said as we did the mending together that night. Or rather, she was mending a pair of Jonah's pants. I was dropping things and breaking thread and trying not to wonder whether he would come again tonight, or whether I had waited too long and he would—*oh, no, please don't let him hurt anyone else.*

"Sorry, Mamm."

She laid the pants leg down in her lap. "What is it, *liewi?* Can you talk about it with me?" I shook my head. "Is something wrong?"

Only everything. I picked up a sock with a holey heel and stared at it. For the life of me I couldn't remember how to start darning it.

"Is it that you're still angry with us about making you and Gabriel wait?"

Wait for what? It took me a second to realize what she meant. "Oh. No. It's not that at all. It's nothing. Must be an east wind, that's all."

"There is no wind this evening. Sophia, tell me the truth. Are you nervous about becoming a bride? About being a wife?"

I choked down the urge to laugh. Once I got started, I wouldn't be able to stop. "No. We had that little talk last winter, remember? Unlike poor Katie. I don't think she knows a thing about it but what she reads in books."

"You're changing the subject."

Was I? I took a deep breath. "Maybe it's a good thing you and Dat asked us to wait. I—I think I might be getting cold feet."

"Are you, now?" She picked up the seam ripper and began to pick out the hems. "Well, I have to say Gabriel seems to have everything all planned out for how he's going to run the farm. He was over Friday night—came quite late, but he was happy to sit with us and have a cup of cocoa and visit."

"Quite ... late?" When had Deputy Palermo been hurt? What was he doing around my family when I wasn't there? Choosing his next victim? "How did he seem?"

"Well, he was missing you, though you'd only been gone a few hours. He was in good spirits. Laughing, joking with the boys. And he told us a little about his family."

"Oh? What?"

She glanced up at me, then concentrated on the width of the hem. "Just little things, about how his father owned a lot of land there in England, and he was familiar with farming. Sounds like a big old place they have."

"Langford Hall," I said faintly.

"That was it. Imagine naming your house after yourself. Vanity and vexation of spirit." She shook her head at the vagaries of worldly people. "He's only got a sister left, but he doesn't like her husband much, so they don't speak. A shame. I don't think she'll be coming to the wedding."

"What's his sister's name?"

She looked up. "Don't you know it?"

"I forgot."

"Charlotte Bellingham. I don't remember the brother-in-law's first name."

My stomach turned to ice. *Upon having him declared legally dead ten years later, his sister Charlotte Maria Langford Bellingham inherited the property.* "What else did he tell you?"

"Just that he still misses his parents, and then Dat asked him why he had cash money to buy the farm, and he said he'd done some speculating. 'Played the stock market,' he said. I said I hoped he planned to give that nonsense up, and he said he had, years ago. Though if that was true, he must have been a precocious child. I don't know what these worldly families are thinking with their computers and whatnot. Imagine a boy buying and selling things over this Internet and his parents not knowing."

A stockbroker in the forties. Rennie was right—if you were going to spin a story, you'd better leave as much truth in it as you could.

My dinner heaved at the thought of these proofs that kept confronting me—proofs that no one would believe but me and three college students in Council Bluffs. I put the sock and unused needles back in the basket. "I don't feel well, Mamm. I'm going upstairs."

She gave me a narrow look as I passed her. "Time for one of my tinctures, I think. I don't like the look of you since you came home."

"Maybe in the morning." I'd welcome a tincture. Because that would mean I'd survived the night.

I waited until I heard Mamm put Miriam down and go to bed, and then even longer until Caleb came in. When I heard him and Jonah both snoring, I tiptoed down the stairs with Hannah's cell phone. I didn't trust my shaking hands not to drop it if I went out to the creek, so instead I used its glowing face as a flashlight and crossed the yard to the barn. I could only hope that two sets of solid walls would be enough to keep the sound of my voice from Dat's sharp ears.

The number to the apartment was the first one on her list inside the phone. It rang three times and then I heard Gordo's voice. "Hello—"

"Gordo, this is Sophia. Is Hannah—"

"—you've reached the lair of Gordo, Rennie, and Hannah. If you're a friend, leave a message. If you're not, go throw yourself at a Sarlacc at the sound of the tone."

The phone beeped in my ear. An answering machine.

"Hannah? This is Sophia. Are you there? Please pick up. It's urgent." I waited. *Please, please* ... Nothing. "I, um, bad things are happening. Deputy Palermo was attacked just like Cara and Uncle Paul. He's in the hospital. And Gabriel came over Friday night and told Mamm his sister won't be coming to the wedding. His sister *Charlotte*." I gulped as my throat threatened to close altogether. "Hannah, stop being mad at Gordo and Rennie because they're right. They have been all along. I'm so scared. I need to talk to you, okay? Please call m—"

Beeeep. Click. Buzz. I had talked too long and the answering machine had hung up on me.

My face heated, and tears sprang to my eyes as I shone the phone's face over to the wall where Dat kept his tools, all hanging neatly on a perforated board with hooks on it. The lamp hung on one end. By the time I'd lit the wick, tears were streaking my cheeks in earnest, and I'd wakened the chickens on top of it all. Confused, they shifted and murmured on their roosts inside their wire enclosure, blinking at me in the dim but unexpected light.

"It's all right, girls," I said hoarsely. "It's not morning yet." Maybe it never would be morning. No, I couldn't think that way. Maybe he wouldn't come.

Sophia.

My breathing shuddered into silence.

Sophia.

Maybe I was a thrall. Because no human voice had said my name.

The barn door quivered and then slid open a couple of feet, and Gabriel stepped inside. "There you are. What are you doing out here?"

I slipped the phone into the deep pocket in the side seam of my skirt as he turned to push the door shut. "I knew you would come."

"I came the other night, but you must have been sleeping too deeply." He held out his arms. "I'm glad to see you."

I thought I might be sick. But I had to act normally, or he might ... what? What did I really think he would do? I stepped closer and he hugged me. My arms went around his waist just like they had always done, and then I felt what I had hoped—prayed—dreaded—to feel.

"Your hands are cold." I had never noticed before, because I hadn't been looking, but a tremor coursed through them, too. Just enough so that I could feel it— the way Mamm got sometimes if she went too long between meals.

He had not hurt anyone. And the effects of poor Deputy Palermo's blood must be wearing off.

"It's a cool night," he said. "You can help me warm them up."

How was I going to begin this conversation? Did words even exist to ask the man you loved if he had killed? If he was a monster? And how could I force them out when he was standing there, a soft smile in his eyes just for me?

But I had to. Under my reasoning about Dat hearing me talking on the phone was a deeper urge. I'd come out here to wait for him, away from my family and anyone who could get hurt.

Now I had to put my trust in God and go through with it.

"What's the matter, Sophia? Have you been crying?"

With the heels of my hands, I scrubbed at my cheeks. "A little. Last weekend was hard."

"Is it your sister?"

I nodded. *Stick to the truth as much as you can.* "I don't think she's ever coming home. She and her roommate are courting."

"Roommate? They're living together?" He looked shocked.

Better that than trying to kiss me.

"Not like that. There's another boy living there, too. In that college everyone lives four to a room, boys and girls."

His forehead wrinkled in a frown. "I hope you haven't told your father this."

"Oh, no. He'd never get over it—and he'd never let me visit her again."

"I wouldn't blame him. So you spent the night there, with these two other men? I don't think I like that, Sophia."

What else was I supposed to do? Sleep out under a tree? "There was a fourth bedroom. That's where I stayed."

"But still. It was indecent of your sister to put you in that position. What if it got out among God's people that my wife-to-be had spent the night in an apartment with two men—worldly men, at that?"

My mind had been so full of bigger, more awful things that this hardly seemed worth answering. "How would it get out? I'm not going to say anything. And she didn't put me in any *position*. I had a room all my own, and the door had a lock, if that's what you're worried about."

His pale skin turned even whiter. "Did you use it?"

"I don't remember. I don't think so. Gordo and Rennie aren't exactly the type, and anyway, they were busy, um, doing research on a project of theirs half the night."

"You didn't lock your door? An open door is an invitation to any man, of any type."

He sounded almost jealous. "Not to those two. Are you trying to pick a fight?" I had trusted him even when Cara had told me point blank she had plans to see him the night she died. I had believed his word over hers—and that had been my mistake. If David had really seen what he said he'd seen, we'd all believed the wrong person.

"I am not. I am trying to understand how my fiancée could spend the night with two strange men."

How dared he take that tone with me—that superior, I'm-righteous-and-you're-the-sinner tone that my uncle had used when he'd mocked me in my helplessness. I wasn't helpless. And he wasn't any better than me.

This was the first time, I realized with a sense of shock, I had thought of him on those terms. Always before it had been, *I'm unworthy of you* and *Why did you choose me?* But not any more. I was still human. Still a child of God. I could not say the same for him, and it grieved me to the soul.

Lord, use me to save him, if it's Your will. Let your love work through me because it's stronger than mine.

"Well, then, since we're on the subject, maybe you can help me understand what you were doing with Cara Troyer the night she died."

His gaze didn't leave my face. "What do you mean?"

"You were seen meeting her on the road late that night."

"By whom?"

"By—" Just in time, I stopped. If I said one more word, would David's be the next body we found with those great, gaping wounds? I took a deep breath, controlling my tongue and the nausea that rose under my ribs. "It doesn't matter who it was. The fact is that you told me you hadn't seen her since the afternoon."

"You sound exactly like that pestilent deputy. It's very unbecoming in a woman, Sophia."

Yes, and murder was most unbecoming in a man. How dared he turn this around and make this about my faults? "Why is he pestilent? He's just doing his job."

I couldn't read his eyes. And he had not answered my question, either.

"He's interfering, and I will not brook interference." He flexed his hands. "It doesn't matter, anyway. He won't be back to bother us again."

"Not for a while, anyway. Not until he recovers."

Gabriel went absolutely still. "Recovers?"

"He's in the hospital."

"Alive? He's alive?"

"The lady at the sheriff's office said so. Why do you look so surprised? And why won't you answer me about Cara?"

He was already moving toward the barn door. "I have to go."

"Where?"

"Never mind where. A matter of unfinished business."

Oh, no. No. "You can't, Gabriel. Leave him alone."

"I must. He will destroy everything I've worked to build. He's a ravening wolf and he'll destroy our lives together if I don't stop him."

My decision to keep him pacified and talking vanished in a twist of desperate fear for the helpless deputy. If I didn't stop him, he'd kill again, and again, until there was no one left standing around me. "So that's why? You're going to kill him, too? Just like you killed Cara and Uncle Paul? Because you think they'll hurt us?"

He stopped tugging on the heavy door and turned slowly. "What did you say?"

"It was you, wasn't it? You've been doing this. Killing them. To protect me. And to—" But even I couldn't voice the last part. *To keep yourself alive.*

"I do not kill." His complete belief in his own words broke my heart. "I present them to God as a living sacrifice."

The last of the scales fell from my eyes and I saw him as he really was. A demon. One who lied to himself so he could keep doing what he was doing. "But they're not living." My voice shook, and I tried to control it. "They're dead. Like you."

He looked at me as though I had said it in Latin. "My darling, you are overwrought. I am not dead. I have been translated by the God I love into eternal life." He frowned again, just a tiny wrinkle between his brows. "Though sometimes His will puzzles me exceedingly. The sacrifices I make to him are necessary in order for me to live. I don't know why that is, but I accept His will." He smiled at me, as if this explanation should satisfy any doubts I had left.

"Gabriel," I whispered, "this isn't eternal life. You're immortal. There's a difference."

Those eyes. I had loved them once, loved the expression in them when he gazed at me. He had made me feel special, beloved, blessed among women. But now, I knew that I had held all those gifts myself, all this time. Gabriel had not given them to me. God had—and because He had, it meant I was worthy of them.

This fresh realization dazzled me a little. I was worthy of love because God loved me. Period. It had nothing to do with men in general or Gabriel in particular. It had to do with me and my Father in heaven.

I blinked and came back to myself to find his gaze pinning me like a hay fork—lifeless and deadly. "What did you say?" he asked quietly.

"You're immortal." My voice caught in my throat, and I steadied it. "You have been for two hundred years. All those things you told me—your parents dying, your sister, the school you were sent to—all that happened centuries ago."

"Yes, I know." His expression said, *Why are you pointing out the obvious?*

"You kill people because you have to drink their blood to stay alive. That's what vampires do."

"You're insane," he said flatly.

"No." I took a breath. "You are."

Insane. A murderer who told himself these stories to survive in his mind. And now I was spoiling his story by dragging in the truth.

As if I hadn't spoken, he said, "You're insane and you're telling lies."

"Look at yourself. You're—"

"Lies!" He was looking at me—through me—back into himself. "You're a liar and a slut and you've betrayed me with those men your slut of a sister lives with."

"Gabriel!" My heart reeled from the cruel words, stinging like a slap.

You are worthy. Those words don't mean a thing.

Now he focused on me abruptly. The blood stopped moving in my veins and time froze. Words were one thing, but they weren't all I had to be afraid of. Why hadn't I moved toward the door when I had the chance?

"You're going to tell everyone that I've killed when I haven't. I sacrifice to God. Why don't people see that? Why do they scream and chase and hunt me from town to town when all I'm trying to do is serve the God I love? Why is eternal life such a torment? All I want is to be left in peace to serve Him!" With every word, his voice rose.

Would Dat hear?

Oh, no. He would hurt my family if they came running out here. I had to do something.

"It's a torment because it isn't eternal life." I kept my voice low, soothing. The voice I used with the chickens. "You've got to stop ki—sacrificing people if you want to find peace."

"But I get sick." His voice spiraled down, like a pathetic child worn out from a temper tantrum, and he slumped against a stack of hay bales. "I have to feed on the sacrifices. It says so in the Bible."

"Those were cows, Gabriel, not people."

"Cows don't make me as strong." He looked around the barn, but the cows, thankfully, were in their stalls on the other side of the wall, next to the milking pen. "Human blood is best. It's God's will." That rambling gaze focused on me. "Human blood is best."

Gott in Himmel.

"I had hoped to spend my life with you, Sophia." His voice returned slowly to normal, that cultured, lovely voice that I had once listened to with such pleasure. Now it chilled me. "I made the blood sacrifices of the wolves to protect His helpless lambs, but you show no gratitude. I was mistaken in you."

I backed away. "No, I just—"

"You don't love me. You'll go running to the elders with your crazy stories and then I'll have to leave again, just when I'd gone to all that trouble to make a home for you."

"No. I promise I won't." I would call the police and they would lock him up, first.

"I don't trust your promises. You must learn to serve God. You must sacrifice." He leaped for me, but I ducked under his arm. I felt a tug, and looked frantically over my shoulder to see he'd grabbed my apron. The pins pulled out and I slipped out of it, whirling for the door.

But he anticipated me. With two long-legged steps, he cut off my escape. "You must be willing."

He was weak. I pinned my hopes on that and backed up, feeling behind me. Dat's bench, littered with tools and pieces of leather and wood. Did I really think I could hit him with something? I couldn't. It was against God's will to raise a hand against another. But what about now, when it meant life and death? What were the rules then?

"Stop this, Sophia. You'll only hurt yourself." He gripped my shoulders with fingers that didn't feel weak at all.

"Let me go!"

"I will never let you go. You are mine. You will be a sacrifice to the Lord—and part of me forever."

He held me just like my uncle had, so he could spew his ugly intentions in my face. Always *their* intentions— desires—needs. Never mine. I never got what I hoped for, but they always did.

Well, I was not going to be prey for anyone, ever again. I was worthy of love, not this contempt.

Besides, I'd learned a thing or two in my escapes from Uncle Paul. Gabriel might be a vampire, but he was still a man. I kneed him in the groin as hard as I could, and he cried out and staggered back, doubled over.

"Thou shalt not kill," I said, my voice harsh. I tried to soften it. "It's not too late, Gabriel. Ask forgiveness of God and stop this."

When he lifted his head, I knew I would never see the beautiful man I had loved again. Eyes flat—inhuman—he looked at me not as the girl he'd laughed with on moonlit nights, but as a creature who was a source of blood. A *thing*.

Thou shalt not kill. Except Gabriel was already dead. So who would be the first to break the Sixth Commandment—him or me? And would it really be breaking it if the *thing* you killed was not alive?

I flung myself at the wall where Dat's tools hung. How did you kill a vampire? Did stakes work? Rennie had told me, but I couldn't remember. A filleting knife? A scythe? What?

Footsteps on the planks of the barn floor, rushing at me. I whirled, flailing for something, anything—and grabbed the first handle that my frantic fingers touched. Something tore loose from its hook and I swung it with all my strength.

Dat kept his tools in perfect working order, as though usefulness were the next thing to godliness. The razor-sharp tip of the hay sickle sliced through Gabriel's white shirt and deep into his side. He grunted in surprise and looked down at himself. I yanked at the blade, but it had struck bone and I couldn't get it out.

Somewhere I heard a kitten mewling. Had to save the kitten. He would drink its blood, too.

With a shock like cold water, I realized the noise was coming out of my own mouth. Tugging hard, I got the sickle loose, and he looked up.

For an endless moment, we froze, he with his hands pressed to his side—which was not bleeding—and me with the sickle swinging loosely in front of me. In that face, once so beloved, the shock of my attack had brought back a spark of emotion—grief that I had tried to hurt him—and love—and pain.

"Sophia," he whispered. "Why does it hurt so much?"

Whether he meant the wound or his life, I could not answer.

And in those few frozen seconds, I remembered what Gordo said had to be done. But I couldn't heft that sickle and swing it at his neck. I could not kill the man I had once loved, even though in the next moment he might kill me. Because in killing him, I would kill everything he had loved in me. That God loved in me.

I'm worthy. I am. And I would not do anything to diminish that.

He saw my decision in my face, and in his eyes, I saw him make his decision, too.

"There is another way," he said, the words rasping in his throat. "If you come as a willing sacrifice, you'll have eternal life along with me."

"You'll kill me," I whispered.

He shook his head, slowly, as if his neck hurt. "The others were unwilling. If you let me drink willingly, you'll die, yes—but only temporarily." His eyes pleaded with me. "On the third day, you'll rise again, dearest. Like I did. And then we can be together for eternity. Living in our house, loving each other forever."

"That's not eternal life. That's turning me into a vampire, too."

His face clouded with disappointment in me, and disgust. "I will sacrifice you. I'm stronger than you are. Willing or unwilling, God will reap your life." He paused, breathing heavily. "Choose, Sophia."

No. I would not allow it. I would not be the one lying here on the barn floor when my father came in for milking. There had to be another way.

In the silence, far off, I heard a sound. A roar.

It was an enraged animal, bellowing its fury and pain.

No, it was a thunderstorm, racing through the darkness, riding the wind toward the farm.

No.

It was a 1967 Chevrolet Impala, with its gas pedal rammed all the way to the floor.

21

Gabriel heard it, too. In that single moment when he was distracted, trying to identify the sound, I darted for the door. With a roar of fury and frustration, he pounded after me, but I slipped through the gap he'd left open and flew out into the yard.

The big car tore up the lane, its engine filling the night like the shouting of a crowd, and slewed to a stop, tires spewing gravel, not two yards away from me. Dust and exhaust curled up like smoke in the beams of its headlights, reaching out for me.

Thank you, Lord. I am saved!

With a grunt, Gabriel grabbed me around the waist, making me drop the sickle. He swung me off my feet and yanked me back into the barn.

"Help!" I screamed.

Doors slammed. Someone—Gordo, I think—yelled, "Hang on, Sophia!" and two figures piled in through the door, then halted as though they'd run into a wall.

Gabriel's arm was like a vise around my ribs, and I could feel the coolness of his body against my back. "Get out of here," he snarled at them. "Whoever you are, you're not wanted here."

Where was Hannah? Had they come without her?

Rennie stepped forward. "Let her go, Gabriel. It's over."

"She is marked as a sacrifice to God. Leave now, or you will be marked as well."

"Rennie." I could barely speak past his forearm against my throat. "Don't let Dat or the boys out here. They heard the car."

The entire county had heard the car. But if my family came out, Gabriel would hurt them for sure, and unlike me, they wouldn't fight back. My father had never raised his hand to anyone in his life. And now was not the time to explain that vampires were real and wouldn't hesitate to kill.

Rennie glanced at Gordo. "I can't leave you, man."

"We'll be fine," Gordo said. "Keep the civilians out of here." Rennie slipped out and Gordo focused on Gabriel. "Do I have the pleasure of addressing Gabriel Charles Langford of Langford Hall?"

"You do," Gabriel said between his teeth. He backed up a step, closer to the workbench. "You have the advantage of me, sir."

"Gordon Dunleavy the Third, of New York. I challenge you to a duel for the life of this lady."

Behind me, I felt Gabriel rear back in surprise. I stumbled, stepping on his feet, but he didn't react. His attention was riveted on Gordo. "Under what conditions? And with what weapons? You are sadly outmatched in strength and experience, I fear."

"Winner gets the girl," Gordo said. "And no weapons. Fists only."

Gabriel's arms relaxed just a fraction. Great heavens above, he was really going to do it. "Are you a pugilist, sir?"

"I am. Do you accept?"

"On the condition that Sophia gives me her word she will stand here and wait for the victor. She will not scream or try to run."

Were they playacting? Had I stepped into a dream? Gordo nodded at me. *It'll be all right.*

"Yes." I could barely get the word out. "I promise."

Out of the corner of my eye, I spotted a movement in the hayloft above the chickens' enclosure. I circled to my left, so that Gabriel could keep an eye on me—and so that at his back, the one person in the world who had never let me down could move to the edge of the loft without being seen.

Hannah carried the sickle I had dropped outside.

Gordo and Gabriel circled, each taking the other's measure. Gabriel feinted, and Gordo reared back, then swung his right fist. Gabriel ducked and came at him low, aiming for his stomach. Gordo stepped out of the way, and in the split second before Gabriel could recover his balance, Hannah leaped down out of the loft onto his back, flattening him in the sawdust.

She might as well have been one of the hens. He reared up on his knees and shrugged her off as though she weighed nothing, and she landed on the plank floor with a thud and a cry of pain.

"Hannah! No!" I forgot my promise and dashed toward her, only to see her try to get up and fail. She must have hurt something in that jump, because her foot turned under her and she grunted, collapsing to hands and knees.

Gabriel grabbed her as if to roll her onto her back, and I shrieked, "Take your hands off her!" He would slash at her neck, I knew it—he would try to drink her to give himself strength. "No! I won't let you!" I flew at him and wrapped my arms around his neck, pulling him off her with all the strength of love and desperation.

Off to the side, I caught a glimpse of movement as Gordo snatched the sickle off the ground, where it was partially buried in hay.

"Sophia! Hannah! Down!" he shouted, and automatically I obeyed. I dropped to the ground, missed my footing, and went down hard on my rear. In the space of a blink—a breath—the lovingly sharpened, curved blade flashed in the lamplight before Gabriel could even turn to meet it.

And as suddenly as it began, it was over. Gabriel's sightless eyes rolled toward heaven.

I rolled over and retched onto the floor.

Still on hands and knees, Hannah crawled to me, grunting with pain, and took me in her arms in a fierce hug. "Are you okay?"

I wasn't ever going to be okay. How could a person live with an image like that stamped on their memory?

"Sophia, did he hurt you?" She shook me.

"No," I croaked. "I'm fine. But you're hurt. Hannah, he was going to—he would have drunk your blood. I had to do something. I couldn't let him—"

"Guys!" Gordo's voice was so frantic that we both whirled. Could Gabriel put his head back on and resurrect himself? "Look!"

Voices sounded outside—panicked, angry, protesting voices. Dat and the boys had run Rennie over and were on their way. But as I stared at Gabriel's mutilated body, it began to desiccate, to sift away, as two hundred years caught up to him in a matter of seconds. By the time Dat had wrenched the barn door open and demanded, "What is going on out here?" the body of the man I had loved— skin, heart, bones—had crumbled into dust.

The wind came in past my father's feet and lifted a wisp of it gently, whirling it in the current, blowing it across the floor of the barn until it disappeared into the darkness.

22

Four months later

People think that autumn is a time of endings—of fruit and grain being cut down and harvested, of animals being slaughtered for winter meat—but I always think of it as a time when things begin. The scholars begin their daily trek to the schoolhouse. As fast as we can empty the canner and boil water, Mamm and I preserve fruit, pickles, and onion relish. Hannah began her sophomore year at college and told me in her last letter that she had added kickboxing to her class schedule.

You never know when you'll need a little self-defense. Sometimes I wake up in a puddle of sweat, dreaming about that night. I don't know how you can go out into the barn at all, Sophia. Anyway, I don't ever want to feel that helpless again, so I joined Gordo's class.

Speaking of the G-man, he's been asking about you, when you're coming up again, have I heard from you lately. If you ever get to that band hop you were talking about, he says to tell you he still wants to go. Should I say forget it? I mean, Englisch boys are one thing when you're running around, but if you're planning to join church it's probably best not to lead them on. Gordo is a nice guy, and I can tell he likes you. Of course, the whole unrequited love thing probably appeals to the drama queen in him. And not every girl has that "loved by a vampire" vibe going for her.

You're unique in more ways than one.

The air is still warm and golden in the late afternoon, when I finish the baking and take her letter out to the barn to reread it. When I get to the "loved by a vampire" part, my skin chills just the way it did the first time.

Gabriel never loved me. I've thought about it constantly for weeks, and that's the conclusion I always come to. He was the predator, and in the beginning, I was the prey. Oh sure, he could pretty it up by saying he was my protector, but in the end, I was just something else for him to consume in order to live.

Fortunately, God has other plans for me that don't include being somebody's prey. Ever. Along with His love, he gives me strength, and that helps me hold my head up, even on days when all I want to do is curl up under my quilt and cry for what I've lost.

I turn over a bucket and sit next to the nesting boxes, and the hens come over to investigate. It's hard to believe that only a few months ago these birds were tiny fluff-balls that would fit in my hand. They're looking positively matronly since they began laying. One of them, a little gold Orpington, jumps in my lap and snugs herself under my left arm, for all the world like a chick under its mother's wing.

Through the open door, I hear a car roll down the driveway. The family is still at the auction in Myerling, but I decided not to go. I'm happy to stay home and look after things. Scooping up the hen, I carry her over to stand in the sun at the barn door as an old red car cruises to a stop. Deputy Palermo climbs out, slowly, hanging onto the door as a crutch.

"*Guder mariye*," I call, and he limps toward me. He is dressed in jeans and a T-shirt, with an old barn jacket tossed overtop.

"Hi, Sophia. Um, friend of yours?" He nods at the hen sitting peacefully in my arms.

"She is. Sometimes they like a hug, too." And since the hens are officially my business, I can hug them if I want and Mamm won't say a word. I still might need her next spring, though, if we get any cross-beaks in the hatch. I have my limits.

"I wondered if you had a minute to talk," he says. "This is an unofficial visit, as you can see." He nods over his shoulder at the car as he follows me into the barn.

"Do you like old cars?" I put the hen down and she goes to join her mates at the feeder.

The deputy draws in a sharp breath as he tries to make himself comfortable on a bale of hay. "I didn't used to think so, but my brother talked me into this one because his wife won't let him have it. It's a 1954 Mercury Sun Valley—not a car you see around a lot. Rob saw it sitting by the side of the road out in Furniss with a For Sale sign on it. Apparently the farmer was storing it for some guy who just stopped paying space rent. I came along with cash in hand and that was that. Runs like a clock. The guy will probably be sorry when he comes back and finds his car gone."

It's the most I've ever heard the deputy say without stopping in all the time I've known him. Men are so funny about cars. Adam Hertzfeld would probably give ten years off his life just to take it for a spin. He got his license this summer. Goodness knows where he found a car to practice with for the driving test.

"Probably," I agree. "How are you, Deputy?"

A shadow crosses his face as he shifts on the bale. "I'm okay. Still weak, and this leg is gimpy. I lost some muscle during—when it happened, so that means lots of physical therapy. Doc tells me I can eat all the liver and red meat I can handle, though, so I can't complain. I'm on desk duty in the meantime." He raises his head, and in his brown eyes I see honest concern. "What about you?"

I can't meet his gaze. "What do you mean? I'm fine."

"He's gone, isn't he." It's not a question. "We're never going to bring him to justice."

"You could say that. He's dead."

He tries not to show his surprise, but I see his lashes flicker and his Adam's apple move up and down before he speaks. "Are you sure?"

I can't help it—my gaze moves to that spot on the floor that has been swept and bleached and cleaned a dozen times in the last months. But the image is still there, and probably always will be until I leave this farm for good.

"Yes, I'm sure." I cross to where I keep the hens' feed, and pull an envelope out of the cupboard. "Here."

Dear Sophia,

By the time you read this it will already be too late. I can no longer live with what I have done. I have broken God's commandments and have damned myself, and my only hope is that you might pray for me. I killed Paul Gingrich and Cara Troyer, and I tried to kill the deputy. I deserve God's punishment, and so I will not wait for man's.

I have already given your aunt the money for the farm. As my fiancée, it belongs to you now. Do with it as you will. All I ever wanted was your happiness. I hope that now this will be possible. Good-bye.

Gabriel

Deputy Palermo looks up. "Is this for real?"

Of course it's real. Rennie worked hard on it, using sheet after sheet of paper until he could render a perfect imitation of Gabriel's old-fashioned script.

I nod. "We found him out here, as a matter of fact." I look up at the rafters. "We buried him with only a graveside service. Family and close friends."

It took nearly an hour that night to convince my father that Gordo, Rennie, and Hannah had just come by to pick me up to go to a band hop. He still mutters about carousing in the middle of the night, even when I'm careful to get home from Singing at a reasonable hour. But after he and Mamm and the boys went back to bed, we swept up the floor and took Gabriel's mortal remains up to what I had once thought of as our spot on the hillside, at the edge of the copse.

Dust thou art, and unto dust thou shalt return. The wild rose stands guard over him now.

"He hung himself?" The deputy sounds skeptical. "In your barn, where you could have found him? Not the most considerate act in the world."

"He wasn't sane, deputy," I say softly. "Who knows what he was thinking?"

"Mind if I keep this?" He folds the letter up. "To close out the file?"

I nod. I've been saving it for him. "I came to visit you, you know." Time to change the subject. "In the hospital. But you probably didn't know I was there. And I was praying for you."

He nods. "I appreciate that. Still would, if you don't mind." He clears his throat, clearly uncomfortable with something that's as familiar to me as breathing. "So. What did you end up doing with the farm?"

I shrug. "My aunt didn't want it back. She read the letter and told me it was Gabriel's to give or not give. So my dad and brothers are working it for now. And I look after the garden." It delights me to move things and dig and plant and make the old place look alive. I may never live there—may never come to love it—but I do like the garden. I let my aunt's chickens out into the safe, fenced yard every day and all of us rejoice in our freedom.

But these aren't the kinds of things you can tell a policeman.

"And you're okay with that?" He's gazing at me again. "You seem different, if you don't mind my saying so."

I smile. Lately it's become easier to do that. Sometimes I wonder how, after all I've been through, and then I think a thing as simple as a smile must be a gift from God. And I'm not about to refuse it.

"I feel different. I think it's just taken awhile to come to grips with the fact that I loved someone who ... who was damaged. He thought he was protecting the church, you know." I meet his eyes at last. "Killing the wolf who was hurting God's lambs."

He nods. "I know. That's one of the last things I remember, him saying that. Before he attacked me. Though I have a hard time believing he saw that little girl as a wolf." He looks at the folded letter and sighs. "If it wasn't for my being in a coma I would have ..." His voice trails away and he looks at me apologetically. "Well, I guess that's all I came out here for, then. To see that you were all right."

Out of uniform and away from that big police car, he's not nearly as imposing and scary as I once thought.

"We're both all right," I say. "I'm glad about that. We're both survivors. It can only get better, can't it?"

He slides off the hay bale and holds out his hand. I take it, and find his grip is the grip of a policeman, not an invalid. "I think you're right," he agrees. "It can only get better."

I lean on the barn door in the sun and the little gold hen follows me outside. She tugs on my skirt with her beak and I pick her up as Deputy Palermo gets into his Sun Valley. He backs out of the driveway and gives me a wave as he turns onto the road, gunning the motor just like Gordo does when he takes off from a light.

The sound recedes into the distance as I stand there, cradling the warm, trusting little hen. The air smells like apples and cut grass, and the sun falls on my face like happiness.

Like a blessing.

THE END

A Note from Shelley

Dear reader,

I hope you enjoyed reading this book as much as I enjoyed writing it. Be sure to watch for the next two books in the Immortal Faith trilogy, *Twice Dead* and *Everlasting Chains*.

You might leave a review on your favorite retailer's site to tell others about my books. And you can find the print editions online.

Do visit me on my website at www.shelleyadina.com, which includes all my releases, including the Magnificent Devices steampunk series and the heroine's personal correspondence in the "Letters from the Lady" series on my blog. I invite you to sign up for my newsletter there, too.

And now, for an excerpt from *Lady of Devices*, the first book in the Magnificent Devices series, I invite you to turn the page ...

Excerpt

LADY OF DEVICES
BY SHELLEY ADINA
© 2011

1

London, 1889

To say the explosion rocked the laboratory at St. Cecelia's Academy for Young Ladies might have overstated the case, but she was still never going to hear the end of it.

Claire Trevelyan closed her eyes as a gobbet of reddish-brown foam dripped off the ceiling and landed squarely on the crown of her head. It dribbled past her ears and onto the pristine sailor collar of her middy blouse, and thence, gravity having its inevitable effect, down the blue seersucker of her uniform's skirt to the floor.

LADY OF DEVICES

Shrieking, the other students in the senior Chemistry of the Home class had already flung themselves toward the back of the room and away from the benches directly under the mess. "Ladies!" Professor Grünwald shouted, raising his arms as if to calm the stormy waters, "there is no cause for alarm. Collect yourselves, please." His gimlet eyes behind their gleaming spectacles pinned Claire in place like a butterfly on a board. "Miss Trevelyan. Did I not, just moments ago, tell you not to add the contents of that dish to your flask?"

"Yes, sir." She could barely hear herself over the squawking of her classmates.

"Then why did you do it?"

The truth would only net her another grim punishment, but there was no other answer. "To see what would happen, sir."

"Indeed. I seem to remember you gave Doctor Prescott the same reply after the unfortunate incident with the Tesla coil." His jaw firmed under its layer of fat. He addressed the back of the room, where the others huddled against the cabinets in which he kept ingredients and equipment. "Ladies, please. Adding peppermint to an infusion of dandelion and burdock will do you no harm. You may adjourn to the powder rooms to rearrange your toilettes if you must."

Several of the girls stampeded from the room, leaving behind Lady Julia Wellesley, Lady Catherine Montrose, and Miss Gloria Meriwether-Astor, who watched her humiliation with as much wide-eyed delight as if it were the latest flicker at the theater. Claire straightened her spine. She should be used to this. Fortitude was the key.

Another gob of foam landed on her shoulder. Behind her, Lady Catherine stifled a giggle.

"And are you satisfied with your newfound knowledge?" Professor Grünwald was not finished with her yet.

"Yes, sir," Claire said with complete truth.

"I am delighted to hear it. In future, when I tell you not to do something, I would like the courtesy of obedience. You are here to learn the chemistry of the home, not to engage in silly parlor tricks."

"But sir, it would be helpful if you had told us *why* the compounds should not be mixed."

In the ensuing moment of silence, she heard an indrawn breath of anticipation from the gallery.

"I am sorry to have incommoded you in your quest for information." His sarcasm dripped as unpleasantly as the substance now forming a sticky mass on her clothes. "By tomorrow morning, you will provide me with one hundred lines stating the following: 'I will obey instruction and curb my unladylike curiosity.' Repeat that, please."

Claire did so in a monotone as faithful as any wax recording.

"Thank you, Miss Trevelyan. You will now go and inform the cleaning staff that their assistance is required here."

"Yes, sir."

"And you will stay for the remainder of the period and help them."

Claire clamped her molars down on the urge to further defend herself. "Yes, sir."

"Ladies, class is dismissed. Thank you for your patience."

Patience? He was thanking *them?* Claire kept her face calm above the storm in her heart as she turned toward the door, the heel of her boot slipping several inches in the foam. Lady Catherine giggled again—Claire suspected she couldn't help herself, being the nervous sort—and the other girls followed her out, careful to keep their clean skirts from touching hers.

"Nicely done, Trevelyan," Lady Julia Wellesley whispered. "We have a half period free thanks to you."

"I must say, that brown substance suits you." Lady Catherine's overbite became more prominent as she smiled. "It's the exact color of your hair."

"Next time, perhaps you'll be less inclined to show off your superior intellectual powers," Gloria Meriwether-Astor added, her flat vowels emphasizing a colonial drawl.

Claire tried to keep silent, but this was just too much. She turned to glare at the new heiress from the American Territories, who had fit in with the other girls from the moment of her arrival like an imperious hand in a kid glove. "I don't show off at all. I—"

"Oh, please," Lady Julia waved her fingers. "Spare us the false humility. But tell me, how on earth do you expect to attract a husband looking like that?"

"She's trying to impress old Grünwald." Lady Catherine giggled. "He's single."

He was also forty if he was a day, overweight, and his receding hairline perspired when he was under pressure, which was nearly all the time. Besides which, marrying anyone below the rank of baron was out of the question, never mind a man forced to earn his living by teaching the next generation of society's glittering lights.

Not that these particular glittering lights wanted to be taught anything but how to embroider a handkerchief or pour a cup of tea. Though if there were a class devoted to the art of landing a titled husband, she had no doubt every one of them would sign up for it and never miss a moment. Of course, Lady Julia could probably teach such a class. Rumor had it that as soon as she descended the platform on graduation day next week, Lord Robert Mount-Batting would go down upon one knee on the lawn and propose. Claire rather doubted that rumor had its facts in order. Lady Julia would never miss her presentation at court in two weeks, nor any of the balls and parties to be held in her honor afterward. If there were to be lawns involved, it would probably be the one at Ascot, or the one at Wellesley House, sometime before the shooting season began in August.

Julia, Catherine, and Claire herself were to be presented to Her Majesty during the same Drawing Room. Claire's imagination shuddered and refused to venture there. Who knew what fresh humiliation those girls could dream up in that most august company?

Finally ridding herself of the maddening crowd, Claire went to Administration and sent a tube containing Professor Grünwald's request down to the offices of the staff. No point in cleaning herself up or changing her clothes if she was to be doomed to pushing a mop for the next thirty minutes. This benighted school hadn't the wit to obtain the services of a mother's helper to take care of the worst of the mess. Armed with a ladder, mops, and buckets, it took her and the two chars the rest of the period to clean the sticky foam off the ceiling, benches, chairs, and floor of the laboratory.

Thank goodness the professor had retired to his office. She was able to laugh at the chars' comments on his marital prospects with impunity.

After Claire helped them carry the equipment back to the basement, she changed into her spare uniform in the gymnasium dressing room as fast as she could. Still, she arrived at her French class late with half her blouse's hem sticking out of the waistband of her skirt, much to the amusement of Lady Julia and Gloria.

"Never mind them," Emilie Fragonard whispered from the desk behind her as she reached forward and tucked in the offending article. "You're all right now."

Dear Emilie. Though her friend's hair was drawn back in an practical braided bun instead of a flattering pompadour, and her spectacles were, in Claire's opinion, too heavy for her delicate features and hid her fine eyes, she was the soul of kindness. And kindness, heaven knew, was in short supply at St. Cecelia's.

After class and before the midday meal, Claire and Emilie took refuge in the dappled shade under a grove of trees on the far side of the lawn. Over the ten-foot granite wall that separated the sheltered young ladies from the bustle of London, the rattle of carriages and jingle of harness could be heard on the road, along with the voices of passers-by and the occasional distinctive chug of a new steam landau. When she heard that sound, Claire could hardly contain the urge to run to the gates and stare.

They were such fascinating engines, each one different, yet operating under the same marvelous principles.

"Don't even think about it." Emilie's tone told Claire she'd been caught. "Ladies do not gawk after steam landaus or those who drive them."

"I don't care about who drives them. I drive one myself. I just like to look at them."

"You do not. Drive one, I mean."

"I do indeed. Gorse is teaching me."

"Claire Elizabeth Trevelyan!" Emilie put a pale hand against the trunk of the largest of the elms for support. "I thought your escapade with the quadricycle was bad enough. You cannot tell me you are actually piloting one of those dangerous things!"

"They're not dangerous, if you know their proper operation. Which I do. One's speed and direction are merely a matter of the correct application of steam. The explosions of the first models are a thing of the past."

"That's lucky, knowing how you are about explosions."

Claire's good spirits cooled like a fire left too long without fuel. "You heard."

"The entire school heard. Honestly, dear heart, you've got to curb this unhealthy tendency to blow things up."

"That ridiculous excuse for a professor wouldn't tell us what would happen. How can I be blamed for the silly man's stubbornness? If there's anything I hate, it's someone telling me 'don't' without saying why."

"And one must know the reason why for everything."

"Not everything. But certainly something as simple as why one cannot add a peppermint to dandelion and burdock. One adds peppermint to cookie batter and tea with no harmful effects whatsoever."

"Thanks to you, everyone in school now knows why. And by breakfast tomorrow, everyone at Heathbourne will, too."

Heathbourne was the equivalent of St. Cecelia's on the other side of the square—and where she would have gone had she been born a boy and her father's heir. "I don't care about the opinions of schoolboys."

"You will in a few weeks, when you're at your come-out ball at Carrick House and none of them ask you to dance."

"You sound exactly like my mother." Why had no one told her the bow on the front of her middy blouse was lopsided? She pulled it out and began to retie it.

"In this she's correct, and you know it. Claire, please consider." Emilie's tone became gentle. "It's a fact universally acknowledged that a young lady of good fortune must make a suitable marriage."

"Do not quote the mores of our grandmothers' generation to me. Besides, not every young lady wishes that." Her own appearance taken care of, she reached over to anchor a celluloid hairpin more securely in Emilie's bun. If it could not be lovely, at least it should be secure.

"Every one who wishes to be received in good society does. You don't want to be one of those dreadful Chelsea people, like poor Peony Churchill, do you?"

As a matter of fact, Claire coveted and envied the intellectual explorations found in the salons and lecture halls of the Chelsea set, known in the papers as the Wits. It was led by Mrs. Stanley Churchill, Peony's mother, and populated by explorers and scientists from the Royal Society of Engineers as well as artists, musicians, and the most independent thinkers of Her Majesty Queen Victoria's empire. Their philosophy that the intellect trumped the bloodline flew in the face of most of society. But no one could argue that the Prime Minister himself was one of them. The fact that a scientist or explorer could be granted lands and a title when noble bloodlines were getting more inbred and in some cases dying out altogether was an indication which way the wind blew.

And Claire had always loved the wind. Was it mere coincidence that the family estate in Cornwall was called Gwynn Place, from the Cornish *plas-an-gwyn*, meaning *manor of the wind*? Perhaps not. Perhaps it was a sign.

A shadow blotted out the sun and she and Emilie looked up to see not a cloud, but an enormous airship passing far overhead. The eleven-thirty packet to Paris had left its mooring mast at Hampstead Heath exactly on time.

Deep in the marble and sandstone halls of the school, a bell rang. "There's lunch," she told Emilie, turning from the wonderful sight of the ship and neatly evading the answer to her friend's question. "Come along or we'll be late."

ABOUT THE AUTHOR

The official version

RITA Award® winning author and Christy finalist Shelley Adina wrote her first novel when she was 13. It was rejected by the literary publisher to whom she sent it, but he did say she knew how to tell a story. That was enough to keep her going through the rest of her adolescence, a career, a move to another country, a B.A. in Literature, an M.F.A. in Writing Popular Fiction, and countless manuscript pages.

Shelley is a world traveler who loves to imagine what might have been. Between books, she loves playing the piano and Celtic harp, making period costumes, and spoiling her flock of rescued chickens.

The unofficial version

I like Edwardian cutwork blouses and velvet and old quilts. I like bustle drapery and waltzes and new sheet music and the OED. I like steam billowing out from the wheels of a locomotive and autumn colors and chickens. I like flower crowns and little beaded purses and jeweled hatpins. Small birds delight me and Roman ruins awe me.

SHELLEY ADINA

I like old books and comic books and new technology ... and new books and shelves and old technology. I'm feminine and literary and practical, but if there's a beach, I'm going to comb it. I listen to shells and talk to hens and ignore the phone. I believe in thank-you notes and kindness, in commas and friendship, and in dreaming big dreams. You write your own life. Go on. Pick up a pen.

Available now

The Magnificent Devices series:
Lady of Devices
Her Own Devices
Magnificent Devices
Brilliant Devices
A Lady of Resources

Caught You Looking (contemporary romance, Moonshell Bay #1)
Peep, the Hundred-Decibel Hummer (early reader)

To learn about my Amish women's fiction written as Adina Senft, visit www.adinasenft.com.
The Wounded Heart
The Hidden Life
The Tempted Soul
And in 2014, the Healing Grace series beginning with
Herb of Grace

COMING SOON

A Lady of Spirit, Magnificent Devices #6
A Lady of Integrity, Magnificent Devices #7
A Gentleman of Means, Magnificent Devices #8
Emily, the Easter Chick (early reader)
Caught You Listening, Moonshell Bay #2
Caught You Hiding, Moonshell Bay #3